JJ CARPENTER

The Corner of Her Eye

Book Three: The Forgotten

First published by JJ Carpenter 2024

First edition

ISBN (paperback): 978-0-6486376-9-1
ISBN (hardcover): 978-0-6486376-3-9

Editing by Greg Cox
Cover art by Evgeniia Gurcheva

This book was professionally typeset on Reedsy.
Find out more at reedsy.com

"I stood by the grave where the dead girl lies
When the sunlit scenes were fair,
And the white clouds high in the autumn skies,
And I answered the message there.
But the haunting words of the dead to me
Shall go wherever I go.
She lives in the Marriage that Might Have Been
Do you think that I do not know?"

HENRY LAWSON

Contents

Series Recap

This is not a synopsis of Books One and Two. This is a short memory-jogger of some of the key premises and themes comprising Charlie's supernatural world. If you haven't read Book One, *The Keeper*, and Book Two, *The Road*, I strongly encourage you to do so before reading Book Three. The below contains all sorts of spoilers, but still won't give you a full sense of the stories.

* * *

Charlie White is a Keeper. A *"Guardien du Purgatoire"* as her best friend Tess would say — a Keeper of Purgatory.

In her mid-forties, Charlie's life was turned on its head by an adult-onset medical condition. Traumatised, she ran from Sydney to the small town of Greenfields, near Newcastle, New South Wales, searching for stability and safety. Instead, she ran into something even more peculiar: a supernatural world between life, death and whatever comes beyond. Everyone dies, but not everyone is ready to move on when it's their turn. Purgatory — or the Waiting Place as Charlie likes to call it — is a place for these spirits to wait, processing the good, the bad and everything that *should* have happened to them in life. Only then will they be ready to move on.

Purgatory is a world of hierarchy and order. More than anything else, it is a place of Balance. In the Waiting Place, spirits are categorised by colour, according to what it is they need to experience in limbo. Blues, for example, are usually the spirits of children who need to experience innocence, childhood and play a while longer. Greys are the spirits of people who experienced significant pain and fear in their lives, and need to process this before they can move on.

Yellows — also known as the party spirits — lived through significant hardship, often physical, and in limbo, they now have the opportunity to experience real pleasure and leisure. Quite often, for the first time in their lives. Purples were repressed during their time on earth, and in purgatory, they have the chance to explore their freest selves. This often earns them the name 'temptresses'.

Some of these spirits are common. The Greys and the Blacks (who are spirits who have been betrayed in life), are two of the most widespread types. An unfortunate reflection of the state of the world. The Reds, who should have been great leaders in life but were robbed of the chance, are among the rarest spirit. Another rare type of spirit is the Whites — or, more aptly put, Keepers, like Charlie.

The role of a Keeper is to maintain the Balance of purgatory at all costs. When something has happened to a spirit that shouldn't have, or that is keeping them from moving on, the Keepers' role is to mend this imbalance. To help the spirit to either accept its fate and move on, or to enter limbo. Marie — the first spirit Charlie helped, and who still haunts her cottage — was imbalanced because she was being hunted by a Grey spirit. The same man who had murdered her in life. While Marie was supposed to be a Blue, the Grey's interest risked her becoming a Grey herself and upsetting the Balance. For the Yellow spirits of the Great North Road, it was their tether to the Red that stopped them from being able to experience their 'party' in limbo.

Spirits and Keepers aren't the only ones in purgatory. Wisps are memories, or sometimes even fragments of a person's soul, left behind. They are responsible for many of the 'unintelligent' hauntings on earth. Unlike the spirits, wisps are completely colourless, drawing their form from the world around them. Charlie and her friends have also just been introduced to the Shadows. Like the wisps, they are not spirits. Unlike the Wisps, they are in no way human. They draw their being from the shadows around them, and their only purpose is to help maintain the Balance. That's all Charlie knows so far.

When Charlie enters purgatory, she calls this 'entering the Dream'. This can happen to her while she is sleeping; spirits can find her and call to her, pulling her to them in her sleep. Charlie can also *will* herself to the Dream, searching for answers, and often finding herself in the past or even the future in her search for answers. Time has no meaning in the Dream, which can cause all sorts of havoc with Charlie's own perceptions. After all, a Keeper is supposed to only exist in the Dream where time doesn't matter. But that's not the case for Charlie.

In Book One, Charlie had accepted her fate. She had been ready to die, to protect Tess, to save Marie, and to maintain the Balance. Instead, she had lived. Why? Because Charlie is tethered to Tess. Tess is literally Charlie's anchor to the real world and the reason she hasn't let go of her physical body. Tess is Charlie's closest friend in this world. A French domestic violence survivor, who stayed in Australia with her now-adult son, Leon, after escaping her Australian partner. We also can't forget Trent, the loveable local librarian, who has a thirst for local history. While not a tether, he does give the best hugs.

The Dream — purgatory — is a place of hierarchy. You can think of it like this: The wisps are the bottom-ranking. Mere shadows or memories of people's former lives; barely conscious and unable to communicate fully. The spirits — the Blues, Blacks, Greys, Purples, Reds, Yellows and others — are full human spirits. The souls of the departed, who need to move through purgatory to whatever comes next. Each type of spirit has a Guide (the next step up on the hierarchy) who is supposed to help them through their journey and keep their various coloured spirits in check. For example, for the Greys, their guides are called Lam. Lam may seek out souls it believes should be a Grey and help them transition. It might also become involved if a Grey steps outside of bounds: becomes too violent, for example, or interferes too much in the human world.

Keepers may be a type of spirit (the Whites), but they are also so much more. They are, in effect, a Guide as well, but they also sit above the coloured Guides in this supernatural hierarchy. Their role is to help *all* the spirits, regardless of their colour. In so doing, they maintain the Balance and keep things in their proper order. The final character you need to remember is

Maryanne, the 'psycho psych'. Maryanne is what she calls a Seeker. Seekers are impartial offshoots of this purgatory hierarchy; they do not interfere. Their purpose is to find Guides, or Keepers like Charlie, and help them come to terms with and accept their purpose. The purpose, above all else, to keep the Balance in the Dream.

Trigger Warning: Amongst its supernatural and morbid content, Book Three of *The Corner of Her Eye* series contains references to domestic and family violence.

1

Alone At Last

It was dark, again, like it so often was in the Dream. It wasn't just the black of night that swallowed her this time, though. This blackness was deeper, wider, thicker. She could almost feel herself absorbing it as it cycled through her, tainting her, before spewing back even darker into the world around her.

Charlie knew where she was. Not the precise location, but certainly the type of place. The grey headstones spreading around her in all directions were a clear giveaway. This was a cemetery, and an enormous one. There had to be thousands of graves here. Tens of thousands. Those closest to her were crumbling, the ground collapsing down to swallow broken stone, the faces of the headstones cracking away, the angels a little darker than they should be.

It wasn't just the dark that unsettled Charlie. A tightness in the centre of her shoulder blades, tingling like painful pins-and-needles, reminded her she was not alone. She couldn't see them, not yet, but she could *feel* them watching her. Their eyes bore into her back. She spun again, her own eyes hopping from stone-to-stone, seeking out the spirit she knew had drawn her here. Drawn her out of her slumber, from her bed, across who knew how far a distance.

She urged herself forward and flew by stones in a flurry of marble and granite. It all looked the same. Rows and rows of burial ground, interspersed by tall, fully mature palms and other trees. The presence followed her, still not making itself known. The feeling in her back grew, spreading through her as an icy chill. She could comprehend temperatures in the Dream, but this was more than just a wintry day. Soft layers of ice seemed to descend on her entire being, slowly sinking into her until the chill was enough to burn her. *Show yourself*, she willed, as her eyes fell on a tiny cherub. Once pale white, it was now entirely blackened by age. The only white remaining was that of its eyes, staring seemingly into her soul. The cold deepened in her and she felt herself shudder.

A glimmer of movement at the edge of her vision grabbed her attention. Part of the blackness had definitely moved, sliding between the graves in fluid motions. Despite the fear and nausea that rippled in her, she moved towards it. This time, as Charlie was pulled forward, she found herself at a different cemetery landmark. She was inside a small, ruined building, standing amongst rotten, broken wood and crumbled bricks. Two red brick walls stood intact, right down to the small, pale framed windows. Before her, the third wall had collapsed halfway down. Behind her, the wall had completely vanished, two metal beams crossed over in its place. In her current state of alert and agitation, the rubble felt oppressive. Like the decay was infecting her through the soles of her feet.

Just as she was ready to move away, she saw it. Through one of the windows, three of its four panes cracked and broken, she caught it watching her. Its eyes glinted like shining coins in the moonlight, silvery and clouded. It reminded her of the darkened angel she'd seen just before. But their glint was even brighter, sitting in its blackened and smoky face. This was the deepest black she'd ever seen. This was no shadow. In place of its nose and mouth were a sharp protrusion. Almost beak-like, but too angular, too curved, too harsh. It didn't move like a bird, either, as it pulled its face back and out of view. It was more like a snake, sliding through mud: smooth, slick and frightfully fast.

Before her determination could dissolve, she pushed herself to follow. This time, she flashed forward to a small church. She assumed that's what it was, anyway. It was immensely tall. The pointed, angled ceiling reached for the heavens, the cross atop it barely visible from this angle. Elaborate arches and columns were engraved around its edges in the same deep red brick. A large, double, wooden door stood at odds with the rest of the building. Its plain white simplicity seemingly not belonging within its elaborate frame. The cold deepened even further here and she shuddered, chilled more so by how this spirit could touch and affect her than by the temperature drop itself. As she readied herself to pull back from the Dream, having had enough of this morbid hide-and-seek, the ground in the front corner of the church moved.

The dark shadows around the building grew deeper, blacker. Writhing like slimy, frenzied worms. Inky veins reached out, before speeding back to the mass as it formed shape and literally loomed upwards out of the dark. Blacker than black. The spirit grew upwards like an ancient tree, its narrow trunk shooting to the skies before its arms reached outwards like wizened branches. The spirit was now taller than the church, dwarfing her, its beak of a face protruding sharply, its moon-eyes glinting. As one spindly arm reached out to her, she stumbled backwards and out of the Dream.

* * *

Charlie shot up in her bed. She quickly scanned every corner of her bedroom, making sure the spirit hadn't somehow followed her here. This, she knew, could easily happen. Only empty walls looked back at her, illuminated by the early light of day creeping around her curtained windows. A stack of colourful cushions was piled in the corner, where they'd been for days. Tess's cushions. Assured she was alone, Charlie took a deep breath and reached out to the bright white energy that coursed through the Dream, reinvigorating herself after her ordeal. She'd learnt how to do that just months before, when helping a group of convict spirits to move on. The effort had nearly killed her, until she realised that the energy of the Dream was at her full disposal as well. Without thinking, she pulled that white light and energy into herself like a shield, willing herself to be cordoned off from that crazed spirit.

My first Black spirit, Charlie thought forlornly, rubbing at the sleep in her eyes, massaging her cheekbones as she did so. While the spirit seemingly hadn't followed her through the Dream, its chill certainly had. Her skin felt like it had been rubbed all over with ice, as though she'd woken caked in a layer of frost. She pulled the throw from the edge of the bed and wrapped it around her shoulders. *Of course this happens now, when Tess isn't here.*

The past two months had passed so quietly. Since Charlie had freed the Red spirit and his Yellow companions from the Great North Road, it was like the universe had given her a break to recover. In those weeks, the only spirit to have called to her for help was a Purple. A man this time, a homosexual who had repressed his true nature his whole life, until death took him, and it was too late. Most people might think the agony and trauma of Charlie's role as Keeper would be enough to bring her down to the same depths of depression in which she found some of these spirits. Sometimes, Charlie feared that possibility herself. But releasing souls from their imbalance, helping them to realise what they needed in order to be fulfilled and to move on peacefully, was beautiful.

The Black had felt anything but beautiful. She picked up her phone from the bedside table to check the time: 6:42 a.m. Too early to call Tess. She'd only been gone a week, but those days had dragged. With the house empty — aside from the lingering spirit of Marie of course — Charlie had felt so alone, rattling in the walls of her 1920s cottage like a ghost herself. Time was meaningless, and dragging. It was a dramatic thought, she knew. Tess had gone to visit her son, Leon, in Sydney to help with his wedding planning to his fiancée Ella. Ella and Tess seemed to actually be getting along now, which was a miracle. On her way home, Tess was picking up a second-hand 'tiny house' on wheels to start fulfilling her vision of a small BnB empire on the property. It was a routine visit; normal. Charlie wasn't abandoned, despite her heavy feeling.

It must be this recent encounter. It had shaken her enough to believe the distance from Tess was dangerous. Or perhaps it was her own feelings of isolation that had drawn the spirit to her. *Malevolent.* She knew it must be. The way it had watched her, almost stalking her, hadn't felt friendly. She couldn't stand this feeling of solitude any longer. She unlocked her phone and went to messages, clicking on Trent's name. He, at least, was physically closer to her. She tapped at the keys quickly: *'Hey Trent. Are you free today? I could really use some company. Spooky stuff.'* She didn't want to alarm him, despite how loudly alarm bells were ringing in her own skull.

I have my appointment with Maryanne tomorrow, she reassured herself. Maryanne had rescheduled it to Thursday for some reason. Something she had *never* done before, normally keeping to their strict Friday schedule. Charlie was grateful in this case. *Tess is back on Saturday. Only three more nights. I can do this.* Her phone pinged, and she fumbled as she picked it up again. It was Trent, surprisingly. He was not usually a morning person.

'Of course', the text read. *'Hope the spooky stuff isn't too spooky. Let's meet at Dot's at 4 after I clock off?'*

The chill that had been caressing Charlie's skin sunk deep into her stomach. Not only because she had to wait almost nine hours just to leave the house for Greenfields Town and the local favourite, Dot's cafe. But also because she'd be seeing the café owner there, Dot. A woman she now thought of as her friend. It wasn't only the convict spirits that Charlie had helped two months ago. There'd been another — Ru. The three-year-old boy who'd died presumably of brain cancer. And Dot's grandson. The catch was that Ru hadn't even been born yet. The Dream was funny that way. Because time didn't matter after death, it wasn't just spirits who had died in the past who could seek out Charlie. While less common, the future sometimes intruded into Charlie's world as well. She truly wished it hadn't in this case. It was hard enough helping the spirits of those she'd never met — and never would meet. It was almost impossible when these things impacted the people she knew and loved.

Charlie had helped Ru's mother — and Dot's daughter — Taylor, as well. The mother who had been so distraught with grief that she'd gone catatonic, her soul literally fragmenting and scattering across the Dream. Part of her spirit — the absolute grief of losing her only son — had followed Ru's spirit, keeping him from moving on. In helping Ru, Charlie had also needed to help Taylor. Reconnecting at least part of her spirit together and bringing her back to her parents in the real world. Dot wouldn't just have to face the loss of her only grandchild, who she was so excited to meet already. She would have to face further pain and trauma for her daughter, who had already been through so much.

Charlie's morbid curiosity had overcome her concern at first. In those first weeks after she'd realised Ru's identity, she'd asked Dot and Trent at any appropriate moment for more information about Taylor. Turned out Taylor was bipolar and had been since her teenage years. She'd grappled with self-harm and even one attempted suicide. She struggled to hold down a job, continuing to live with her ever-loving and doting parents, who never blamed Taylor for what afflicted her. They only ever offered love, support and understanding, or at least an attempt to comprehend. Taylor also had manic episodes, cycling through an endless sea of sexual partners. The cause, Charlie assumed, of Ru's conception. Charlie had grappled with this picture that Dot and Trent had painted of Taylor; contrasting her with the woman she'd met repeatedly in the Dream. She understood why Dot felt Ru would be such a blessing to Taylor. Finally, some good. At least for a couple of years.

Charlie gulped before she replied to Trent: '*sounds good*'. She swallowed the bitter lie as she hit send. She hadn't been able to bring herself to tell Trent what she'd discovered. Trent, who knew both Taylor and Dot far better than she did. Tess had figured it out for herself, of course, and seemed to find it even harder than Charlie to visit Dot's café.

"No cowardice now, Charlie," she told herself curtly, swinging her legs over the edge of the bed, the throw still draped comfortingly around her shoulders. "If they can live through it, you can be part of the sideshow."

2

Latched On

Charlie arrived at Dot's early, eager to get away from her empty house. She'd sat in her sewing room most of the day, Marie's spirit occasionally shifting the threads and fabrics on her desk. Marie had been more active that day than Charlie had sensed for a while, perhaps picking up something of the Black spirit Charlie would soon have to help move on. As Charlie walked across the road to the small, white, tin-roofed café, she saw Dot heaving outdoor chairs upside down and onto the table. "Hey, let me help!" Charlie yelled out, jogging the final few metres across the road. Dot jumped slightly at Charlie's voice, her large stomach and backside jiggling as she stood straight.

"Oh, Charlie," she sighed in a flustered voice. "Sorry, dear, I'm lost in my own world." Dot squeezed Charlie's hand affectionately, before turning back to the chairs. Her hand was freezing cold, as though she'd been standing outdoors in the chill Autumn air for hours, not just popped out to pack away. Her face was pale except for a slight flush to her rotund cheeks, seeming to confirm Charlie's theory that Dot had in fact been standing outside for some time. Resting a hand on the chair she'd just replaced, Dot turned to look at Charlie again. "Oh, I suppose you'll be wanting this table, dear?"

Charlie nodded, placing her hand atop Dot's. "Are you okay? I thought you didn't close up until 4:30?" Visions of Ru's death and Taylor's gaping, catatonic eyes flashed briefly through Charlie's mind and she shuddered slightly as well. She knew this couldn't be what had Dot feeling so down, but the images came to her unbidden.

"Oh, you know me…" Dot trailed off, placing the last chair back on the ground and removing a towel from the pouch of her apron to wipe at invisible streaks of dirt on the table. "I'm an over-thinker!"

"What is it today?" Charlie said with a smile, marvelling at her ability to feign casualness. She pushed the memories of what had yet to happen further back in her mind and pulled out the chair Dot had just replaced. She motioned for Dot to sit in it. "Trent won't be here for a while, so I'm a free and willing ear."

Dot chuckled a little as she took Charlie's offer, once again jiggling ever so slightly as she moved. The chair creaked as she eased her weight into it. "Oh, it's Taylor and the baby again…" Dot waved her hands as if waving away her own worries. Despite the clenching in her gut, Charlie lay a hand on Dot's sleeved forearm and nodded for her to continue. "She just won't stay still! She hasn't slowed down at all. If anything, she's just sped up! Why, just the other day, she went *running* with some new friend of hers. *Running!* And afterwards, they drank *caffeinated* coffee and *ate soft cheese!*" The bubbles of worry in Charlie's twisted stomach popped in mirth at Dot's words. A small smile creeped out from the corner of her mouth and Dot — seeing this — pulled her arm away and started waving her hands in dismissal again. "I know…I *know.* I'm being overprotective."

"Haha, no!" Charlie said in a voice light and unforced. She reached for Dot's arm again. "Worrying about these things is perfectly *normal!*" Not that Charlie would know, she supposed. Having never had children, and never wanting them. Still, she was refreshed to find Dot's concerns so benign and easily addressed. "I have a *very* strong sense that everything is going to be okay with this pregnancy."

"You do?"

Charlie gave a fierce nod. "Yes! I know that baby is going to be born healthy and happy, and be surrounded by so, so much love. You are going to squeeze that child with affection until his eyes pop." Dot laughed, and some of the brightness returned to her face.

"You really think so?" She smiled and leant back in her chair, resting her hands on her stomach. "You're a rational girl, Charlie. You know we can't tell these things, but thanks for saying so anyway. And you're right, I shouldn't worry."

"I have a very good sense of these things actually." A genuine smile popped through Charlie, and this time memories of Ru's happy, if short, childhood seeped in as well. "Trust me. There's no point worrying now. You just enjoy every beautiful moment with that kid. He's going to be very special."

Dot smiled and then flicked her eyes as she looked up to glance behind Charlie. Charlie turned to see Trent and Brent approaching. She felt some of her agitation return when she saw Brent tagging along. She liked Trent's boyfriend almost as much as she liked Trent, but he wasn't someone she could discuss 'spooky stuff' with. Trent had been very clear on that. "Slacking off, hey?" Trent teased Dot as they reached the table. Brent gave her a hug and peck on the cheek, while Trent flopped into a chair next to Charlie.

"Well, I *was*! No chance of that now *you're* here."

Brent laughed as he moved around the table to give Charlie a quick peck on the cheek as well and sit opposite her. "True. Trent is always demanding when food and coffee are involved."

"Well, I'll go get started on your coffees then." Dot pushed her chair back and braced herself with her arms as she went to stand. "Pancakes too?"

Trent started nodding but stopped at Brent's raised eyebrow. He ran his hands self-consciously over the slight gut poking over his pants. Trent was far from fat or even plump. But with Brent's movie-star good looks, he had a lot of living up to do. "Ah, just the coffee this afternoon, honey. Brent is trying to convince me to join him on a diet." Dot arched her own eyebrow as she ran her gaze over Brent's taut frame, but said nothing as she turned to bustle into the café.

"Good luck with that," Charlie jibed as the boys made themselves comfortable. "Good to see you both. Thanks for sparing me from another day all on my lonesome." Even though Charlie couldn't open up to Trent about her most recent fright just yet, the afternoon was still a welcome reprieve from the jitters that had plagued her since the Dream. It was almost 5:30

p.m. when Dot finally poked her head around the door to let them know she'd closed up the café and to replace the chairs when they were done.

"Ooh, it's getting a bit nippy, isn't it?" Trent said several minutes later as a chill began to pick up in the air. The light was slowly fading as dusk approached and he shivered dramatically to give his words good effect. "Doesn't seem like summer lasted long this year! I'm not ready for it to be this cold just yet." Charlie was nodding in agreement as the temperature dropped even further, despite the stillness around them. Her breath seemed to push rather than flow into her throat, as if the cold had swollen the air. The fine hairs on her arm stood straight as goosebumps began to prickle her skin.

She recognised the sensation mere moments before she saw it. Standing at the corner a few blocks down from them, its round moon-light eyes focused and unblinking, was the Black. Once again, its form billowed around it in veiny protrusions that infected the pavement and walls like a fungal growth. This must be what it felt like to stare into the abyss of a black hole, devoid of all colour, all light. Simply empty.

A sharp squeal pierced her reverie, sucking the breath from her and setting every nerve ending buzzing painfully. What happened next passed in moments, like brief flashes from a picture roll. The tyres of a car screeching and skidding, leaving black marks on the road. A woman's gasped scream as she jumped off the footpath on which she was standing, and out of the path of the swerving vehicle. An impossibly loud crashing sounded as the metal of the passenger-side door buckled and tore, wrapping itself around the concrete lamp-post. *Thank God the driver had been alone in the car.* The woman, who had so recently stood by that lamp-post, collapsed to her knees in shock. Breathing heavily, Charlie took in the sight of the near-miss, Dot rushing from the door behind them, and the Black now nowhere to be seen.

* * *

Charlie knelt by Marie's grave in the final light of day, the blue-tinged horizon almost glowing. With the excitement of the evening, she hadn't

10

been ready to head home just yet. Somehow, in an empty street, on a clear and fine day, the driver of the car had lost control, skidding across the road and almost hitting a nearby pedestrian. She couldn't help but feel the Black was involved, having appeared just before the near-misfortune. Charlie absently brushed the dirt and loose stones from atop Marie's grave, rubbing a palm gently over the headstone. "What do we do about this spirit, hey Marie?"

Marie had never haunted her own grave, but Charlie still felt a morose peace sitting by her final resting place. Perhaps she'd come here today because she'd met the Black in a cemetery, somewhere in Australia. Was that where the Black had been buried? Was that the place he haunted now? How would she find it? As she pondered these questions the temperature dropped yet again, falling over her like a fine frost blanket. She stood quickly, heart pounding slightly, as the shadows from the graves stretched long before her. These were the longest shadows of the day, right before the light disappeared and everything turned to shade. She shook the morbid thought free as she made her way back to the small metal fence and her car.

As she reached the fence and pushed the gate free, using a little extra grunt to shift it over clumps of unmown grass, she began to shiver. Perhaps it hadn't been such a good idea to come here in the evening after all. A deafening crack sounded above her. Charlie automatically looked up as a corner of the church's roof broke free and tumbled violently to the ground. She squealed, then lost her balance and tumbled. The roof crashed right besides where she'd been standing. It landed so heavily it didn't even bounce, dust and dirt spraying into the air. It eerily reminded her of the near-miss at the café just an hour before.

She put a palm against her chest to try to calm her heaving breaths. "Fuck!" she whispered in fear, fumbling for the keys in her pocket. She kept her eyes on the stone that had fallen free as she stepped backwards towards her car, feeling across each key for the remote that would open her black RAV4. It was now so dark she was struggling to see where, if anywhere, the Black might be hiding. "It fucking followed me after all..."

Her hand finally wrapped around the right key just as her back hit the driver's side door. Unlocking the vehicle, she swerved inside and slammed the door shut. Once again, she pulled at the white light from the Dream. She willed the white energy to form around her like a shield, to keep her safe in her car. She paused only a moment before starting the engine. She peered out the windscreen to search the church grounds for the Black. With the interior light still fading in her car, her eyes struggled to adjust, and she saw nothing.

Charlie hit the favourite's button for Tess on the car dash as soon as she could pull away from the church. *"Bonjour, ma chère!"*

"Tess!" Charlie practically shrieked as she sped a little too fast away from the church. "Another one of them's found me." There was a brief pause on the other end of the line.

"Are you okay?" There was hesitancy to the question, and Charlie cursed herself for spoiling Tess's time with Leon. She drew a deep breath before she continued, more evenly.

"Sorry, yes. It just gave me a bit of a fright is all. It's a Black. My first Black."

"Fils de pute... Do you need me to come back?" Charlie could hear the thinly-veiled disappointment in Tess's voice and took another deep breath, trying again to ease the tension in her voice.

"No, no. Sorry, no. Of course not." A tear threatened at the edge of her eye and she swallowed harshly, pushing the emotion back. "I can protect myself. That white light — that energy I can pull from the Dream — it seems to work like a shield as well. I don't think the Black can hurt me." She remembered the squealing car brakes and the broken church roof and shuddered. She began in a more measured voice. "Maryanne brought our call forward to tomorrow too, so I'm sure she'll be able to give me some good advice. Timing, huh?"

"You're sure...?"

"Yeah, totally."

"Is it one of those things from the bush? You know, those shadow people that watched you release Harry's spirit?"

Charlie thought for a moment before answering. "No. Those things were literally like shadows. The opposite of wisps, pulling their form together from the shadows around them instead of the colours. *This* Black was its own creature. It didn't need anything to help it draw its form. And it was in no way a shadow. It was so *deep*, so complete a colour."

"Charlie..." Tess's voice was hesitant.

"Yeah?"

"Whatever you do, just *don't* enter the Dream without me there."

3

The Shadow People

Charlie sat in her car, hands on the steering wheel, staring at her darkened veranda, the front door just visible from where she was sitting. She had shivers so deep in her flesh she could feel the skin pull tightly across her scalp and temples. *White light*, she thought to herself. *White light, all around me, all around the house. It's not welcome inside...* She remembered the screech of those tyres. The thud of that stone falling from the church roof. A crack sounded behind the car, causing her to jump, her chest clenching, and those pins-and-needle shivers again digging into every nerve fibre. It was the branch of one of the many gum trees, groaning as it settled in for the night. She knew that and yet she still couldn't unclench her teeth or loosen her shoulders.

White light... Charlie thought one last time before uncurling her fingers slowly from the wheel. They ached slightly as they released. She breathed out all the air from her lungs in a long, soft blow. Then shoved the car door open and ran to the house. The night air gripped onto her tightly; the abnormal cold reminding her she hadn't come home alone after all. She heard her heart thumping loudly in her ears as she slipped her front door key into the lock. The gum trees behind her creaked again, their leaves rustling slightly as though also alive to the presence that suddenly found itself among them. She slammed the door behind her, picturing that protective white curtain once again. She hadn't felt this way in her own home since the Grey had pounded on her front door. Since it had stood in the corners of her room. Had climbed on top of her in her sleep. The Grey, at least, Charlie had been able to command to leave. She wasn't so sure that would work where a Black was concerned.

She switched the lights on as she turned, inspecting the interior of her cottage. Just as she'd left it, except perhaps for a dining chair facing the wrong way courtesy of little Marie. The warmth of the room soothed her too, melting some of the ice that had settled on her — in her. "I'm safe in here," she sighed loudly, rubbing at her temples to ease the last of the tightness in the skin. Even if she couldn't send this spirit away, at least she'd figured out how to create a safe haven for herself. She dropped her bag by the front console and made her way to the kitchen, pushing the dining chair back around as she passed, and heading straight for the kettle.

A warm cup of black Russian Caravan tea in her left hand, Charlie balanced her laptop on her knees with the other. She sat on her couch, a light blanket thrown across her lap. She'd been tempted to start a fire in the fireplace, despite the fact it was still weeks until ANZAC Day. She laughed to herself at the stubborn persistence that she not use any heating until the twenty-fifth of April. An obstinate streak she'd inherited from her father who, every year, had insisted that no matter the temperature, the twenty-fifth was the first day any heating was allowed to be turned on. After a long sip of the warm, gentle tea, Charlie put the mug on the coffee table and turned the computer on. Even with Maryanne able to answer some of her questions tomorrow, she didn't want to wait. Months ago, Maryanne had told her that Blacks were almost as common as Greys. That they could even be perceived by sensitive ordinary humans *as black ghosts*. So surely, there must be *some* information available online.

In amongst advertisements from various alcohol stores offering 'black spirits' like whiskey and rum, she found the threads of conversation she was searching for. Some accounts claimed scientific explanations — akin to the sleep paralysis demons the doctors were convinced Charlie's Grey visitor had been. These asserted that those, like Charlie, who saw black spirits must be under the influence of deliriant substances or suffering from a mental illness like schizophrenia or bipolar disorder. Others dismissed the scientific 'evidence', talking instead about malevolent, evil entities: tragedy, betrayal, lovers-to-enemies, demonic presences, powerful despair, energetic parasites…even *those rejected from heaven*. Charlie tried to remind herself that internet searching about the Red spirits hadn't been all that helpful. But even those results held snippets of truth; they'd talked about Reds being spirits of incredible power. The Reds certainly were that, even if they weren't all evil. Charlie's searches about the Blacks were, just like their name, *dark*.

Charlie stopped typing as another result caught her attention. 'Shadow people'. The first account claimed there were three types of 'shadow people': troubled human spirits who were just pretending to be evil to antagonise the living; ancient and evil spirits that were never human; or demons. She shuddered again, the chill this time trickling from the back of her neck and running down her spine. Armed with the knowledge Maryanne had already shared so long ago, Charlie knew the spirit that had latched onto her was human. At least, it used to be human. There was no doubt it was a Black, and so must have suffered serious betrayal in its lifetime. Her mind turned again to the shadows that had pursued her, Tess and Trent in the bush those months ago. The ones who Maryanne said were watching, driven only to maintain the Balance; "…never human…". Perhaps these search results were more accurate than she'd wanted to believe.

She decided to open one last webpage before trying to turn her mind to mundane things, like what to have for dinner. This was a chat-thread. Charlie picked up her cup of tea again as she read with determined concentration.

Paranormal_Norman - *What are shadow people? I see them. Other people see them. But they don't seem to do anything but watch us. What are they, really? Are they evil? Are they good?*

MoonStar686 - *In Middle Eastern lore, shadow people are djinn, or demons. It's believed they live on earth, much like us humans, but in a different dimension. They LOVE abandoned places. There's heaps of* *evidence of any abandoned building being infested by shadow people. In terms of Middle Eastern lore, they're supposed to be about as intelligent as animals.*

Wisp26212 - *I'm from North Africa and we have shadow people in my lore too. I don't know about them being unintelligent though? In my culture, only certain people can see them and we call them 'they who see Jins'. As well as being able to inhabit abandoned homes, we believe Jins can reside in people, and so possess them.*

RavynMadd - *Interdimensional beings, no doubt. They cross over to our plane of existence and take on the appearance of shadows. They can't harm us but do feed off our energies. I think of them as harmless scavengers.*

DezRawk - *I agree, I don't think they can hurt us. I'm not sure what they are. I kind of use them as a warning. I would see them if I was slacking off at school. Once I quit slacking, I also quit seeing them.*

Charlie sighed and closed the lid to her laptop. Schizophrenics. Anxious teenagers. Middle Eastern sensitives. What did they all have in common with her and with the Blacks? One thing she'd decided after reading all of this: Maryanne was right about regular people (even sensitive ones) having trouble perceiving what they did. And perhaps there were more than just human spirits at play here.

* * *

Charlie tapped her pen on her lip as she re-read the notes she'd made ahead of her call with Maryanne. She wondered if this was a habit she'd picked up from Maryanne and made a conscious decision to place the pen down firmly on the table. She'd slept poorly and woken early, thoughts of djinn, demons, shadow people and the Blacks swirling in her head. She'd tried to sew clothes in the morning (for her fledgling, oft-forgotten, online clothes 'business'), but had broken *two* needles and needed to rethread the machine half a dozen times. She normally only broke one or two needles a year. Eventually she'd thrown her hands up in defeat, made a cup of tea, and gone back to the desk — blanket draped across her shoulders — to tidy her notebook and await the call with Maryanne.

Charlie shrugged and loosened her shoulders as a notification popped up on screen that there was an incoming call. She smiled as she answered, ready for the obligatory salutation. She paused mid-greeting, her mouth hanging open, as not only Maryanne's screen popped up, but a second screen as well. "Good morning, Charlotte," Maryanne said in her even tone, her chin resting nonchalantly on her interlaced fingers. "Thank you for taking my call a day early."

Charlie's eyes flicked between the relaxed Maryanne and the second screen, her eyes popping as widely as her still open mouth. The second screen was glitchy and dark, as though coming from a very poor connection. She squinted as she tried to better observe who was there. She could just make out what looked to be a dirty, unmade bed, squished on either side by wooden cupboards. The walls were claustrophobic. She jumped as a man suddenly sat in front of the camera, just as dishevelled as the bed behind him. His long-sleeve jersey hung loosely and lopsided from one shoulder. His jeans were also loose and baggy, revealing the tops of 'Bonds' underwear as he sat. A mat of dark hair stuck out at odd angles on his head. While Trent's untamed mane was endearing, this stranger's looked like he'd just tousled out of bed. He was also very lithe, tendons popping out of his slim neck, wrists and hands. A horrid, unkempt beard — largely black — hid most of his face, though a very large Adam's apple still protruded easily beneath it. As Charlie took all this in, the call glitched again, his features once again blurring.

"What the fuck?!" Charlie finally found her voice.

"Charlotte, this is Rafael. Rafael, this is Charlotte." Rafael smiled then, his white teeth gleaming more brightly than his rugged exterior might have suggested. Unkempt, but clean at least.

"G'day, Charlotte," he said in a thick Australian accent, saluting her with two fingers and a head tilt as he spoke. "But it's Raff, not Rafael. Raffa at a push."

"And it's Charlie," she mumbled, before turning her full attention to Maryanne once again. "What is this?"

Maryanne took a deep breath and fixed another fake smile to her face. Charlie now knew her well enough to tell the fakes from the real deal. "Rafael is having a problem that we think only you can help him with." Maryanne's tone was even and slow, as though explaining something to a child. "I wasn't sure if you'd agree, so I decided this was the best way forward." Charlie's mouth fell open again as she looked between them.

Wasn't sure if I'd help...?! Indignation hit first and then curiosity. *Would I?*

"Rafael is a Guide, Charlotte. You remember me telling you about the Guides, right? Each type of spirit has its own Guide; like their supernatural leaders. Rafael is one of the lucky ones, like us Seekers, who gets to keep on living while carrying out our duties. His particular spirits often interact violently with the real world, so it's important he can do the same."

Maryanne paused to let this sink in. Charlie remembered Maryanne explaining the Guides. They were entities sort of like herself. Like the spirits, they were human or had been once. Like Keepers, Guides helped spirits to accept their purpose in purgatory — but they weren't as powerful as the Keepers, who could interact with any spirit, no matter its colour. She internally chastised herself at the thought of 'power', though hierarchy was incredibly important in the Dream. Charlie realised she was still frowning at the two of them and rubbed at her forehead a tad aggressively to try to loosen the muscles. She noticed as her hand fell that all she'd achieved was leaving a large red mark.

"What spirit?" she asked, though sensing she already knew the answer before Raff gave it.

"Blacks. I've been doing this gig for about eight years now, and I've never needed help before. But something's not right with this one. It's not just a little out of whack, it's...imbalanced. As a Keeper — that being *your* job and all — Maryanne thought you might be able to help." Charlie bristled at the emphasis he put on his words and the frown returned.

Maryanne stepped in. "I know you haven't had any experience with the Blacks yet, but—"

"Actually, I *have*." Charlie interrupted stubbornly. "And I don't like your insinuation that I wouldn't have helped, or *his* insinuation that this is somehow my responsibility. My fault." It was Charlie's turn to pause and let her words sink in. "A Black arrived the night before last, pulling me through to it from my dreams, and ever since then it seems to be following me around. Causing all sorts of chaos!" Maryanne and Raff's gaze both flicked away, and Charlie realised they were examining each other's expressions.

"It could be the same one," Maryanne conceded, and Raff shrugged back. "What do you mean chaos?"

"There was nearly a car accident in town, for no apparent reason. A large part of a church roof fell and nearly hit me. My sewing machine keeps malfunctioning. Just, little bits of bad luck." Raff nodded at the explanation.

"Blacks have more impact on the world when they're imbalanced," Maryanne explained. "A balanced Black might make you feel uneasy, give you the occasional scratch, make you vomit, but not be able to do real harm. An *imbalanced* Black, on the other hand, can cause some real damage. Even deaths, on occasion. It's a little bit like Marie. When she was imbalanced, she was a more violent poltergeist, damaging your actual house. But now that you've helped her, she is more placid, only moving the odd item around, and never violently. Blacks can cause a lot of misfortune when they're off-balance. It can be quite dangerous."

"And you think this spirit I'm seeing is Rafael's spirit?" Charlie asked. Maryanne tilted her head and squinted her eyes in thought.

"It'd be a bit weird," Raff finally answered, seeming to be conversing more with Maryanne than Charlie. "Normally only one Guide can connect with any spirit at a time. Possibly there could be two of them? But who knows...? I've never had so much trouble with a spirit before." Raff's own eyes narrowed and he ducked his head slightly as he turned his gaze and stared intently at the screen.

"What...what are you doing?" Charlie finally asked.

"Willing a connection between you and my unbalanced Black, of course." Raff had said it as matter-of-factly as Maryanne might. A jolt struck Charlie at the thought of *two* of those things getting their hooks into her and the chill descended again. Without thinking she grabbed the computer mouse and clicked to disconnect the call.

"Fuck!" She ran her hands through her hair aggressively. The chill wouldn't leave her, even with the connection lost. Finally, she raised her head, her eyes catching on something through the window. It was here. Watching her. The Black, with its round moon-eyes, was right outside.

4

Into the City of Woe

Charlie jumped up so quickly her chair fell backwards, clattering noisily to the floor. Still, she couldn't tear her eyes away. The Black was a stone's throw from her house, standing under a large, old gum tree. The tree's silvery trunk, patterned with layers of circular bark, stood out starkly against the spirit's black flesh. Perhaps this was even the same tree that had been creaking the night before. The creature's tendrilled body twisted out, latching onto the trunk and branches as if it were fog come alive. Its hooked face was completely still, those huge eyes gleaming in the sunlight. It was like some horrid monster from the forums she'd been reading the night before.

Her computer beeped again and Charlie tore her eyes away, just for a moment, to see if Maryanne might be trying to call back. Not a call, but a message notification appeared on the screen. She turned back to the window, but the Black was already gone. Nothing there but the gum tree, swaying slightly. At least, she couldn't see it anymore, though she knew it was still out there, waiting and watching. Still shaking, Charlie clicked the message box open. *'I know that was unsettling, Charlotte. But you know as well as I, it won't end as easily as a phone call. I've given Rafael your number. He'll be in touch. I'll see you next Friday.'*

Charlie closed the laptop angrily, kicking the desk chair as she did.

* * *

Charlie jerked her head back as once again she nearly nodded to sleep in her chair. She'd paced the floor after ending her call with Maryanne and Raff, feeling sick to her stomach at the thought of the Black spirit watching her from outside. Potentially Black *spirits* now that Raff had tried to sic a second one on her. Whatever they were, they seemed unable to enter Charlie's house. Whether because it was one of their quirks, or because Charlie willed it to be that way, she didn't know. And she hadn't had the opportunity to ask Maryanne. That grated at her almost as much as Raff's attempt to unleash a Black on her had. She'd been looking forward to a chance to get more information from the psycho-psych, perhaps some much-needed answers. Instead, she'd gotten Raff.

She had managed to prove one of her theories about the Blacks lingering outside by attempting a walk in her hills. As soon as she'd stepped outside, she'd felt its eyes on her again, pinching into the centre of her back. She'd tried to ignore it, setting out for her walk, despite the clouded skies and threat of rain. If nothing else, Charlie was stubborn. She willed the world to fit within her own definitions (including of what the Black could do) with sheer determination. The sensation, though, had never left her, and at every third step she'd have the overwhelming urge to turn and look over her shoulder. Expecting to see those moon-eyes staring at her. She'd breathed far more heavily that walk than the hills had demanded of her, at least physically. The feeling had vanished as soon as she'd closed her front door behind her. That proved it. Unlike a Grey spirit, she couldn't *will* the Black away. She could, though, keep it outside of her house.

Despite being tempted to call Tess, Charlie decided — whether gallantly or stupidly — not to ruin her friend's time with Leon. Instead, she'd watched movies, read books, cooked, cleaned — anything to put off sleep, and the risk of the Black — or Blacks — finding her while she was dreaming. She ignored when the TV glitched or glasses fractured in the sink. Now on the other side of midnight, the TV blaring, her head began to nod again.

* * *

Charlie found herself in the Dream, thankfully in a bright afternoon day. She felt awe as she took in her surroundings. Dozens of sandstone and red brick buildings spilled out in front of and behind her, on either side of a large pale road. Cables ran above the road, with wooden trams rattling along shallow ruts. She felt herself jump as a horse and buggy swept behind her, the horse whinnying loudly and the people atop the carriage laughing and calling loudly to be heard over the din of the young city. A large building on the corner drew her attention straight away. It had beautiful details carved atop its every palisade. An ornate clock tower loomed above it all, the highest point of any surrounding building by far. A lovely rotund gazebo-style pinnacle topped the tower. She instantly recognised it from her own days living and working in this very city. Sydney Town Hall, but not as she'd ever seen it before.

The air was thick with smoke and smog, blocking any view of what might have been a pale blue sky. Men, for the most part, hurried through Sydney's streets, wearing grey, blue and tan wool suits with crisp white shirts, matching vests, and straight, thin neckties. The collars were oddly pointed only at their very tips. Each man also wore a stiff hat or, less often, a loose cap upon his head. Those wearing loose caps tended also to wear less impressive suits and more crumpled shirts. The thickness of people's blazers and coats let her know — as much as her own senses — that the weather was frightfully cold whenever it was she'd found herself. Another horse passed by her, this one pulling a full carriage, the windows hidden by thick, green curtains. It diverted her attention up and to the arched covered entrance to city hall. This was one part of the Town Hall she couldn't remember from present-day Sydney. The entranceway extended well into the road, a line of well-dressed people making their way inside.

Did my Black spirit pull me here, Charlie internally questioned, *or did Raff succeed after all? Did he send me to this part of the Dream?*

"Come along Beryl," a clipped voice ordered, distracting her. Charlie turned to see two women hurrying along the road to the Hall, dark umbrellas in hand, and ornate white lace gowns peeking out from behind their long, thick woollen coats. Each wore an immaculate, huge white hat atop her head. These women didn't look like they'd stepped out of an historic fair or re-enactment. They looked so much more: comfortable, at ease, gliding with short, brisk steps towards their goal. While both were dressed alike and were close enough in looks Charlie figured they must be related, they were a distorted reflection of each other. Beryl was a slim, soft woman with lips the colour of roses, the perfect button nose, and a youthful glow to her skin. Her honeyed hair curled in playful ringlets, despite the tight bun in which it had been placed. Charlie couldn't help but notice, even under that coat, that Beryl's figure was deliciously curved.

The first woman, however, while also slim, had harsh and stocky lines to her figure. She was slightly shorter, with a heavier chin, sharp pointed nose, and deep dimpled cheeks. Her dark blonde hair showed none of the shine or curls of Beryl's. "Don't fuss, Addie," the other woman said in a softer, if similarly clipped, voice. "See? There's our entourage now." She skipped happily the last few steps to a couple of gentlemen standing at the edge of the road, who were obviously relieved the women had finally arrived.

"Good stuff, ladies." The first tipped his hat and offered his arm to Beryl.

"We thought you wouldn't make it," the second said in a thick accent, taking Addie's arm in his, slightly more roughly than his fellow. Like some of the more random convicts in Charlie's most recent major encounter, these two men were blurred. Their features indistinguishable, indicating to her they weren't who she was here for. She was here for Beryl or Addie. Perhaps even both of them.

Is one of you my Black spirit? Or Raff's?

The four joined the throng of people moving into the Town Hall and Charlie followed behind. Although she'd been to Town Hall before, the sight of it at this point in time filled her with awe. The panelled ceilings and ornate archways along the walls she knew, but the brilliant lights that lit up the grand hall, the fine red curtains and carpets, and the hundreds, if not thousands, of chairs positioned not only on the floor but up in the balconies stunned her. The atmosphere was positively electric, excited murmuring and laughter vibrating through the air. Addie, Beryl and their escorts quickly found their seats with the help of a finely dressed usher, towards the left of the stage and in the centre of the room. The girls had offed their coats on entry to the building, and now sat delicately, patting scented handkerchiefs to their nose as they waited for proceedings to commence.

Charlie tried to focus on the two girls, but her attention was soon diverted by what unfolded that day. An organ struck up loudly, its reverberating echoes humming deep in her soul, at once reminding her of church. Or at least of something ethereal. A man, oddly dressed in what at first looked like red pyjamas, introduced the main event, speaking at length about the wonders of Italian cinema. This, it seemed, was a showing of the movie, *Dante's inferno.* When the silent black-and-white film started, accompanied by the organ and narration of the would-be devil, the crowd fell so silent it was as though they were dead themselves, and awaiting their journey *'into the city of woe'.* The narrator's strong voice, paired with the deep, thrumming and trilling of the organ, pulled Charlie — along with the other spectators — into those ever-deepening layers of hell.

Images of writhing, often-naked, human bodies soon filled the screen against a backdrop of dramatic mountain landscapes. The actors were drama personified, each movement deliberate, exaggerated. Their acting reminiscent of a shout when a whisper would have worked just as well. The flourishes were jilted, staccato, which Charlie realised quickly was due to the low frame rate. All along, as the scenes unfolded, the devilish narrator boomed, *"Dante imagines himself lost in a dark and gloomy wood..."*

When the intermission brought the masterpiece to a momentary pause, silence hung for several heartbeats. Then the crowd erupted into cheers and applause, turning to each other to begin their excited recounts. "I've never seen anything like it!" Beryl breathed, clasping Addie's hand in hers. "When those damned souls were blown around in the winds of hell... Well, it was almost as if I was there. How ever did they manage to make them fly around?"

"I for one found it unrealistic that carnal sinners would be so lightly punished, in that very first circle of hell," Addie said. "So close to the unbaptised babies and uneducated pagans... Surely they should have been deeper, at least deeper than the misers!" She flinched as her companion laughed loudly at her summary.

"Oh Addie," he said. "You are a prude."

"I thought it was *romantic*," Beryl breathed, squeezing a program in her gloved hands and bringing it to her chin in joy. "Poor Francesca."

It was Beryl's companion's turn to laugh this time, though more softly. He gently took the program from her. "Trust you to find the beauty in amongst all that horror, Beryl!" He began to read from the program, which Charlie realised as he did so contained the narration to the film. "One day for our delight we read of Lancelot, how him love thrilled, alone we were and no suspicion near us. Then he at once my lips all trembling kissed..." Beryl blushed and Addie scoffed, fanning herself with her own program and staring back towards the stage.

Beryl smiled not so shyly as she batted her eyes at her companion and recited back, "The stormy blasts of Hell with restless fury drives them on."

5

One Man's Trash…

Charlie opened her eyes slowly, staring up at her darkened living room ceiling. Her throat grated when she tried to swallow, and her lips at first stuck together and then pulled apart in tiny pinches of pain. She rubbed her hand across them and found them dry, flaky. She sat slowly, a pain instantly building behind her eyes and across her forehead. Her vision faded to white at the edges for a moment. *Fuck, not again…* She fumbled in her pocket for her mobile phone to check the time and cursed, aloud this time, when she found the battery completely depleted. *How long was I stuck in the Dream this time?*

She wobbled to her feet and stumbled to the kitchen, her legs spasming slightly and feeling much heavier than they should. She grabbed a glass from the kitchen sink, filled it with water from the tap, and drank slowly. Her stomach unclenched as the water made its way down her barren gullet. Leaning on the bench, she checked the time on the microwave oven: 22:33. She'd obviously been in the Dream for the rest of Thursday night and all of Friday. Almost twenty-four hours. "Fuck," she whispered to herself again, her voice catching slightly on her roughened throat. She refilled her cup of water and walked around the island bench to take a seat at one of the stools there. Staying so long in the Dream had only happened once before, when she was still learning the importance of intent and control. She'd been so scared of heading into the Dream with the Blacks. *Did I do this to myself? Or*

28

is Raff to blame? Her fear of the Blacks didn't seem so warranted now; at least, not after what she'd just experienced.

After another cup of water was downed, she made her way to her bedroom to retrieve her phone charger (via the restroom) and set herself back up on the couch. Aside from a photo message from Tess — of her, Ella and Leon trying wedding cakes — Charlie hadn't missed anything much. She went straight to her phone internet browser and typed the quote she most clearly remembered from the film, *'The stormy blasts of Hell with restless fury drives them on.'*

"Dante's Divine Comedy…" she read aloud. "The vision of Hell…"

She kept tapping at her phone, *'Dante's Divine Comedy Sydney Town Hall 1900s'.* The first result was an online newspaper archive and exactly what she was looking for: *'Dante's Inferno at Town Hall, 29 June 1912'.* She spent the next few minutes, until her stomach urged her back to the kitchen for food, learning about *L'inferno*, the first full-length Italian movie. A horror that had been met with rave receptions worldwide following its initial release in 1911 after three years in production. She spent an hour watching the black-and-white movie on YouTube, marvelling — though perhaps not so much as Beryl and Addie had — at how much better the special effects were than she expected for a film so old.

Is one of you my Black spirit, Addie and Beryl? she thought to herself. *Or Raff's?* Before drifting back to sleep, this time Charlie made her way to her bedroom, setting an alarm for the morning. *Thank God Tess is back tomorrow.*

* * *

Despite her fears of being sucked back into the Dream, Charlie woke early Saturday morning from a restful, dreamless slumber. A misting rain fell against her bedroom window as she flung open the curtains, staring out at the pale grasslands, laced with a light fog. She felt a ball of anticipation and excitement form in the pit of her chest, between her ribs. *Tess is home today.* It hadn't been that long apart, and she'd always been the fiercely independent type until now, but she still couldn't wait to not be alone in this house anymore. *Well...at least not isolated from* living *companions. I suppose I'm never truly alone anymore.*

From this window, Charlie could just see the gum tree at the front of the house under which the Black had stood a couple of days before. There was nothing to be seen of it today. Just beautiful, misty Australian landscape. A parakeet trilled happily from its hidden perch and Charlie took this as a good omen and rushed to shower and to tidy the living space before Tess, Trent and Brent arrived. The latter two eager to see this 'house-on-wheels' Tess was bringing back with her.

A pot of coffee was brewing, her tea steeping, and a batch of scones cooling in the oven, when Trent and Brent arrived bang-on time at 9:30 a.m. "Smells bloody good." Trent smacked his hands together as he stepped into the cottage. Brent followed behind with a bulging brown paper bag in one hand, and his recently removed scarf in the other. He gave Charlie a peck on the cheek before making his way to the kitchen like it was his own. "Brent brought just a couple of little somethings for brunch too." Charlie walked over to investigate as Brent removed a large Tupperware container filled to the brim with large, flaky croissants.

"Shut the fuck up!" Charlie said happily as she popped the lid and took a deep breath, the scent of the still slightly warm croissants caressing her face with buttery fingers. "You did not make these did you?" Brent chuckled and shrugged one shoulder with self-deprecating affirmation. "Oh, you suck up." She gave Brent another kiss on the cheek before heading to the fridge for her small selection of jams and a pot of whipped cream. "You make my scones look like crap."

"They look good to me." Trent had pulled the oven door slightly ajar. "Can I get them out?" Charlie nodded and motioned with her head to a wooden bowl she'd already pulled out of the cupboards. "Ooh, they're fluffy!"

"My secret ingredient is lemonade," Charlie winked at him. As they pottered in the kitchen, Charlie heard the unmistakable crunch of car tyres on her gravel driveway. She perked up immediately, feeling her eyes widen with anticipation and the smile tugging at her mouth. "That's Tess then!" She headed to the door with almost as much of a skip in her step as Beryl had at the Sydney Town Hall, flinging the door open to see Tess's beaten-up Subaru sedan pulling in front of the house, a terrible looking 'tiny house' dragged behind it. It certainly was tiny, only just over two metres long and a little less than that wide. Its tin roof was badly rusted, the windows boarded up, the wooden frame so badly peeling it had less paint than not remaining, and the dust shield over its tyres also showing more rust than metal.

Charlie hopped down the steps of her veranda as the car and the monstrosity behind came to a stop. "What the fuck is that?" Trent said slightly too loudly, and undiplomatically, as Tess stepped out of the car, also beaming.

"Welcome home!" Charlie threw her arms around her friend, squeezing her tightly. She smelt like bodywash and rain, and was nicely warmed from the interior heater of her car. Charlie relished the feel of Tess's now shoulder-length curtain of dark hair brushing across her cheek and shoulder. Tess's smooth skin had darkened slightly over summer, making her bright blue eyes stand out all the clearer. Days of working in their gardens had slightly hardened her previously soft arms and hips, though not unpleasantly — at least to Charlie. She doubted Tess could ever look unpleasant in her eyes. Charlie's heart twanged momentarily, longing for the type of romantic relationship of Lancelot and Francesca from *L'Inferno*, but equally knowing that could never be. Tess was more than a friend, true. She was family, a sister, and now Charlie's tether to the living world. Never would it morph into anything more romantic, though, no matter how hard Charlie's heart might secretly long for that. Tess was as straight as the Mormon Tabernacle Choir.

"*Salut, ma chère.*" She kissed Charlie on each cheek before looking up over her shoulder to Trent and Brent. "*Bonjour, mes amis!*" She skipped up the stairs to hug and kiss the boys before spinning dramatically, and with an air of strong satisfaction, to gaze out at her tiny house. "Isn't it spectacular?!"

"That's one word for it," Trent muttered, followed by a loud grunt as Brent cleared his throat. "Needs a bit of work, honey!"

"I have all the plans sorted, *mon cher*, don't you worry your pretty little head. Come and see?"

"Why don't we have those delicious scones and coffee first, love?" Brent turned to go back inside, Trent eagerly following. Tess showed only a moment's hesitation and then Charlie's hand was on her arm.

"It is *so* good to have you home."

* * *

Bellies full, and a second pot of coffee already nothing but dregs, the four of them had investigated Tess's tiny home. It was even worse on the inside, the old single-bed frame seeming to have rotten, the floor spongy and sagging underfoot, and the rest of it gutted. There were harsh scratches and ruts in the walls where cupboards had evidently already been removed.

The most surprising thing upon opening the double doors had been a second, unplanned purchase. A 4WD buggy sat on the floor, fixed in place with blocks and wedges temporarily drilled in place in front of and behind each tyre. It barely fit in the tiny house; Charlie pictured Tess and the person she'd purchased it from awkwardly shuffling and pushing to get it inside. It had two seats, the covers torn with yellowed fuzz poking out. The canvas tarp was also ripped in several places and hanging loose.

"Does it even work?" Trent had said in a voice so quiet Charlie wasn't sure Tess had been meant to hear.

"You bet! Blows a bit of smoke but runs fine. And he threw it in so cheap!"

"I wonder why…" Trent had again muttered, receiving an elbow jab in the ribs from Brent.

Back at the dining table, the conversation had revolved around Tess's plans for the tiny house, and the septic toilets she'd been researching. They'd agreed to set up an Air BnB empire near the ruins of the old stockmen's quarters at the other end of Charlie's property. The quarters were a collection of buildings from the late 1800s, now fallen into significant disrepair, but laced with history. They were also the location that the terrifying Grey — the spirit of a murderous and murdered swagman — had haunted. Trent excitedly threw in his ideas for information boards for the ruins, filled with some of the town's and the homestead's history. A loud bang at the front of the house instantly silenced their conversation, with Tess calling out in shock at the sound. It had been as though a large stone had been thrown at the window, reverberating through the walls of the cottage.

"What the hell?" Charlie got to her feet and walked slowly to the window, her heart hammering as she once again remembered the Black. The spirit she hadn't yet been able to warn Tess or Trent about. *Not here, not now, not with Brent...* She frowned as she got to the window, noticing a slight crack not quite deep enough to run the full width of the pane. A small smear of deep red blood marred the surface. Her racing heart now sent shivers of numbness down her fingers. She peered through the window carefully, not wanting to press her face up against it.

Crumpled at the foot of the house, its wings bent, its neck arced unnaturally, its clawed feet frozen, and its white eyes staring, was a crow. A dead one.

6

Omens

"What the fuck…" Trent retracted the stick he'd used to poke the dead bird. "That thing must have been flying pretty fast to off itself like this." Tess had her arms around her chest, squeezing tight and shivering as she looked nervously at the bird and all around her. Charlie, standing just behind Trent, trembled too. It wasn't just that the Autumn air brought a bite with it. She could feel them again; those moon-eyes boring into her back. She wondered if Tess could feel them too, the way she kept on fidgeting. Brent — evidently the smart one of the bunch — had opted to stay inside rather than poke at a crazed dead crow with a stick. "This is that spooky stuff you mentioned the other day, isn't it?" Trent had obviously seen the agitation in Charlie's face. She nodded briskly, looking up at the window to make sure Brent wasn't in earshot.

"We're still keeping all this secret from Brent?" she asked. Trent nodded solemnly. "It's my first Black spirit." She paused for dramatic effect, filling in the blanks when they each stared at her blankly. "The spirits of people who have been betrayed or abused in life. It's not like anything I imagined, though. Whatever this spirit is, it's not like the others. It's…*malicious*… I want to say evil, except…" Her voice trailed off as she remembered Addie and Beryl enjoying the cinema. "…except they're victims, I suppose. Or at least, they were. God knows what they are now."

"What else?" Tess asked firmly. Charlie quickly recounted the near misses

34

at Dot's and the church, the sensation of being watched, and seeing the Black standing outside the house. She felt heat rising from her collarbones as she debriefed on her call with Maryanne and Raff, and his attempts to unleash a second of these spirits on her. Tess's cheeks grew in colour too.

"Because of the cinema, we know we're dealing with a spirit, or sprits, from the 1910s. Or at least, they lived through the early 1910s." Charlie paused as Brent came to the window, tapping to get their attention and see what was taking so long. The three of them waved and started to slowly make their way back to the front of the house.

"I'm afraid a couple of women named Beryl and Addie who passed through Sydney in 1912 isn't much to go on…" Trent scratched at his ear and then ran his hands through his hair, making it stand even more on end. "You know me, I'll help when I can. Just keep me looped in."

Charlie squeezed her shoulders tighter together as the sensation of being observed grew deeper. She shivered uncontrollably as they approach the front door. She twisted slightly to look behind her, expecting to see the Black looming over them, and instead reeling as a dark blur sped at her. She felt herself falling backwards. Her chest burst as it was hit with adrenaline. The shriek that accompanied that flash was so close it was like someone had screamed directly into her ear. Her hearing instantly began to whine, blurring yet another of her senses as whatever it was plummeted past her. Tess screamed next and then there was a thud, even louder than before, rattling the wood of the front door.

As she spun, still trying to take stock of what had happened in mere seconds, her eyes fell on it. Another crow. Another twisted, broken, bleeding crow. Well and truly deceased.

* * *

After mumbling about bird diseases, Brent had convinced Trent it was time they went home. That was, after they'd ensured Tess was okay. The crow had scraped Tess's scalp with either its claws or beak as it had barrelled to its death against the front door. It wasn't a deep scratch, but still significant enough to bleed. And with Brent's concerns about plague-ridden birds, it seemed only sensible to thoroughly disinfect the wound.

"Keep me updated," Trent said as he kissed Charlie's forehead, pulling back from a quick hug. "Look after each other." Charlie gave a nod, then waved enthusiastically to Brent, who was hopping into the passenger-side seat. "We'll catch up again soon," he promised, before jogging to join his partner.

"This just keeps getting weirder and weirder," Tess mumbled as the two of them made their way back inside the warm house. With a cup of tea in hand, they took their usual seats on the couch and continued to discuss what had happened with the birds. "And you're sure this thing can't come inside the house?"

Charlie nodded, trying to reassure her friend even though she herself couldn't shake the pins-and-needles in the back of her ribs. "It's like with the convicts on the road. I think by picturing that white light, that energy from the Dream, and drawing it back around the house, it sort of acts like a shield."

"Even better than salt and sage," Tess tried to joke, though from her expression Charlie could tell she was considering throwing them in for equal measure. Charlie's phone pinged and she picked it up without thinking, unlocking the screen.

"Fuck," she groaned as she saw the first words of the text.

"What?!"

"It's Raff." Charlie double tapped the message to open it and read it aloud. *"Charlotte, it's Raff. We need to meet. This Monday, 2 Pacific Street, Newcastle, 11:00 a.m."*

"Can we trust him?" Tess asked, taking the phone from Charlie to re-read the message again herself. "Fucking Maryanne…"

"I don't think we have a choice, do we? There never seems to be coincidences with this crap. First I dream about the Black, and then Maryanne shows up with a Black Guide needing my assistance? It's connected, no doubt about it. And Maryanne's right. As much as I hate to admit it. If I don't help, it won't end. And dead birds certainly won't be the last or the worst of it."

* * *

Charlie frowned as she examined the buggy, which, with some difficulty, she and Tess had extricated from the tiny house that morning. It now sat beneath a gum tree a stone's throw from the cottage. It looked even bleaker in full daylight, with its rust, tears, sags and dents on full display. Charlie grimaced as she grabbed the frame of the buggy and pulled herself into the passenger seat. She'd wiped it down, but she could still feel that yellowed stuffing from the seat scratching against her back and bottom. Tess laughed and swatted at Charlie when she looked over and saw her expression. "Don't be such a wuss! It's fine!"

"I think your definition of 'fine' is different to mine. Must mean something different in French..."

Tess started the engine and as it rumbled to life a cloud of white smoke shot up and out of the buggy, along with the heady pong of diesel fumes. Charlie coughed and put a hand to her mouth. *"Une nouvelle aventure nous attend!"*

Charlie squealed and grabbed at the front of the buggy as it lurched forwards and started rumbling through the grass. Tess just continued to laugh.

They'd decided to hit their problem head on, and for Charlie to enter the Dream with intent. To seek out this spirit and determine what was wrong with it, so they could be rid of it, and quickly. The only hiccup with their plan was that they didn't want to try anything in — or near — the house, lest they accidentally let the spirit inside. They'd waited until morning and were now making their way to the stockmen's quarters ruins. If all went well, maybe they could draw the Black spirit there and leave it to roam the abandoned buildings while Charlie figured out how to help it move on.

Miraculously, the buggy made it to the ruins without any more issues than the puffs of white smoke that trailed behind them. Tess patted the nose of the buggy affectionately as she hopped out, as though thanking a sturdy steed. "I'm going to have to give this guy a name."

"You're going to name your buggy?"

"I think I'll call him *mon canard*."

"*Canard*? Duck?" Charlie asked. Tess nodded and made her way towards the ruins, with Charlie shaking her head and rolling her eyes as she followed behind. The Autumn morning was once again cool, and so early in the day, a light mist still clung to the air, dangling across the ruin's pale stones and caressing the dewy grass. She always felt a thrill at the sight of the ruins; some of the broken walls reached for the heavens proudly, while others barely peeked above the tall grass. Their now-empty windows and doors — those that remained intact — were like portals to an older time. In the mist, they held a sense not just of abandonment and isolation, but also of veneration and taboo. "Maybe we should have come later, when this fog was gone…"

"It does feel a little eerie, *ma chère*." As they crossed over to the largest of the ruined buildings, long grass swishing at their knees, Charlie carrying a picnic blanket, Tess vocalised a thought that had been nagging at Charlie as well. "I wonder what happened to that Grey. He hasn't moved on, as far as we know. So where is he? If Marie is still in the house, then is he still here?"

Images of the Grey who had haunted Charlie all those months ago returned unbidden. The abnormally tall, thin spirit with the piercing white eyes that was drawn to pain and terror, and who revelled in inflicting the same emotions on others. The Greys might be one of the most 'common' types of spirits — a fact her mentor, Maryanne, liked to remind her — but they would never feel common to her. Maybe because this particular Grey — a murderous swagman — had been one of the first spirits Charlie had ever encountered. And perhaps because of all the torment he had caused both Charlie and Marie's spirit. Tess and Charlie hadn't seen any sign of the Grey since Charlie had finally set Marie's spirit free from him. They'd always assumed that these ruins, where the swagman had spent his final months of life, had been his place to haunt.

Charlie pulled her puffer coat more tightly around her and peered through the fog at the outlines of the ruined buildings. "I don't know where he is.

But I don't think he's here. I'm pretty much ready to piss myself with fear, and he wouldn't be able to resist coming on over to soak that up." Morose thoughts still cycling through her head, Charlie asked another question she'd yet to speak aloud, as they made themselves comfortable on the picnic mat. "Can you feel the Black looking at you too? Did you feel it when that crow attacked us?"

Tess tilted her head as she thought, crossing her legs and encouraging Charlie to lay her head in her lap. "I think I felt something," she said, nodding, already running her hands through Charlie's hair to help calm her down. "Mostly unease, like we weren't alone. Just a buzz to the air. Does that make sense?" Charlie nodded.

"Okay, let's do this. No more procrastinating." Charlie visualised her intent as she closed her eyes, trying to relax every part of her body as she prepared to enter the Dream. *What is imbalanced? What is wrong?* Charlie felt herself slipping into the Dream as she held her goal firmly in her mind. She couldn't help but also feel icy tendrils across the top of her shoulders and the backs of her arms as she fell to the Dream. She didn't want to give the Black any more power over her, any more fear, but as she entered the Waiting Place the emotion entered with her. She was once again standing in the off-white, greyish columns, archways and platforms of the Waiting Place. Stairways led off in all sorts of directions and there was a constant sense of movement, worsened as she herself pivoted. It hardened the fear into a little ball inside her. Here in purgatory, she would find her answers. *What is wrong with the Black spirit?* she willed, despite her angst.

The skin at the back of Charlie's scalp tightened and tingled, and she turned, coming face-to-face with the Black. Not just behind her, but mere inches away. This close, its eyes were enormous, glistening so sharply she almost couldn't look directly at them. Instead, her eyes were drawn to that inky blackness, so deep she feared if she touched it, she'd be consumed and fall forever in its darkness. The Black's sharp hook of a face leered at her, so close that if it were to bend just slightly, it would knock the top of her head. *I'm here*, she sent to the creature. Deep, dark energy waved back off it and towards her. She desperately wanted to take a step backwards, to flee, but also feared losing ground. Feared losing sight of it, in case it whisked off again to a hiding place from which it could watch her. *What is wrong?*

The beak split, opening wide, that same white shine of its eyes now beaming through the crack in its bird-like mouth. The shriek it emitted — so similar to the crow's — wasn't just a sound, but a reverberation, an energy in this place. In amongst its call was a word, formed as if by inhuman lips: *liar!* She shuddered as it hit her and she was pulled into her intent and away from the dreamscape.

She found herself in a dark, small room. A smell of mouthwash, copper and bleach hit her as she tried to take in her surroundings. It was too dark to see much more than the vague outline of corners. She felt the spirit's absolute anguish, though, even if she was not able to see it. Its pain let her know beyond doubt that it was present in this space with her. This memory, whatever it was, must be connected to her intent. It must be related to whatever was wrong with this spirit. Grief flowed in waves, but not just sadness. Loss, anger, betrayal — *despair*. A large clack sounded, as if of a stool being shoved, and in the minimal light she caught a glimpse of a shadow, swaying, spasming. The sound of a rope echoed over the stool, snapping taut, and then twisting and groaning as if holding significant weight.

Charlie gasped as she pulled herself free of the Dream and came to, her head still in Tess's lap. She looked up at the cloud-filled sky with relief to be free not just of that darkness, but of that malady of emotions. *"Ma chère?"*

Charlie rubbed at the side of her nose and one eye as she sat. "I think I saw it die..." She puffed out her lips in a half-hearted raspberry, before turning to face Tess, whose eyes were creased in concentration and concern. "It wouldn't show me much. It's like it... wasn't ready? It's hard to explain. I saw no tether though. No other spirit. It's alone. It's full of despair. And it's certainly malevolent."

40

7

Into 'the Hellhole'

The sky had cleared overnight, and only wisps of grey clouds were left to mar the blue sky. Charlie and Tess were once again entering the city of Newcastle. The strong mining and shipping industries, and vibrant economy, gave Newcastle a commercial feel, despite its idyllic beaches and friendly residents. Before they'd left, when the girls had told him where they were going, Trent had been unable to resist sharing another titbit of history. *'You know, they used to call Newcastle the 'hellhole' because it was where the most dangerous convicts were sent to mine coal.'*

Due to how often they frequented Newcastle for their spooky adventures, it was beginning to feel like a second home. First, they'd visited a descendent of stockman Kapiri when freeing Marie. Then they'd been introduced to Zac, who'd excavated the convict dig site. Now they were here to meet Raff, a Guide. The first living, breathing, talking 'human' connected to the Dream, to purgatory, that Charlie would meet in person. She'd never met Maryanne in the flesh, always speaking to her via video call. And the only other Keeper she'd ever visited in the real world, Alex Cooper, had been in a coma. All the other spirits had existed only in the Dream. As much as she bristled at the way she and Raff had been introduced, she couldn't help her intense curiosity and anticipation at meeting him.

The address Raff had given them was certainly not in any 'hellhole', but in the hippiest part of Newcastle, right near the beach. Well-kept gardens lined the street, beautifully maintained heritage buildings overlooked the ocean, and every now and then a colourful graffiti mural stood proudly on an otherwise bare brick wall. "*Chic*," Tess murmured, looking out the window as they circled the one-way streets, looking for a carpark. They found one on the road snaking along the beach's path. Charlie breathed deeply as she exited the car and the fresh, salty breeze ruffled her hair.

"The map says *2 Pacific Street* is just across the road, up there." Charlie nodded up a slight hill, holding her phone in her hands. "Must be that big building?" The building was four storeys tall, entirely red brick, and with what could pass for towers on its corners. It was well-constructed, with tall narrow windows on every façade. From this distance, she guessed it must be some sort of public building. Perhaps office space. As they crossed the road and drew closer, she noted balconies on some of the levels, filled with potted plants and airing clothes on drying racks. "An apartment building?"

"Looks like it," Tess agreed. Their guess was confirmed as they reached it, seeing glass doors leading into a foyer, and silver metal postal boxes on one wall. '*The North Wing, 2 Pacific Street*' was spelt out in crisp white letters on the door. Tess peered through the glass as Charlie took a step back to look up at the building's front. This close, it felt imposing, putting a crick in her neck as she craned to see its roof. The white metal bars across the bottom windows didn't help ease her ill-feelings. "But which apartment is his?" Charlie thought back to the gloomy video call, struggling to match up the scruffy man with these luxury-looking apartments. "And what do you think North Wing means?"

"It was a hospital," a mid-tempo, thickly accented voice spoke behind them. Charlie jumped and squawked as she turned to find Raff standing behind her. Raff looked even worse in high definition. He was wearing the same jersey he had days ago, but this close she could see every loose thread and poorly patched tear. It also had splotches of yellow and brown down the front and on the collar, perhaps from lunch some days ago. His baggy black jeans were far too large for him, and he held them up by shoving his hands into his pockets and lifting up the fabric. His black hair was shoulder-length, straight, wispy and slightly oily. His only redeeming feature, in Charlie's opinion, were his slightly shimmering green eyes.

"Fuck! Don't creep up on me!" Charlie wanted to add 'you creep' at the end of her admonishment, but bit her tongue.

Raff laughed, shrugging. "Hazard of the job." As he held out a hand to her, one side of his pants hung dangerously low, showing the top of yet another pair of Bonds underwear. Charlie swallowed as she took a step forward to quickly shake his hand. She'd feared his smell would match his appearance, but this close, all she could smell was cheap soap with a subtle hint of wood smoke. His hands, while slightly rough, were also clean.

"I'm Tess!" She didn't seem to have as much hesitation as Charlie, smiling brightly as she hurried forward to give him her own hand. "I'm Charlie's tether; we're a double deal these days." Raff arched a dark, bushy eyebrow at Tess and smiled lopsidedly. "So, which apartment is yours?"

Raff burst out laughing, doubling over, and slapping his free hand on the top of his jeans. Charlie felt sorry for anyone who might be walking behind him, copping an eyeful of his tightie-whities. "*HA*! I wish." He shoved his hand back in his pocket, chuckling to himself as he turned and headed across the road. "Nah, we're not going in unfortunately. That would be great! But there's no way I can afford their Air BnB rates."

"So why here?" Charlie jogged to catch up to him as he crossed the road and made his way to the green park on the opposite side.

"It's as far as I've traced them," he said ambiguously, looking at her briefly over his shoulder, as he continued to make his way into the park. From the road, Charlie hadn't realised just how large or beautiful the gardens would be. The same red bricks formed a path, with dark stone shallow walls on each side, and bright green, well-trimmed grass in front of them. Grass for Tess to envy! It was soft and perfect. The biggest Moreton Bay fig tree Charlie had ever seen arched over them like some humongous umbrella. Its beautifully twisted roots spread out nearly as far as its fanning branches. Fallen yellowed and brown leaves made a carpet between the roots, and somewhere above them a parakeet chirped.

"Them *who*?" Charlie jogged again to catch up with Raff, whose long legs spurred him on and to a grassy patch beneath the giant tree. It was only then that Charlie noticed he had a long, thin roll slung over his shoulder. He shimmied it off and opened the clasps to reveal a picnic mat, which he spread on the ground before hiking his pants back up.

He spun and then fell back on the mat with a satisfied sigh, patting the ground beside him in invitation as he answered. "The sisters, of course. Did I manage to get a connection through for you?" Charlie's mouth dropped open and she turned to look at Tess, whose eyes were also widened, but in bright curiosity. She took Raff's invitation first and sat beside him, folding her knees neatly beneath her.

"You've seen them too, then?" she breathed excitedly. "Charlie only just told me about them a couple of days ago. Addie and Beryl. You know who they are?"

"Wait, rewind." Charlie held her hands in front of her, still standing rigid and refusing to sit. "I am *not sitting* until you tell me what the hell is going on, what you know, and who the fuck you are." Tess's eyes widened slightly further and she pursed her lips, but Raff just laughed again. It sounded hollow, forced, fake. She didn't trust him.

"I promise, I don't bite." He patted the mat again but when Charlie refused to move, he continued. "Maryanne did say you were stubborn." She bristled at the thought of Maryanne, *her* mentor, sharing details about her with anyone, let alone this bogan. "I've been seeing Maryanne for eight years now. She's the Seeker who found me, told me what my purpose is. As she told you, I'm a Guide for the Blacks. I keep them in check, stop them from causing too much havoc. Sometimes they push the boundaries, you know? Torment people they shouldn't. Cause a little too much havoc. I calm them down. I can do what you do, at least for the Blacks, and help them to accept their purpose, their fate. At least for this part of their journey. I used to be a carpenter before all this, before…well, before things changed for me."

"How is what you do different to what Charlie does?" Tess asked Raff curiously as she made herself comfortable besides him. Charlie glared at them both, which Tess chose to ignore.

"Most spirits can't hurt ordinary folks, at least not badly. A Black will occasionally scratch someone, pinch them, shove them. All perfectly normal and acceptable behaviour for a Black while they process everything that's happened to them. When something is *off* though, and that's the only way I can think to describe it, the spirit gets thrown out of whack too. Sometimes, they don't accept that they've passed on, or they don't realise they're dead. Sometimes they refuse to accept the cards fate has dealt them. Dying can be pretty confusing!

"I guide the Blacks. Teach them what they need to do while they linger in purgatory. Help them get that revenge they may not know they need. Most often, I coax spirits out of the darkness and confusion. Spirits *very rarely* step out of line, and even then, not in a big way. Hmm…" Raff rubbed his stubbled chin as he thought, reaching for an example. "Last year there was a woman who started breaking bones, which *is* taking it too far. She'd been grounded in purgatory *a long* time though. When I got involved, she actually moved on, out of purgatory and to whatever comes next. Whether to heaven or hell, reincarnation even, I've no idea. None of us knows what comes next. That part is pretty neat, though. It's indescribable, seeing what happens when their work is done."

Charlie hadn't experienced that yet. If she was honest, she hadn't even considered it. Hadn't let herself think about that next step. So far, her experience had been limited to fixing imbalanced spirits. Helping Marie to become a Blue. Helping the Yellows to untether themselves. Helping the Red to accept his purpose. Nudging the odd Purple to accept its fate as well. She wondered how long Marie would stay in the cottage before heaven called her home. She liked to think that was where Marie was destined.

"When a spirit is unbalanced, though, they get more powerful," Raff continued. "It's like Maryanne said. The mischievous Blues can become poltergeists, able to throw the world into disarray when normally they'd only be able to move a cup or chair. A *Black*, well… When they're imbalanced, they can take their revenge too far. Deaths have happened. This is where the Keepers come in." Raff nodded at Charlie as he said this. "When the cases get complicated, and need a little more oomph, Keepers figure out what's wrong and fix it. They've also been known to step in when the Guides don't do their jobs properly, or if the Guides start vying for control or power over the other types of spirits. That hasn't happened in my time, but still… Nasty business when people step out of line."

Charlie thought of the Grey, then, and how it had tried to turn Marie into a Grey rather than the Blue she was destined to be. Perhaps that was the type of thing Raff meant. When a spirit reached too far, for dominance over another type of spirit. Charlie found herself letting her guard down as Raff educated both her and Tess, peeling back the curtains to this mysterious world in a way Maryanne never had. She took a tentative step forward. "And the sisters?" Her mind was a whirlwind of new ideas already. She needed to focus on the task at hand.

"I dreamt about them for the first time a couple of months ago," Raff said. "You do that too, right? See parts of the spirits' lives when they were still human?" Charlie nodded. "Well, that's how it started for me this time. But when I tried to figure out which one was the Black, reached out to the spirit, there was resistance. It felt *wrong*. It felt violent. Well, more violent than normal. It took me and Maryanne a while to figure out the spirit must be imbalanced. That's where you come in. I'm glad I could help you connect with them."

Charlie clenched her fists but finally sat, for which Tess gave her a brief smile. "You and Maryanne said imbalanced spirits can be dangerous? Can hurt people? Is it possible my Black and your Black are the same spirit?" Out of the corner of her eye, she saw Tess tentatively touch the scratch on her scalp.

Raff frowned at Charlie, shaking his head slightly. "Yeah, nah… Nah… That's not how it works. Spirits can only connect to one Guide at a time. *I'm* the one connected to this spirit. It shouldn't be able to connect to you as well. At least, not like that. Glimpses, yeah. I can encourage a limited connection, like what I did through the video call. But you shouldn't be able to bring it to your house."

"That Black spirit that has been watching me at home is this bird-like thing with horrible silver moon-eyes. Is that the same?"

"Hm." Raff again scratched at the stubble on his chin and neck as he stretched back, thinking. "I don't think that's my Black. Interesting… two imbalanced Blacks. You really do have all the fun, Charlotte."

"It's Charlie."

"Charlie then. My Black isn't roaming around anywhere, certainly not to your house. It's not connected to a Keeper, it's not that lucky. Mine will be trapped in the place it's haunting." Raff paused at Charlie's look of confusion. "What, Maryanne hasn't told you this yet?" He laughed his same forced laugh and shook his head again, his mop of hair swinging around his ears. "Tsk tsk, Maryanne. Sloppy. Spirits can't normally just move all about however they please. At least, not human spirits. They're usually bound somewhere, or to something. Normally to the place they died, or somewhere that meant a lot to them in life. Sometimes to where they're buried, but not often. I even helped a Black spirit that was connected to a locket once. That's when you might get spirits moving, when they're tied to an object and the object itself moves. Think haunted paintings and mirrors."

Charlie played Raff's words over in her head. It made sense. Outside of the Dream, the only spirit who continued to stick around her was Marie, who haunted the house she'd once lived in. The spirits of the Great North Road had been tethered to where the Red had died. And all those others — those Blues and Purples — she'd never seen them again outside of the Waiting Place. The only ones that didn't make sense were the Black and the wisp of Ru's mother who'd followed her home. "But...?" she probed.

"*But*, for a Keeper, it's different. You're not like the rest of us Guides. You can connect with all spirits, not just one type. And once you connect to them, they can move with you. Follow you. Maryanne really should have let you know. I mean, I guess normally, you wouldn't be *walking* around the real world. You'd be off floating through the Dream somewhere. So maybe she didn't put two-and-two together."

"And so why are we here?" Tess jumped in, with the shock silencing Charlie for a moment. "You tracked them here?"

"Yup. They worked here at some point. The Royal Newcastle Hospital, at least when it still was a hospital. I haven't been able to get in, and they haven't presented themselves to me. I'm hoping you, the all-powerful Keeper, will be able to help. That you'll be able to tell me if *this* is where she's haunting."

8

Simples

Charlie lay on the mat with her head in Tess's lap. Raff sat to the side, staring down at her with his head on a slight tilt. "It really is strange seeing one of you in the flesh," he said after a moment. From this angle his Adams apple looked even more obscene as it bobbed and weaved under his throat beard.

"I feel strange doing this in public," Charlie breathed in reply, looking instead at the leaves above her. The fig leaves filtered the light beautifully, not so much through them as it would if this were a gum tree, but around them.

"You get used to it," she heard Raff say. "I did, anyway. Plus, when you look like me, not many people come and tap you on the shoulder to check if you're okay when you're staring into space." Charlie felt a little uncomfortable at Raff calling out his own appearance, and closed her eyes, preparing herself to enter the Dream, focusing her intent on this hospital and Addie and Beryl. Blocking out the uneasy thoughts. For the first time in a long time, the Dream resisted slightly. She pushed back, reaching for the sisters. "Focus on the hospital…" she heard Raff from a far distance, whispering into her mind almost like the spirits would, without words so much as resolve. "I'm willing a connection again."

Who lingers at Royal Newcastle Hospital? Charlie found herself straddling what felt like several worlds at once. She could see the Hospital as it stood now, an apartment building overlooking a vibrant, bustling harbour. But it flickered, as though she were peering through an old zoetrope, a spinning circle of individual pictures that together, with tricks of light, blurred into motion. One moment, all was as it was in the present day. The next, the red brick buildings spilled out to the right of the North Wing, dwarfing it at least four times over, each structure more elaborately detailed than the last with beautiful pinnacles atop the pointed rooves. The next moment, the visage was more like it was now, but with horrid concrete buildings replacing those delicate spires. A smokestack burnt behind the North Ward, spewing smog, both behind those beautiful buildings and the concrete monster.

Then the North Ward was completely gone, a tiny cottage in its place, and the beautifully pointed building with its spires was back. It flickered, some moments large and long, others halved or even quartered in size. The most confronting of all was when nothing stood there at all, excepting small gum trees and squat salt bushes amongst the native grasses. The ocean rolled against the shore in clear view. She squinted as another building occasionally disturbed that scene, sandstone and squat, a single door and two windows, single chimney, and Union Jack flag flying high atop it. *"Focus on the time now..."* This was Raff's voice? *"The 1910s..."*

She was back to that spired building, the North Ward vanished again. She counted three spired, pointed rooves, another two buildings further along, and that cottage standing where the North Ward should be. *Are you here, Addie? Beryl?*

"They were here, I can sense her..." Focusing in on Raff's voice she matched her intent to what he was experiencing.

Take me to them. Charlie blinked as she found herself in a wide, open room. White, thin tables ran down its middle, and white beds along each wall. The beds were narrow, small, something she herself would struggle to fit in with her height. The floor was dark, but the walls a pale cream. Lights danced across the ceiling and along the floor from a series of half-bowl lanterns, suspended from the ceiling above every second bed. A woman in a pale blue, long-sleeved, stiff cotton dress was bent over one of the beds, replacing the sheets. She wore a white apron that covered her entire front, crisscrossing on her back. Her honey-coloured hair was pulled up into a tight bun. Several

49

other nurses and patients were present, Charlie knew, but they blurred so much to her it was easy to ignore them. *Beryl?* Another nurse bustled into the room, wearing the same uniform, her darker hair in an identical bun.

"Beryl!" Addie confirmed, speaking in whispered, urgent words as she sped across the room, her black heeled boots clicking on the ground. "The Matron wants to see us. *Now.* In her office." Beryl's cheeks coloured slightly as she turned to her sister.

"Did she say about what?" Beryl asked. Addie grabbed her sister's elbow, nodding to the other nurses as she pulled her along.

"Of course not. But you know it's not worth dilly-dallying when *she* calls after you." Charlie followed them through the hospital until they came to a small office, with a single window and a dark walnut desk. An older woman sat there, not a wrinkle to be seen on her dress, or a mark to be seen on her apron. Every hair was tidied, held back in place in her perfect white cap. Her eyes and the corners of her lips were the most wrinkled of her features, giving her a pinched and fierce look. The flickering lanterns and candles in this room deepened the lines of the woman's face.

"You asked for us, Matron Hartley?" Addie said politely, her head poking through the door. The Matron silently motioned them inside with a single curl of her finger, then stood slowly and made her way around the desk to where the two girls were standing. She eyed them carefully, walking slowly around them, picking at imaginary lint from their uniforms.

"How long have you been with us now?" she asked in a rasping voice that spoke of too much tobacco.

"I've been here three years, and Beryl two months shy of that."

"Mmhmm, and I've only called you to my office a handful of times in that period."

"Yes ma'am." The Matron nodded, finally finished her inspection. She returned to her desk, placing her fingertips atop its surface.

"I'm told you both have a satisfactory academic record." Matron Hartley opened the top drawer of her desk, extracting two neatly folded white caps. Beryl gasped slightly before she could catch herself and Addie's eyes widened. The Matron smiled, easing some of the frown lines in her face.

"I thought you might want to do this together before we make things official. Congratulations, Miss Beryl Morgan. Congratulations, Miss Adelaide Morgan. Nurses, you may now put on your bows."

* * *

As it so often did, the Dream had left Charlie with a lot more questions than answers. Questions she wanted to throw at Trent about the hospital and what sort of interaction she'd just witnessed as soon as she could get him on the phone. And answers she wanted to wrangle from Raff, though she was still struggling to phrase her questions in her mind. The Dream had felt different this time, more devoid of information. Like watching a video of history, rather than living that history for herself. Before the three of them had debriefed, they'd purchased hot chips and coffee from one of the nearest cafés. They sat by the seaside, the fast food spread in front of them. Charlie stared at Raff. Perhaps glared was a better word. Trying to figure out where to start and if there was anything she was missing in what had just happened.

"That was your voice in the Dream, wasn't it?" she asked. "Helping me to drill down where I needed to go?" Raff paused, a large handful of chips halfway to his mouth. He shoved them in, chewing loudly with his cheeks extended like a chipmunk, before starting to answer her around the half-chewed potato and grease.

"Yup." He paused to lick some of the salt off his fingers. "I wasn't fully in the Dream with you, but I knew it might be hard for you to track down a spirit that's connected to me, not you, so..." He took a loud slurp of his coffee and leant back on one elbow, brushing the crumbs from his beard and onto his jersey, but missing quite a few of them. "I was so hoping they'd be there, but there was no sign of the Black spirit. Just an echo of its life. At least we found out it's not there anymore. Just a few lingering memories. Back to the drawing board!"

Charlie thought this through, grappling to hold onto concepts Raff seemed to have no trouble with at all. It seemed to come so naturally to him. Was that because he'd been doing this for eight years already, or was it simply because he was a natural? Charlie thought about the vision she and Raff had shared. Normally, when a spirit pulled her into the Dream or she reached out to connect, she could almost feel their intent and emotions. Even if she didn't understand what she was seeing in the moment, she knew it was part of the puzzle. In this instance, however, all they'd seen was a memory. It had held no spirit, no substance.

"We have their full names now though," Tess added, eating her chips one at a time in delicately pinched fingers. "That'll help us find out more about who they are, and maybe where they are now."

"Oh, I knew their names already." Raff reached for another huge helping of chips, some of them falling to the mat as he pulled them towards him. "And that they were born in Newcastle, in the late 1800s, less than a year apart. Two of *thirteen* children. Knew they were nurses too."

"And you didn't think to mention this before, because…?" Charlie deliberately picked her food from the bucket of chips Raff hadn't touched. Registering this, Raff reached for that same bucket next.

"Well, it's not normally all that important, is it? All that family and history stuff. Blacks are usually pretty straightforward. They're betrayed or abused, usually by someone they were close to, and now their spirits need to exact some delicious revenge before they can move on. Simples."

"*Casse-couilles…* Things are never simple where Charlie is involved." Tess smiled and winked at Charlie as she said this to take some of the sting out.

"If you need more information, I've got some back at my place. It's how I found out the sisters trained to be nurses at this hospital. It's all in Adelaide's journal, if you want it." Charlie's mouth dropped open, thankfully with no food inside.

"*Yes*! Yes, of course! Of course I want it. Why didn't you say so before? What else does it say?"

Raff shrugged and sat up straight again, pulling at a crick in his neck. "Dunno, I never read it all. I'm not really big on reading. Or history. I was kinda hoping this hospital would be bang on the money. If you like all that boring shite, you be my guest."

* * *

Tess was soon driving her and Charlie out of town, following Raff in his old and rusting Toyota Landcruiser to a random pin-drop he'd sent to Charlie's phone. It hadn't filled her with confidence; neither did the fact it would apparently take them fifty-three minutes to get there. It looked like it was in the middle of nowhere. She could picture Raff as a serial killer, even though Tess seemed to be getting along fine with him. No accounting for her taste.

Charlie stared out the window at the passing streets and cars, thinking how much Newcastle must have changed over the past two hundred years. Thinking of those visions of the Royal Newcastle Hospital and how much it had altered over the decades. It was a shame the oldest building, the one with its pointed spires, hadn't survived. As she was staring out the window, she caught glimpses of tombstones through the gum trees. A cemetery, and a large one, was passing by on their righthand side. Charlie was about to turn her gaze to the other window when something else caught her attention. A red-bricked church, tall and pointed, with a crucifix barely visible through the trees above it.

"Oh my God, Tess, *stop!*" Charlie shouted. Tess jumped and started swearing, swerving slightly as she looked for the imaginary obstacle or danger she'd evidently missed. "Tess! It's the cemetery, *the* cemetery. Where I saw the Black. *Stop!*"

9

To Live Like This

Tess — perhaps a better driver than Charlie — hadn't screeched to a stop on the fast-moving highway. Instead, she'd turned right at the next set of traffic lights, which thankfully took them around the other side of the enormous cemetery. They passed the first red brick gate, Charlie's heart thumping between her ears as she read the sign 'Sandgate Cemetery'. They passed a second red gate, still unable to turn into the cemetery with the large grassed and fenced island splitting the road in two. Charlie pulled at her seatbelt, shifting to the edge of her seat, trying to see if she recognised anything more. The cemetery extended all the way down the road, a large blue sign at its end repeating what had been marked on the gates before 'Sandgate Cemetery, Sandgate Cemetery, Sandgate Cemetery'.

Tess made an illegal U-turn at the lights, to the irate beeping of the car behind her, and then pulled into the first gate, parking beside two other empty cars. Charlie unbuckled her seatbelt as soon as they passed the red bricks and was opening her car door before Tess could even come to a full stop. She inhaled deeply as she saw the same sights she had in her dream. Hundreds, thousands, of graves spreading in all directions. She saw the palm trees, oddly misplaced, lining the central path. As she moved forwards, Tess came beside her, tugging on her shoulder. "We'd better let Raff know we stopped, *ma chère*." Charlie nodded absently, pulling her phone from the side pocket of her jeans and passing it to Tess. Tess knew the passcode as well as her own.

Scanning the morose landscape, Charlie saw something else she recognised. Moving to a jog now, she weaved her way through the simple dirt and gravel paths towards the small, ruined, red bricked building. She paused as she saw it, cordoned off by large temporary fencing, signs warning 'ASBESTOS' on every edge. She laced her fingers through the fence, holding tightly as she pulled her face closer. It was exactly the same. The crossed metal beams across the missing wall. The rubbish strewn across its foundations. The two windows, through which she almost expected to see the Black staring back at her.

"I called him," Tess said as she joined her, tapping Charlie on the shoulder with her phone so she could take it back from her. "He's turning around. What is this?"

"I have no idea," Charlie breathed, turning to look at Tess. "It still gets me, every time. Seeing a place from the Dream, where I've never been before, in real life." Reminding her that all the craziness was, if still mental, then at least real. "He was right there..." she pointed to the window before unlacing her fingers from the fence and turning to look at Tess again, who was swatting at her arms and legs.

"What's with all these fucking mosquitos?"

Charlie noticed them then too. Black, with white stripes, dozens of them, swarming around every exposed patch of skin, resting on the thin fabric covering her arms. It was odd seeing the blood-sucking insects when the weather was so cold. The cemetery was full of damp, though. The perfect breeding ground. She began swatting too, able to hear their whining now they'd been pointed out to her. She took in the cemetery in more detail. The water puddled in some of the graves. The cracked and crumbling headstones. The weeds sprouting in the poorly tended plots. Decay, everywhere. Small midgy bugs joined the mosquitos, dancing in the damp, cold around them. Cockatoos screeched from the palm trees and other imported British trees, perhaps standing-in as Australia's cemetery ravens.

"It's pretty run down, isn't it?" Charlie said aloud as she inspected some of the headstones more closely. If they weren't blackened with age, then they had turned orange, covered with lichen. Some no longer had headstones at all. She looked further afield. Some of the graves had cracked in the centre, bending inwards as if the ground were trying to swallow them up. Others were thrust outwards, as if rejected by the very earth on which they sat. Or perhaps their inhabitants were looking for an escape. Peering down, she could see thin splinters of stone — the faces of the headstones which had crumpled, taking with them the names and eulogies of people long passed. As she looked down, she caught sight of more mosquitos, resting on her arms, and swatted at them.

"Do you know which grave you're looking for?" Tess spun to take in the thousands of plots around her. "Did you see?" Charlie looked as well. Most were single plots, tightly crammed together, though there were also mausoleum-style graves occasionally dotting the rows and rows. Or fenced areas, no doubt holding the burial sites of multiple family members.

"No." She sighed the word out, feeling the weight of those thousands of bodies pushing down on her. She could wander in here for hours. Days! If she had to read every tombstone. Or at least, the ones that still had visible names. She perked up slightly as she remembered one other prominent feature from her Dream, and what she'd seen from the road. "The church, though. *That* I remember clearly. I saw it from the other side. Come on." They began their trek to the opposite boundary of the mammoth grounds. When they walked under the cool shade of trees the mosquitos swarmed in even greater numbers, and their hands were constantly moving to slap at their faces and arms. At one point, passing a huge old tree draped with ancient cobwebs, they saw a mummified spider, which made them both shiver even more. Eventually, they moved back to the main road through the centre of the grounds. At least here, the bugs thinned out and the air didn't feel quite so sorrowful, cold or oppressive.

It took them almost fifteen minutes to reach the church, which they caught sight of as soon as the road bent to the right. It was just as Charlie remembered it. Small, but domineering, reaching to the sky, surrounded by the unending sea of tombs. Its crucifix was the highest reaching point, and a pale path led between the graves to its bright white front door. "This is the last place I saw it," Charlie whispered as they stood in the church's shadow, feeling even colder, shivering slightly.

"It's Catholic," Tess said with confidence, laying one of her hands on the red bricks. "I'm certain. This must be the Catholic section of the cemetery."

"So the spirit was Catholic?"

Tess didn't answer the rhetorical question, but Charlie hadn't expected her to. She placed her own hand on the cold, rough bricks as well. Hoping to feel something, find some hint or clue. At first all she felt was chill clay, but then an avalanche of sorrow smashed into her, taking her breath away. She blinked as her eyes went dark, momentarily almost seeing a figure kneeling over something, wailing, crying. "You okay?"

"Y-yeah..." Charlie shook herself and removed her hand. "Just an impression. They were so miserable...so sad..." She craned her neck to look at the church, past its red bricks, past its shallow and darkened alcoves, to the cross that stood proud against the blue and cloudy sky. "They lost something. Maybe a child? I want to say a child." She shook herself. "It's gone, I don't know."

Tess placed a cold hand on Charlie's shoulder, her icy fingers seeping through the thin cotton. Tess obviously hadn't expected to spend so much time in the cold Autumn air and hadn't dressed for the weather. She grimaced as she looked around them. "Do we have to look through *all* of these graves?" She sounded less than enthused, and Charlie shook her head.

"No, no. That would be pointless. I don't know the name of my Black spirit. And even if we found Addie or Beryl, we can't be sure which one of them is Raff's Black yet. At least we know where they might be buried. Trent can probably dig up the rest for us." Tess arched an eyebrow at her. "Oh, God! Pun *not* intended."

* * *

Raff had been waiting for them at their car when they'd returned, leaning against the front door of Charlie's Rav4, one leg bent, dirty shoe marring the paintwork. Charlie — through a pinched frown — had quickly explained to him why they'd stopped, to which they'd received a "Bugger me" response, but seemingly no deeper interest than that. Before long they were back on the road, heading out of Newcastle with the bustle of cars and trucks speeding along the highway. Though the city was soon behind them, and nothing but trees on either side, the business and bluster of the coastal town seemed to follow them along the road.

Charlie's feelings didn't improve as they turned off the highway and began making their way through the trees. They were all tall, their branches reaching for the sky, almost in competition with each other. Every trunk was either pale, almost white, or dark, almost black. It was a forest like any other in New South Wales, except Charlie couldn't fight off the feeling she wasn't welcome here. Didn't belong amongst these ominous trees. Rubbish on the side of the road, either black bulging garbage bags or rotting furniture, ironically rested besides 'report illegal dumping' signs. This didn't make her feel any better.

The road became worse the further they travelled, recent rain having washed ruts into the path. She was glad she had a 4WD with high clearance as they bumped the final way down the path. There were no signs here. If not for that pin drop, and the muddied white Landcruiser bumping along in front of them, she'd have no clue where to go next. They pulled into what she assumed was a large campground, again with no signs, no facilities, just a large open patch of dirt amidst the trees. A caravan as beaten-up as Raff's 4WD was pulled to the side of the road, not far from a burnt-out car and dumped, soiled mattress. She couldn't help her pinched lips and curled nose as she jumped down from her own vehicle and surveyed the scenes around her. Native birds made a pleasant noise in the surrounding trees, though they were instantly overtaken by the roar of an aeroplane flying somewhere overhead.

"Home, sweet home!" Raff said as he passed them and headed to the caravan, a set of keys jangling from one hand. He patted the door fondly as he twisted the key in the lock, grunting a little as the door stuck and he pulled it free. Tess poked her head inside after Raff, even taking a tentative step inside, while Charlie stayed as far back as she could. She recognised the messy bed taking up an entire side of the caravan from that gloomy video call with Maryanne. To the right was a squished kitchenette, with a sink, microwave oven, and two cupboards. Both were peeling paint, the corners chipped to reveal cheap plywood. The smell — like dirty socks soaked in vinegar — was enough to encourage her to retract her head as soon as she'd dared to glance inside.

Raff soon exited the caravan, a thick, aged and leather-bound book in one hand. He flicked his oily hair out of his eyes and sat on the caravan steps, the whole thing swaying as he did so. "Adelaide's diary," he smiled as he held it out for Charlie. He held onto it as Charlie tried to take it from him, smirked, and finally released it as she tugged it.

"Where'd you get this?" Charlie flicked it open carefully and glanced at the finely scrawled words, in perfect looped cursive. The pages were slightly yellowed as she'd expected, but still very much legible. Dates helpfully lined the top of each entry, which she gently and reverently traced with her fingers. Raff just shrugged. "Seriously, where?"

"Does she always ask this many questions?" Raff ignored Charlie again, turning to Tess. "Doesn't bloody matter, does it?" He glared at Charlie a little stubbornly and she relented, closing the book and holding it tightly in her hands.

"Why do you stay so far out of town?" Tess asked instead, deflecting Raff's own deflection with another question, one hand on her hip, and the other motioning around them. "Surely there's places in town with… facilities…"

"This is free." Raff kicked his feet out. "It's quiet. I don't have to explain myself to nosy families who ask too many questions, or who call the cops because they think I'm a homeless bum." He raised an eyebrow at her with a small smile, and Tess sheepishly smiled back. "Charlie should be able to tell you. It's a lonely life. Normally, anyway. And it's better this way."

"What *is* it like being a Guide?" Tess leant against the caravan now, looking sideways at Raff. "Maryanne answers our questions to a point, but doesn't exactly go too deep into the details."

"Nah, fair dinkum. She doesn't, does she?" The ocker accent made Charlie bristle, but she listened carefully as well, unable to help her curiosity. "Not much more to tell, though. I live like this! Travelling wherever the spirits pull me, staying away from living people as much as I can. The nightmares, you know? It's bullshit having to explain that crap — why you're waking up screaming — to strangers over-and-over." He paused as he looked Tess up and down. "Charlie's lucky to have you." He then turned to stare directly at Charlie. "Lucky to be here at all."

Tess yelled out at that moment, and Charlie broke off her staring contest with Raff to see her fall to the ground, instantly rolling over and curling up to grab at her elbow. *"Ça me fait chier!"* she groaned as she rolled over and onto her knees, still clutching at her arm with a pained expression.

"What happened?!" Charlie yelled as she ran to help her friend sit up. Tess was not the clumsy type. Between Tess's whitened fingers, Charlie could see that her elbow was red and grazed, thin beads of blood starting to appear where the skin had been rubbed free. Raff had stood, but didn't get any closer, his expressionless face unreadable.

"Something fucking pushed me!"

10

Beginning January 1909

Charlie settled into the living room couch, a cup of hot tea steaming on the coffee table. Neither Raff nor Charlie had seen what had pushed Tess down the previous day, though she suspected it was her own Black spirit. Whatever it was, it had been enough to encourage the two of them to leave soon after. With Tess nursing her bruised elbow, Charlie had taken the keys, eager to leave Raff behind in his rusted caravan in the middle of nowhere. As she'd started the car, Tess had wound down her window and Raff had leant against the roof on that side. "Thanks for everything," Tess had said, smiling up at him. Raff had shrugged, and then Tess had said something completely unexpected. "You should come and stay with us. We have plenty of space at the property. I mean, until this is all over."

Even though Raff hadn't agreed, telling Tess he'd think it over, Charlie had still been steaming on the drive home. "Why would you do that? We barely know him."

"You were the one who wants this over quickly, *ma chère*," she'd said. "It makes sense to work together." Charlie hadn't been able to argue with that, but for whatever reason, it still hadn't sat right with her.

Reminiscing over, she blew on her mug, taking a slow sip. The hot liquid slid pleasantly down her throat to nestle in her belly like a warm ember. Tea always had a calming effect on her. She reverently picked up Adelaide's diary, unlacing the leather ties around it, and carefully opening it. In the centre of the first cream page was written: *'Diary of Adelaide Mable Morgan. Beginning 10 January 1909.'* The handwriting was beautiful. Cursive in style, though thankfully still legible. She could differentiate each letter, despite the beautiful loops. And so, she began to read.

* * *

Sunday 10 January 1909

The day is finally arriving. Tomorrow, I shall depart for Newcastle to begin my three-years study as a nurse at the Royal Newcastle Hospital. After church today, I ensured my trunk was neatly packed, my train ticket safely ensconced in my purse. This journal is my parting gift from my Mama and Papa. My brothers and sisters are no doubt jealous. However, as the eldest, it is only right that they mark the occasion of my parting. And besides, tomorrow is my birthday.

My sister Beryl shall have to take over my duties at home, minding the younger children. She shall have Sophie to help her I suppose. I expect the older boys shall be little use. This task will become all the more important, with Mama expecting another baby in the Fall. I do so hope this shall be the last of them, as much as I adore my brothers and sisters. She seems weaker every day.

It is due to the loss of young Grace last year, and Ava just some months gone, that I expect Mama is pining for another babe to wrap her arms around. We all feel the loss of my dear sisters keenly. Consumption is a beast! Their deaths, indeed, are a good part of what has driven me to this profession. I think of them now as I write, and as I prepare to make this journey.

Monday 11 January 1909

The weather this morning was fitting for my departure. The sun was fierce, but a cool breeze took away some of its heat. Papa walked me to the station, with dear Beryl, Finn and Mary trailing behind. The others stayed back to tend to Mama, who took unwell again last night.

I am here now, with the other nurses in training, at the Royal Newcastle Hospital. The building is quite something to behold. I find myself fearing I shall become lost in its endless halls. Each ward looks so alike, each room. I don't know how anyone finds their way. Some of the other nursing students seem to know each other already, and so I find myself at somewhat of a disadvantage. This far from home, I've never found things to be so busy and yet so lonely. I miss Beryl and the others terribly.

The new students were introduced to Matron Hartley on arrival, who at once admonished several girls for having their hair loose or dresses wrinkled. I found her to be magnificent, if somewhat daunting. I do so hope we'll get along. Some of the older girls whispered over dinner how strict she is, saying she made them pay for broken syringes out of their own wages. I shall mind my step, as I must keep every shilling safe to send back to Mama.

* * *

Charlie found herself skimming the next several entries, which spoke of the chores and lessons that Addie was subjected to. The entries, which had started almost daily, started to stretch to weekly. Addie seemed to have difficulty making friends, or at least didn't write of any in her journal entries, preferring to describe the weather of all things. It was when Charlie reached March 1909, and a screwed-up docket from Woolworths supermarket, that she realised she'd read as far as Raff probably had. Thinking, no doubt, he'd found the answers. She threw the receipt to the side and continued reading.

* * *

Monday 1 March 1909

I had the most unexpected surprise today. I am working the day shift at present, and when I returned to the nurses' quarters this evening, who should I find waiting for me but my own dear sister, Beryl. I have never been so shocked and so happy. I'm relieved to no longer feel alone. She claims to have written to me at the hospital advising of her decision to follow me into the nursing profession. However, if such a letter exists, I am yet to see it.

Of course, I do now worry for Mama. Beryl tells me she takes to her bed most days, barely strong enough to last more than an hour or two on her feet. This baby is taxing her. Sophie is only nine, and Mary seven. They will struggle to wrangle the other six children, with a seventh now on the way. Nicholas and Connor, then, the oldest boys, shall have to step-up at home.

While I am of course worried for my family, I am so pleased to have Beryl here. I am also pleased she has decided to follow my example. We shall make such a difference in this world, together. I shall look out for her, and she for me. So far, I have avoided the ire of the Matron and, with luck and each other, surely we shall continue to do so!

* * *

Charlie was about to start on the next entry when an almighty crash rattled the windowpanes. She felt the vibrations shuddering up her legs and through her chest, building as the crunching, crushing noise grew in intensity. It was followed almost immediately by a whimpered cry. "Tess!" Charlie dropped the journal, shuffling and rocking as she attempted to extricate herself from her comfortable position on the couch and rush to her friend's aid. She stumbled to the door and down the veranda towards the garden where Tess had been working.

At first, Charlie saw nothing as she frantically scanned the yard. Just the hedges and trees that Tess had planted. Then Tess whimpered again and Charlie spotted her, crumpled to the ground, barely visible behind the greenery. Charlie ran down the back veranda steps and around the shrubs to find Tess cowering with her hands covering her head, and the concrete bird bath she'd only just set-up smashed to pieces beside her. "*Ça m'emmerde...ça fait chier...quesquecette merde...*"

"Tess! Tess!" Charlie crouched beside her, gently taking her head in her hands and turning her towards her so she could see if she was hurt. Blood rushed over one of Tess's eyes from a large cut across her eyebrow, already swollen red and tinged dark purple. The blood pumped with each beat of Tess's heart, spraying over her lip and splattering her shirt. "Oh my God, Tess!" Tess's hands were shaking as Charlie gently pulled them away from her pale face. "We've got to get you checked out. *Fuck...*" Charlie shrugged her light cardigan off her shoulders, balling it up to hold to Tess's head, not caring that the fine beige cotton would now be ruined beyond repair. "Can you stand?"

"*Oui..* I think I can." Charlie supported Tess under one armpit, while holding the makeshift dressing with the other. She stumbled slightly against her.

"What the hell happened?"

"It's after me, *ma chère*. I don't know what I did to piss it off, but I saw it just before that bird bath crashed onto my head.' She whimpered again then, squeezing her eyes shut. "Your Black is after me."

* * *

Trent met Charlie at the small Greenfields Hospital. He'd left the library as soon as Charlie had called him, once they'd hit phone reception fifteen minutes out of town. So he was ready and waiting when Charlie pulled into the emergency drop-off bays. He pushed a wheelchair towards the car, which caused another flurry of French profanity to spew from Tess.

"It's just a precaution, Tess," Charlie said stubbornly, turning off the ignition and opening her car door. She'd move the car later and risk a ticket. This was an emergency after all. She made it round to the other side of the car in time to help Trent practically pull Tess into the chair. He'd neglected to put the break on, and so the wheelchair spun back and forth as they eased her into the seat.

"Fuck me," Trent whistled at the site of Tess, blood soaking the cardigan and splashed down her face and onto her white shirt. His face turned a pale shade of green. "What happened?!"

"That stupid concrete bird bath fell on her head."

"How the hell does that even happen?" Charlie and Trent continued their quick-fire conversation as Charlie pushed the wheelchair along the concrete path to the glass sliding doors, which whooshed open as they approached. There were only two other people in the waiting room — a young Mum and her wriggling toddler. She had a spew bag in her lap and her phone blared the latest children's TV show. The nurse beneath the 'want to see a doctor?' sign got to her feet as the three of them bustled in like a circus side-show.

The nurse disappeared and then reappeared quickly through a side door, walking calmly but determinedly to meet them in front of the admissions window. "Looks like a nasty bump to the head, love. Who have we here?" Charlie tumbled over herself to explain what had happened as the nurse calmly checked Tess over. "Ah yes, you'll need some stitches, love." She looked up at Charlie then, adding a reassuring, "heads tend to be dramatic. They always bleed a lot. We'll get her through to the doctor next. You alright, Trent?" The nurse smiled up at him as she stood, reaching for the nearby hand sanitiser.

"Never better, honey." Trent smiled automatically, and the nurse swiped her card on the reader by the door to let herself back in.

"I'll get you the admission paperwork. You just make yourself comfy. It won't be long."

11

The White Plague

Trent had gone back to work by the time Tess and Charlie finished with the doctor. Tess had been given six stitches. After telling Charlie how to keep the wound clean, the doctor placed a hand softly on her elbow and leant in close. "Do you have a moment to talk in private, Miss White?" Charlie flinched in brief shock before nodding quickly and letting the doctor guide her from the room.

"I won't be long, Tess. Just rest up." The doctor took Charlie a few steps down the hallway and into an empty room close by. Light danced through the windows on the freshly made bed, and the smell of antiseptic was heady. "Is everything okay?" Charlie continued to whisper despite their now complete privacy.

"Was there anyone else at the house with you this morning? Does Tess have a boyfriend, perhaps, who visits?"

Charlie shook her head slowly, maintaining eye contact with the doctor whose gaze was fixed directly on her. "No, she doesn't. Why?"

"Perhaps a secret boyfriend…"

"I would know. She tells me everything. And even if she didn't, it's kind of hard to sneak into my place. I'm in the middle of nowhere." The doctor nodded his head in slow motion as if deep in thought. "Why?" Charlie emphasised as she repeated her question.

"There are marks on your friend's shoulder and back. Scratches and bruises where someone has grabbed her firmly. And from the look of her elbow and knee, this isn't the first time she's been pushed down recently." Charlie pinched her lips, trying to keep her expression otherwise neutral.

"She fell the other day."

"Yes, that's what Miss Boucher said too. But you're *sure* the bird bath just lost its balance today?" Charlie didn't answer. "Look, if you or Miss Boucher ever need to talk to anyone, or if you ever need help, it's okay. I've seen Miss Boucher's public health records. I know this isn't the first time..." He slipped a card into Charlie's hand and squeezed it briefly, before exiting the room. He paused at the door to say over his shoulder, "You don't have to be alone in this." Charlie stood there a moment before uncurling her hand and reading the orange and black text on the white card: *'National Domestic Family and Sexual Violence Counselling Service'*.

* * *

By the next day, Tess's right eye was so swollen and purple, it looked like someone had swung at her with a cricket bat. She'd pulled a loose woollen cap low over her forehead and draped her hair over that side of her face like a partially closed curtain. "Are you sure you're happy to go out?" Charlie had reiterated as they'd gotten to the car.

"Well, I'm not staying home by myself with that *thing* after me. And we need Trent to help us figure out what's happened to this Black — to those sisters — to piss them off so much. So yeah, I'm sure."

Dot had gasped loudly when she'd caught sight of Tess, reaching out on motherly instinct to pull the cap back and inspect her more closely. Tess had winced at Dot's touch and pulled the cap down tighter. "I'll be damned!" Dot breathed. "What happened darling?"

"I'm okay, really. It looks worse than it is. *N'en fais pas trop...Merci*, I'm okay."

"The bird bath fell on her while she was gardening," Charlie explained, when Tess still refused to make eye contact. Dot gasped again and began tsking.

"Well, no coffee for you today, my love. Not good for all that bleeding. I'm going to make you one of my own herbal tea remedies. It will help with the swelling and bruising, mark my words, it will." Dot continued muttering to herself as she hurried inside her shop.

Trent jogged up from the corner at that moment, his satchel hanging over his shoulder, a slight puff in his voice. "Sorry I'm late! Thomas screwed up entering the new books into the library system and I had to show him how to fix it." He gave Charlie a quick peck on the forehead and flinched as he saw Tess. "Fuck me, Tess. You look like you've been hit by a bus!"

"Thanks, *mon cher*," Tess said glibly, putting one hand up to shield her face and her offending eye. "This better not become the talk of the town. Trust me, it's *nothing*. I've had far worse."

"Charlie said yesterday it was *the Black*," Trent whispered as he sat, ducking his head forward. "Did you see it?"

Tess nodded, adjusting her cap and pulling her hair across her face again. "I did… One minute I was pulling out weeds, and the next this dark shape just loomed up out of nowhere. It was sort of like a human, I suppose, but so much taller. Then down came the bird bath on my head."

"You're lucky, really," Trent said. "That thing was a concrete monster. It could have been much worse." Dot came through the front doors with Charlie and Trent's coffees on a tray and a pot of tea that smelt horrible. The vapours wisping from its spout smelt like plastic that had been left in the sun too long, mixed with an acrid bitterness. Charlie took her delicious milky latte a little sheepishly as she watched Tess's face contort in disgust.

"*C'est dégueulasse…*" she whispered under breath before looking up at Dot with a pained, false smile. "What is it?"

"I know it doesn't smell or even taste the best, dear, but it's just the thing to help bring that bruising and swelling down. Green tea, steeped with aloe vera juice and turmeric, and just a little ginger to take some of the taste away."

"*Merci*, Dot." She took a slow and hesitant sip as Dot watched. "Ah, it's not so bad. It smells worse. Thank you." Dot nodded in satisfaction and then was gone to attend her other customers.

"For whatever reason, this Black that's attached itself to me seems out to get Tess." Charlie leant in close to speak with Trent. "First the crows, then being pushed down at that camp, and now this. Plus, the doctor found hand marks on Tess's shoulder and back that she can't even remember getting. *Please* tell me you found something about those sisters? I have nothing else to go on. I just have to hope there's a connection with Raff's Black."

"I did." Trent lifted his satchel and wiped the coffee froth from his top lip. "Any spare moment I got in the library yesterday afternoon and this morning, I spent hunting the online archives." He pushed an old, printed photo towards them first, not black-and-white but shades of brown.

"Is that a service nurse?" Charlie asked as she took the photo, staring at the features more closely. "It's Beryl!" She was slightly older than the last time Charlie had caught a glimpse of her, but definitely the same woman.

"Yes, that's right. She served in World War I, in Belgium and Egypt. I also found records of both of them having trained as nurses at the Royal Newcastle Hospital."

"But that's not where they stayed?" Tess jumped in.

"No. They did stay on there for just shy of a year, but then both of them moved to Waterfall Sanatorium near Helensburgh, south of Sydney."

"Sanatorium?" Charlie asked, passing Beryl's photo to Tess.

"Ah, she's beautiful," Tess cooed as she took it.

"Yeah," Trent answered Charlie. "A tuberculosis hospital to be precise. It was New South Wales's only purpose-built facility for people suffering from Consumption — or the White Plague as it was also known. And in the early 1900s, it was the state's principal tuberculosis sanatorium. The main building opened in 1909, but the female ward didn't open until May 1912, which is when the sisters started working there. I want to keep digging because I honestly didn't find that much in my initial searches."

"Is the hospital still there?" Charlie asked, thinking back to the Royal Newcastle Hospital and how most of it had been destroyed, with the remainder converted into apartments.

"Yeah, it is," Trent said, nodding. "Part of the site was remodelled as an aged care facility, particularly for those with advanced dementia who need to be kept better secured. Most of it, though, is abandoned. The hospital shut down in the 1950s when advances in medicine, in particular antibiotics, meant TB wasn't such a big threat anymore. The old hospital is just fenced off and rotting from what I could see online."

"When did the sisters die?" Tess piped in, sliding the photo back across the table. "And where?"

"That I can't tell you. I did find their birth records — which lined up with the diary entries you told me about Charlie — but no death certificates. Which means they must have died some time in the last hundred years. This type of personal information is protected under New South Wales Law. It doesn't become public information until after the first century. So unless we can find some of their descendants, we won't be able to request that information. And I didn't find any eulogies either. At least not yet."

"So they *could* have worked at that hospital their entire career. Or at least for the rest of their lives." Charlie finished her coffee but held the mug tightly in her fingers as she continued to think. "The records didn't say how long they worked there?"

Trent shook his head. "It was literally a single line entry. Honestly, I didn't find much. But I'll keep at it, don't you worry. I'll have more to share next time."

71

12

Addie's Entries

That afternoon — with Tess comfortably sitting in front of her TV in the living room watching the latest episodes of *Farmer Wants a Wife* — Charlie went to the bedroom to try to enter the Dream. Tess knew to come and wake her if she was in for too long, but they both felt comfortable enough now to do this in separate rooms, if admittedly under the same roof. With Raff's assurances she couldn't draw *his* Black spirit back with her, she reasoned it was safe enough to try to reach out to the sisters. In fact, according to Raff, his Black spirit wouldn't be able to get to the house at all. It would still be haunting whatever place it had ended up stuck. Most likely the place it had died, wherever that was. Charlie's own Black, who had gone suspiciously quiet, still seemed unable to get inside.

Charlie lay back on the bed, the pillow folding around the sides of her face. She itched absentmindedly at the mosquito bites that had managed to pierce her thin cotton top at Sandgate Cemetery, wondering only for a moment what else it was that so many thousands of mosquitos ate in such a lifeless place. Willing her limbs to still, and the itching to fade, she focused instead on the Dream.

Within seconds, now well practiced in this ritual, she was attempting to connect with Addie and Beryl. She willed herself to see what she needed next. Again, the Dream resisted, pushing against her. It was as though the surface of the ocean had suddenly turned solid — repelling her. *Perhaps my*

Black isn't either of the sisters after all...perhaps they are only connected to Raff. She thought back to how Raff had helped her find them last time and tried a different approach, this time slipping into the Waiting Place. She had to hope there was still a connection with the spirit that was attacking Tess. It was the only lead she had to go on. The familiar grey pillars and platforms were now like a second home to her. She looked about herself, wondering — not for the last time — how many other spirits lingered here, and if any of them could see her. Was this *her* Waiting Place or a communal one? Did everyone perceive the Dream this way?

Take me to Raff's spirit, she thought. The Dream shuddered again, but as she took a step, she found herself looking through a small archway and onto an unfamiliar scene. This was the smallest archway she'd seen yet, and she crouched so she could better peer into the memory playing out before her. She reached out a hand but again felt that spongy, resistant surface. Fluctuating as though there really were an ocean beneath it. *Spectator only, then,* she thought, as she peered into the arch.

Addie and Beryl were, once again, in their nurse uniforms and pacing the hallways of the Royal Newcastle Hospital. Daylight was fading from what she could see of the exterior windows, the hanging lanterns now struggling to fully illuminate the passageway. A candleholder was balanced in each sister's hand, flickering as they hastened their steps. "I'm telling you, it scared the life out of me!" Beryl was saying in a shaking voice. "The ward was *empty* aside from Nurse Gladys and I, and the three patients. The door opened on its own. There was *no one* there. Gladys was shaking! And then I turned around and the blanket I'd been fitting to the bed was on the floor. I didn't drop it, and I am *not* going mad." Charlie chuckled to herself as Beryl recounted her supernatural encounter, wondering if it was a real haunting or flights of fancy.

"I was talking to one of the wardsmen and *he* said that *this* hospital was built on the site of an old convict hospital! Almost one hundred years ago. And before they turned it into a hospital, it was a *jail...* Just imagine those convict ghosts rattling their chains around here. It's spooky!"

Charlie continued to watch the girls as they made their way to their sleeping quarters, talking not just about Beryl's convict ghosts, but the wardsmen, with Beryl gossiping about who was shacking up with who. (To Addie's disapproval). Eventually, Charlie pulled herself free of the Dream, sitting up in bed. She supposed she could try and connect directly with her Black spirit, the one that had attacked Tess, but that still felt dangerous. Sighing, she reached for Adelaide's journal on her bedside table instead. She'd marked her place with one of the leather straps and carefully opened the book. She'd now *almost* finished reading about their three years of training, and had already read some of that gossip she'd just heard firsthand. As much as Addie might feign disapproval, the woman had a penchant for sniffing out scandal.

As Charlie opened the journal, something slipped out slightly from between some of the pages. She reached for it, flipping the journal open not to her current place, but quite a few entries forward. The journal fell open to the date '29 June 1912'. The item in her hand was a folded program for *L'inferno*, Dante's Divine Comedy. The coarse and yellowed paper tingled in her hands and she stroked it reverently as she placed it to the side. She not so much read — as devoured — this next account of a moment Charlie herself had at least partially experienced.

* * *

Saturday 29 June 1912

Today, Beryl and I treated ourselves to something quite special. It marked not only the end of our time at the Royal Newcastle Hospital, but the soon to be beginning of our time at Waterfall Sanitorium. We were quite thrilled to spend a little of our savings to see our first ever film. Two of the hospital wardsmen, who took their leave to match our departure, accompanied us. While we promised to write to them from Waterfall, I highly doubt we shall do so. These wardsmen are well-muscled from their labours around the hospital, but their conversation dull. At least to me. Beryl seems to like hearing about their drudgery. Still, they were enjoyable company for a moment.

The film was L'inferno, *an Italian piece of cinematic mastery, bringing to life part of Dante's Divine Comedy. I must say, in the sanctity of these pages only, that the whole thing brought something alight inside of me. I see a lot of nudity in my profession, but on screen it became something else. Something almost forbidden. Some of the tortured souls wore loin cloths, but even then, my mind contorted them to become giant bushes of pubic hair. It made my stomach twist most uncomfortably. Especially surrounded by so many people, in my finest dress, in such a fine place.*

Beryl seemed less shocked. In fact, she seemed to feel sorry for Francesca, who had committed the carnal sin. Giving in to her base desires. Perhaps it is because she engages so well with some of the wardsmen. More a man in a woman's body. Well, both of us have stolen kisses from time-to-time. But it makes me wonder what else she's done. I always thought she would confide everything in me.

For me, I felt most for the condemned man who lost his sight, having been accused of a crime he did not commit. Then he flung himself to his death, only to be punished over-and-over in Hell for ending his own life. Let Beryl feel for the harlots. I'll feel for the wronged.

I have experienced my fair share of death in the halls of the Royal Newcastle Hospital. But never before had I experienced such drama in death. Lucifer's face, devouring tortured souls, shall haunt me in my dreams.

* * *

Charlie joined Tess after the entry about *L'Inferno*, serving them both an early pumpkin-soup dinner in mugs, and suggesting they watch *L'Inferno* on YouTube again. For Charlie, watching it with Addie's journal entry so fresh in her mind, it took on new shape and meaning. Tess, meanwhile, struggled to keep her eyes open. So it wasn't long before Charlie found herself alone on the couch again, Adelaide's journal open on her lap, reading back over the entries she'd skipped.

* * *

Friday 27 January 1911

I received a most awful call today. Billy, one of the wardsmen, was the one to fetch me and take me to the radio room. I hope the words I write are not too blotched, as I cannot keep myself from crying. My dear Mama has left us. The birth of young Ciaran took so much from her. Then the Consumption was true to its word and consumed what was left of her.

She died two days past, and her body has already been interned, for fear of others contracting the illness. My heart breaks. I never had the chance to say goodbye. I knew, from Nicholas's letters, that she had deteriorated, but this news was still so unexpected. Shall all the women in our family who contract Consumption be doomed to perish?

Monday 24 June 1912

I received word today that I am to be transferred to Waterfall Sanatorium, as per my request. Beryl, too, received the good news. I do hope it is good. We truly feel this is our purpose in life. While the rest of Australia runs from this awful disease, or ignores it, Beryl and I shall face it head on. It does seem that the number of cases is declining, so perhaps modern medicine has finally found a way to treat the disease? And with the New South Wales Parliament finally joining the other states in establishing a Tuberculosis Board, perhaps finally we shall overcome this scourge.

I am told the first female patients were transferred to Waterfall Sanatorium from Newington Asylum, a place for destitute and infirm women. Surely, we shall find many of their kind in this establishment. Those who are too poor to go to any number of the rich country estates offering treatment. Beryl and I shall be their angels.

Wednesday 3 July 1912

We have been at Waterfall Sanitorium for two nights now, and yet this is the first chance I have to write my notes. I must admit, I am slightly appalled. While the staff are all acceptable, and Waterfall's Matron is kindlier than Matron Hartley, I find many of the facilities here lacking. I'm told it is because the funding ran low, but the kitchen is so small and so far from the dining rooms that I often find myself skipping meals. Furthermore, electric lights have been shining brightly in

Sydney homes for almost one full decade now, and yet the Government saw fit to build this Sanatorium with only oil lanterns for light. I can understand the Royal Newcastle Hospital taking time to adjust to the new world, as it is at least an old institution, but why not move with the times now?

I also find myself insanely jealous of the wardsmen, doctors, and male nurses here. Unmarried men each have their own quarters to retreat to at the end of the day, and yet Beryl and I bunk in with the rest of the nurses like students once again. I try to be gracious. To focus on why I am here. Beryl certainly seems to be settling in well. Perhaps it is the isolation of this place that has me on edge. We were taken by horse and carriage from the Waterfall Station to this place and saw no-one else other than hospital staff and patients our entire journey. It feels as though Sydney were a dream and I am now lost somewhere in the Australian bush.

* * *

Charlie looked up from the journal as a clap of thunder rattled the tin roof, shaking the walls of the cottage. She snapped the book shut and jumped to her feet. She'd been so absorbed in her reading, she hadn't noticed the rain setting in around the property, and the tinkering of large drops of water as they sprayed across the roof. She checked her phone for the time; just before 9:00 p.m. Perhaps she would join Tess for an early night and resume the journal tomorrow. She planned to finish it quickly so Trent could pick it up; no doubt he'd be able to uncover useful historical facts she'd miss. She smiled at the thought of his goofy grin as he absorbed Addie's words.

She walked to the window, reaching for the curtains to draw them closed for the evening, when she saw a shadow loitering in the yard. Not beneath the gum tree this time, but moving towards the front of the house. The rain sprayed as it hit the dark figure making its way towards the door.

77

13

Invite Me In

Charlie pulled the curtains across the window, her hands fumbling from how much she was shivering. *Was her Black going to try to get into the house? Was it coming for Tess again?* She thought for a moment about waking Tess and then steeled her nerve. What good would submitting Tess to this same terror do? And besides…it couldn't get into the house. *Can it?* Charlie gripped the edge of the curtain. Part of her wanted to retreat, like a child would, pulling the covers over her head. Another needed to know if it was still there. If it had made it onto the veranda.

She flicked the curtain to the side and stifled a scream as she saw a figure there, by the window. Right beside the front door. Dripping from the rain. Barely illuminated in the dim the light that escaped through the cracks in the curtain. A loud bang sounded at the door, and this time she did shriek, dropping the curtain and stepping backwards, eyes focused on the door. She reached out for the bright light from the Dream again, willing it across the front door. The banging stopped.

"Charlie?" Tess's dazed voice wafted down the corridor from their bedroom. "Is someone at the door?" Charlie's voice caught in her throat as she looked between the entryway and the hall behind her, where a shuffling Tess was now emerging. Her blackened, swollen eye even more unsettling in the dim light. "Who is it?"

"Tess, I…"

"Hell*ooo*!" A distinctly human voice sounded from the veranda. "Are you going to let me in? I know you're there, Charlie." The fear in Charlie's chest caught like a hiccup, sending sharp tingles outwards, and bringing a slow feeling of nausea as the anxiety slowly unclenched itself from around her heart. It wasn't her Black spirit after all.

"Raff?" Tess walked to the front door and called again, louder. "Raff? Is that you?"

"Well, who else did you expect at this time of night?" Tess unlocked the door and pulled it open. With the light now flooding across the porch, Charlie could see it was indeed Raff and not her Black. His long hair was plastered to the side of his face, and his dark and baggy clothes were even gloomier now they'd been saturated.

"You look awful," Tess said as she looked him up-and-down.

"All compliments, this one." Raff turned to look at Charlie, pointing a thumb in Tess's direction as he did so. "You going to invite me in? I'm still right to crash here a few days, right?"

As Tess went to answer, Charlie spoke over the top of her. "You can stay, but you'll have to sleep in the caravan." Raff and Tess gave her near identical *are-you-kidding-me* looks, but Raff's broke first. He smiled broadly, holding his hands out wide in a mock bow.

"Whatever you say, sheila. As long as I can have a hot shower, you won't hear a sideways cooee outta me. Have you got a towel?"

* * *

Fifteen minutes later, Charlie and Tess were sitting at their round dining table, black tea untouched in their mugs in front of them. The shower had been going steadily for at least the past ten minutes, as soon as Raff had been able to retrieve a dirty duffle bag from the boot of his car. They'd messaged Trent to let him know what was going on. "I just don't trust him," Charlie said again, staring absently into the swirling brown liquid.

"Why? Because he's a bit uncouth?" The word echoed beautifully with Tess's French accent and Charlie stole a glance at her deep red lips.

"He's just so proud. And stubborn. I feel like he's not telling us everything, and like this is all some big joke to him. Plus. He's a bit derro."

"Derro?"

"It means unkempt. Dodgy. Bogan."

"Derelict?" Charlie snapped her fingers and pointed one at Tess in affirmation. "I think he's just lived a rough life, *ma chére*. Why don't you ask him some questions about the Dream? It's a good opportunity to learn more about everything from someone *other* than Maryanne."

The shower clicked off at that moment and they both bowed their heads over their tea. A few minutes later, Raff was back in the main living area, a fresh (if still holey) jersey and jeans on. These, at least, seemed to fit him better. His bare feet were pale and slapped against the hardwood floors as he walked towards them, towelling his long hair dry. He slumped into the chair next to Tess, brought one foot up besides his bottom, and rested the other foot on the fourth and empty chair. The towel was discarded on the floor, at which Charlie sneered before she could catch herself. Raff ignored her.

"Fuck me, I needed that!" He sighed deeply, wrapping one long arm around his knee and propping the other behind his head. "You have any grub? A beer wouldn't go amiss either."

Tess pushed back and stood slowly. "I'll heat up some leftovers. And Trent left a couple of Tooheys in the fridge I think."

"Thanks, darl." He watched Tess as she walked to the nearby kitchen, then turned his gaze back to Charlie. "You thought I was your Black tonight, didn't you?" He was far too perceptive for her liking. She pinched her lips until she could feel them curling inwards to a thin line. "It did that to Tess, too, didn't it?" He touched his eye for emphasis.

"I think it's targeting her. First she's pushed over at your place, and now this. It attacked her out in the garden. Brought a concrete bird bath down on her head." Raff winced dramatically, but with a slight smile that spoke of some level of appreciation for the Black's antics too. "Why is it after Tess, and how do I stop it?"

Raff stretched out both legs and arched his back, pushing at it as though to stretch out a knotted muscle. As Tess returned, he took his beer, waiting for her to sit back down before answering. "Look, Blacks usually want one thing, and one thing only. A bit of sweet revenge. If this one has taken a shine to Tess, then it's because some part of this—" he motioned at the two of them "reminds it of something that happened to it in its own life. It doesn't have to be exactly the same, just some small element that reminds it of its own tragedy." He pointed the tip of his beer in Tess's direction. "That bump is a nasty one, I'll admit. Usually you'll get scratches, maybe a bruised handprint, and some good old-fashioned mental torment. *This* level of attack is because your Black is imbalanced, like mine. Help the spirit find Balance, and it'll stop. It'll also stop following you around, Charlie."

"Addie and Beryl—" Charlie began, but was cut off

"I still think Addie or Beryl is *my* Black. I don't know who yours is, or if it even has anything to do with those sisters." Charlie sighed and plopped her elbows onto the table, leaning forward floppily to rub at her temples. "We'll figure it out."

"You said you've been doing this for eight years," Tess jumped in. "You must have learnt a lot. It must be tough, though. How do you even, you know…"

"…get by?" Raff arched an eyebrow at her. "As you can see, not all that well. Homeless, jobless, most often penniless. I am a chippie though, as I said."

"Chippie?" Tess asked, standing again as the microwave beeped to retrieve the leftovers.

"A carpenter, a tradesman. Of course, I don't have any current licenses, but you'd be surprised how few people care about that. I tend to be able to pick up a handyman job or two wherever I go, usually a cashie. You know, cash-in-hand. It's not much, but it's enough for fuel, a bit of food, my delightful second-hand wardrobe." He pulled at the frayed hem of his navy, knitted jersey.

Tess grinned as she returned with the food and a fork, placing it in front of him. "Well, I might just have a few jobs for you while you're here too."

Raff smiled, genuinely, behind the strands of wet hair plastered to his face.

"I'd like that."

"What does the Dream look like to you?" Charlie asked, curiosity pushing through as the conversation became more comfortable. "It's like a series of off-white, almost grey, platforms and archways to me. There's a sense of colour to it, but it's hard to explain. And it's never still. It's like it has this-this—"

"—continual sense of motion?" Raff finished for her. "Yeah, I see that too, but no platforms. And my Waiting Place is black, not the colour you described. All different shades of black."

"And you're alone there?" Charlie pressed, desperate now to hear someone else's account.

"For the most part. Sometimes the spirits I'm helping will show up there. Or another Guide, if there's a reason to talk about something important. I like to think of it as *my* Waiting Place."

"Me too…" Charlie breathed the words before she could stop herself. She shook her shoulders, determined not to fall too easily into this conversation. For whatever reason, she didn't want to let her guard down. She didn't want to find herself liking this stubborn, rambunctious hobo.

"I've seen other spirits in the real world too, sometimes," Raff offered without Charlie having to ask any follow-up question. "Not often, mind you. Blues, Greys. They show up quite a lot around the Blacks."

"And have you seen Purples, Yellows, Reds…?"

Raff squinted at her, downing the last of his beer and continuing to devour the leftover curried sausages Tess had brought him. He ate so fast it dribbled down his black beard. "I've never heard of those types. Maryanne obviously never thought to mention them."

"She fails to mention a lot of things," Charlie said. Both she and Tess joined Raff in smirking at this. "A Purple is a spirit that was repressed some way in life, and now gets to live out that part of themselves. Temptresses they're often called."

"Kinky."

Charlie ignored the comment. "Yellows are like party spirits. They've had a hard life, usually manually hard, and get to enjoy and understand a bit of true pleasure before they move on. The Reds are a tough one. They're people who should have been great leaders in life, but never got the chance."

"You come across a Green yet?" Raff put both feet up on the empty chair as he finished shovelling another mountain of food into his mouth. Charlie had to pause and process this before she could decipher what it was he'd said around his rice, peas and sausages. She shook her head. "Nasty lot, those ones. Batshit crazy they are. There's just something *off* with them." He tapped at his temple as he spoke. "I never quite figured out what it was keeping them around, though."

"Well, let's not talk about them, then," Tess said behind a hand, yawning widely and wincing slightly as her bad eye pinched. "Charlie tends to attract anything just by being close enough. We don't want to tempt fate when we've got two imbalanced Blacks on our hands already."

"Fair enough," he shrugged.

"Have you met any of the other Guides?" Tess stood again, picking up the empty beer bottle and wiggling it suggestively.

"Why not, sure. I'll have another." It was Raff's turn to yawn now. "Yeah, I have. Not often, but occasionally we've crossed paths. The Greys are a nasty looking bunch, and they only exist in the Dream so they can conjure up whatever horrible shape they want to appear as. The Greens only exist in the Dream too, I think. I've never seen their Guide though. Now, the Amber Guides… they are full flesh and blood, just like you and me."

"Amber?" Tess asked, and Charlie wished she had her notebook. She'd need to write all of this down before she went to sleep.

"They almost look like fire in the Dream. Crackling in brilliant orange colours. The way they describe it to me, they're spirits who had a sudden or unexpected death. Or some other huge change in their life just before they passed away."

"I think we're learning more from you tonight than we've learnt from Maryanne in months." Tess yawned again, stealing a glance at the clock, which had ticked passed 10:00 p.m.

"Well, we'd better hit the hay. Rain's died down. I'll head out to the trailer."

"Wait," Charlie said as he made to stand. "One last question. Have you ever seen a shadow creature? Here, in the real world I mean."

"What d'ya mean?" Raff hunched over his beer.

"You know those colourless wisps? Those memories or strong emotions sometimes left behind?" Raff nodded. "Well, the shadows are sort of like that. They're not human, that's for sure. They're almost the opposite of a wisp. They seem to have intelligence, but no true form. They draw their shape from the shadows around them. Maryanne said their only purpose is to maintain the Balance."

Raff shook his head seriously. "No." He stood, taking his beer with him. "There's a lot more to this than you or I will probably ever understand in one lifetime." He paused, his hand on the front door handle. "But one thing I learnt early, and you'd do well to learn now…don't meddle with anything that isn't human. Or at least, that's never been human. Trust me on that."

14

Ripples

Charlie rolled over, picking up her phone as the daylight peeked through the curtains and woke her. She hadn't slept well, thinking not only about the Black stalking around the outside of her property, but of Raff in his caravan. The phone informed her it was 'Good Friday', and it was like a light switch flipped in her brain. *Of course,* she put the phone on the bedside table and stretched slowly. *Trent and Brent are going away for the Easter long weekend, to spend it with Brent's parents in the next town over.* She made a mental note to have the boys over for dinner when they got back. Or at least, when this was all over and it was safe again.

"Tess?" Charlie rolled onto her side and reached out to the dark mass beside her. While Tess and Charlie weren't romantic, they had started sharing a bed shortly after Tess moved in — when she was worried Charlie might still slip off into the Dream and never come back. And the routine had just stuck. It also meant the spare bed was free whenever Trent wanted to stay over. Charlie patted the bulk beside her softly and it collapsed in on itself. Nothing but a heap of Tess's prized pillows, throws and blankets. Charlie sat, yanking at the collar of her pyjamas to straighten them. She stood and walked to the bedroom door, realising she could hear the faint sound of talking. And laughter? Crossing her arms over her braless chest, she walked out to the living room in nothing but her tartan PJs and socked feet.

"Bloody oath! No wonder you shacked up here. Fuck me dead. So that's how she did it. A living tether."

"*Morning*," Charlie said loudly — and, she admitted to herself, snippily — as she exited the hallway, leaning on the doorframe. "You two were up early."

"I was just telling Raff here what I needed doing with those decks for the tiny houses," Tess smiled, unapologetically, patting the seat beside her in invitation. "And we got to talking about everything that's happened to us the past few months as well." Charlie lingered in the doorframe, watching the two of them. The way Tess angled her body slightly towards Raff. The way Raff kept looking at Tess's beautiful red lips and the sharp edge of her collarbones peeking over her cotton shirt. "The kettle's only just boiled if you want a cuppa." Charlie pushed herself upright from her slump and walked through to the kitchen, hearing the two continue to talk while she busied herself with the tea.

Bitter jealousy bubbled up through her chest to her throat, making her eyes swim, and her head feel both empty and pounding. *Don't be jealous*, she willed to herself. *We're just friends. Just sisters.* The laughter kicked off again. *And he's just temporary.* She forced a smile onto her face and brought her tea out to join them. "I've got my call with Maryanne today…" Charlie started.

"*Oui, ma chére*," Tess said. "We'll make sure you have the house to yourself. I offered to take Raff out to the stockmen's ruins. He thought he might be able to see if the Grey is still there or not. I know we've only just been, but he said Blacks and Greys are closely connected. It's worth a short, *non*?"

"God, your accent is sexy." Tess flushed at Raff's complement, as did Charlie, but for different reasons.

"Oh, come on!" Charlie couldn't catch herself before the abrupt comment was out.

"Sorry, you're right." Raff held his hands up in mock defence. "I'm *sorry* Tess, Charlie. I promise, I'll be better behaved in your house." Charlie gave him a sharp look and started on her tea.

"Are you sure?" She directed the question to Tess only this time. "I don't mind if you're here, you know that. And Raff has his caravan. Maryanne is never very long."

"*Oui,* I'm sure. It'll be great. I want to show him where I'm planning on putting the tiny houses anyway. He can give me his expert tradesman opinion on the decks." Charlie sighed, but nodded, and went back to her tea.

* * *

"Hello, Charlotte," Maryanne said as their video call connected. Like always, she was wearing her trademark headscarf. Deep maroon with black flower patterns today. She had a long-sleeve shirt on under her tunic today, obviously starting to feel the chill that had arrived early this year. "How are you?"

"Better than last time I saw you."

"Yes, I do apologise for that. I wanted to explain what Raff would be trying *before* he willed that connection on you. He can be…stubborn. And rash."

"I know!" Charlie rolled her eyes in exasperation and flopped back into her office chair. "He's here now, staying at the property. Tess invited him. She thought it'd be better to have him close while we're trying to sort this mess out."

"Not a terrible idea." Maryanne nodded to herself, also relaxing slightly in her seat. She looked tired. Exhausted, actually. The bottoms of her eyes were puffy and purple-tinged. Her skin was sallow and pale. Even her normally rose-coloured lips had lost some of their colour.

"Are you okay, Maryanne?"

"Hm? What? Oh yes. I'm fine. Nothing for you to worry about." Charlie frowned but Maryanne, as always, was not to be distracted. "What have you discovered about the Black spirits so far?" Charlie shared what little they'd been able to uncover. Her confusion over how her own Black spirit might be connected to Raff's. Her frustration and difficulty connecting with the sisters without Raff's assistance. And Raff's theory that her Black was trying to hurt Tess because of some similarity to its own past life.

"That does make sense." Maryanne nodded, jotting a couple of short notes in her book. "It's like the old ghost story about the woman maddened by her husband's abuse. You know the story? The one who killed her children and then herself, and who now continues trying to kill other children in death. Or the woman who was raped and killed on a highway — any highway — coming back as a vengeful spirit to attack any man who travels that same road. Urban legend is full of accounts of Blacks, because they act in similar patterns. Causality doesn't have to be precise for the Blacks to lock on to a target."

"So whoever my Black is, she — or he — was wronged by another woman?"

"Or another woman was involved in some way. Honestly, you could chase your tail for weeks trying to figure out the Black's connection. Keep focussing on the connection between your Black and Rafael's. It's too much of a coincidence, I think."

"I'm trying…" Charlie muttered. "I've been so scared to reach out to my Black in case I let it into the house, and it hurts Tess even worse. So I've been focussing on the sisters, hoping the connection will eventually reveal itself."

"Yes," Maryanne murmured distractedly as she took a few more notes. "I was intrigued by your description of how you used the energy from the Dream to fashion your own shield. Still, doesn't hurt to be careful. A Black isn't as easy to handle as a Grey. With most spirits, you, as a Keeper, can send them away if you will it. A Black, though, has betrayal in its nature. They're not so easy to order around."

"I have another question to ask you today." Charlie opened her own book, turning back to the notes she'd taken from her internet research about the Blacks. "I did some research myself." She hurried on before Maryanne could disparage her. "I *know* it's mostly codswallop, but you yourself said there are grains of truth. When I was trying to find out more information about the Blacks, I came across information about shadow people." A flicker of something passed over Maryanne's face, as though her own shadows were ruffling the surface of her normally unflappable composure. "It said there were three types. Troubled human spirits, which I just dismissed as what we know of as Blacks. But the second two were apparently inhuman. Ancient spirits that never lived human lives. Either interdimensional beings or djinns or demons, or anything like that. Inhuman."

Charlie paused, waiting for Maryanne to respond. When she didn't, Charlie continued. "It made me think of those shadows that were watching Trent, Tess and I when I was helping those convict spirits to move on. The ones who you said were driven by a single purpose: to protect the Balance. The descriptions I found online certainly sounded familiar. Shapes that are formed out of shadows. That can melt away at the corner of your eye. That watch, but rarely intervene. That have a sense of menace. This sounds pretty bang on the money. It is them, isn't it?"

Maryanne pursed and twisted her lips, as though trying to repress a sour taste. "I've already told you. The Shadows are not human and never have been. They aren't even spirits. I don't fully know what they are. They are neither good nor evil, and driven by only one purpose: to maintain the Balance. And..." Maryanne breathed shallowly and swiftly, her voice shuddering in her chest as it whispered past her lips. "And they are only the beginning."

"The beginning of *what?*" Charlie pressed, willing Maryanne to open up. "*Please,* Maryanne. I can't believe I learnt more from that bogan Raff in one night than I've learnt from you in months. *Please*, tell me."

Maryanne blew out a breath, her lips puffing as she did so. "I don't share everything for a very good reason. It's taken decades, *decades*, for me to get to where I am. And some days I still think my mind will snap, will break and fragment into a million pieces. Listen, Charlotte. So long as you do your duty as Keeper, you won't have to worry about the Shadows, or who sends them." Charlie went to speak again and Maryanne held up a hand. "When you had trouble releasing those convict spirits who raped that poor First Nations woman, I told you that if you failed in your duty there were much, much worse things that would happen if you failed."

"Yes..."

"The Balance is *so* important. It doesn't always seem fair to us. Doesn't always make sense to us. But I've heard what happens when a Keeper fails in their duty. I've seen the ripples from it."

Charlie gasped. "A Keeper before me failed?" She gripped the edge of the desk, feeling her fingers beginning to sweat. She had felt this pressure, this tension, to succeed in her duty three times now. With Marie. With Ru, the poor boy whose mother was so broken by his death she had held onto him. And with the convicts, who were tethered together so strongly they couldn't move on. Her palms felt slick as Maryanne nodded.

"The Seeker before me saw it all happen, firsthand. I will not share the full story today, Charlotte. So do not ask me to and do not expect it of me. What I will say, is this Keeper did not just fail in their duty. They rebuked it. This affected not just them, but so many, many spirits around them. It was like a ripple in a pond. A single stone causing waves of pain and imbalance for decades to come. Centuries even."

"Is that what's happening now? Ripples?"

Maryanne squeezed her hands together until the knuckles turned white, visible even through the screen. "Quite possibly. Before your convicts, I'd never known so many Yellow spirits to be trapped at once. Now we have *two* imbalanced Blacks, at the same time, and I'm convinced they're linked to each other. Yes, quite possibly this is a ripple. But if it is or not, it doesn't matter right now. All that matters, is helping those spirits. Restoring what's wrong. That's your only duty now."

"Maryanne, I—"

"That's enough for today, Charlotte." Maryanne sighed, and the tiredness seemed to sink even deeper into her. "I'll speak to you next Friday. Work with Raff. I know he can be obnoxious, but he's not a bad soul. He's been through a lot. Give him some grace. Goodbye Charlotte."

15

Better to be Bored?

Charlie settled into the sofa in the living room with Addie's journal, to kill time until Tess and Raff came back. As she read, she continued to glance up at the window, peering at the swaying grass in case she could spot them returning. She supposed the rough sound of the buggy's engine, and the plumes of white diesel smoke, would give them away. She found it difficult to focus on the words on the page, constantly looking up and through the window, finding herself re-reading the same passages over-and-over.

* * *

Sunday 22 September 1912

I must say, after the weekend Beryl and I just had, I can almost feel those carnal winds of Hell whipping us around the upper layers of the underworld. Waterfall Sanatorium, for all its hundreds of patients, is a quiet place. A restful place. A boring place, most of the time. We two are not the only ones who find it so. While fraternising with the male staff is strictly taboo, Beryl and I find a little risk the most exciting and thrilling of diversions.

I had my first kiss last night. My first proper kiss. Not just a sneaky peck on the mouth. Freddy is the wardsman's name. Slightly younger than I am with a shock of red hair and more freckles than skin. We snuck out into the bush with a small group of the others, and soon had broken off into pairs. His lips were so dry to start with, but as he poked his tongue between my teeth his kiss became suddenly wet. Overwhelmingly and uncomfortably so, but despite how slobbery we both were, it felt like embers from a fire were sparking through me, alighting in the most unexpected places...

Beryl tells me it was her first proper kiss too, with one of Freddy's young friends. I forget his name. I do not believe her, but it is nice she wishes to share this experience with me. To at least pretend that we are joined together in this first as well, as we have been for so many others. Chaps like Freddy and his nameless friend will come-and-go, but not Beryl and I. We two are steadfast.

Friday 8 November 1912

I am afraid what influence this place is having on my sister and I. I consider both of us to be of the highest calibre and character. But this boredom we face, day-in and day-out, at times becomes too much to bear. Tempting us to things we shouldn't. Freddy continues to persist in his affections towards me. I see now why casual flirtation is so frowned upon. Any work situation in which we cross paths is dastardly. I've never felt such discomfort in my life. Perhaps it is still easier for men to be so casual, yet more is expected of us women. Freddy certainly seems to expect more. I find myself regretting the encounter.

Beryl finds it quite amusing. Her flock of suitors is far longer than mine, and yet she fixates on Freddy, teasing me with mocking wedding bells. Ding-dong-dell. Still, she could abandon me for any number of handsome young men with good futures, and she refuses. My loyal sister. I shall forgive her a few poor jests.

And still, Freddy proved useful for one thing. He arranged for a small group of us to leave the confines of Waterfall Sanatorium and explore the nearby town of Helensburgh. We took to a well-worn path through the bush, the boys leading the way to pull back any large branches or sticks. Beryl and I, and the other nurses who tagged along, needed to lift our skirts as we walked, to prevent them getting snagged on the brush. I'm sure this was delightful entertainment for the boys, who looked back far more often than they should! I am so glad we chose our dark skirts today because the mud and burs will take some scrubbing to get out. Imagine if we'd worn our white dresses!

After an hour or so, we came to the town. Of course, Helensburgh is quite small, and the bush still tries to press its way inside and between the buildings. One of the first things I spotted was the train station, though the boys tell me it is not yet connected to Waterfall. But not to matter. Exercise and fresh air is a good remedy for most ills, as we tell our own patients. We took our time exploring the town. I was pleased to see several small shops as well as an emporium that I shall now frequent. The park is quite lovely. Though it was quiet when we visited, I can imagine on weekends it must be full of picnicking families and courting young lovers. I shall be best pleased to return here as well.

What the boys wanted to do, and Beryl as well I must admit, was to go to Helensburgh Hotel. Poor Beryl was most distraught to be denied entry to the bar with the other men. What was she to expect though? This may be a small country town, but it's still illegal to serve women. Some of the nurses were pleased enough to go to the Ladies Lounge. Beryl and I, and a couple of others, took a walk back to the station instead to watch the trains come and go.

I still cannot get over what Freddy told me when we met up and began the walk back to the Sanatorium. Apparently, they'd spotted several of the male patients from Waterfall drinking in the hotel as well. Beryl thought it great fun and burst into laughter. I, myself, was appalled that they should risk infecting others. I suppose it's not just the staff who are bored at Waterfall.

Tuesday 4 February 1912

Beryl departed for Newcastle over the weekend to take her leave. I am still quite disappointed we were unable to take our leave together over Christmas, but such is the nature of this employment. It is most tiresome without her here. With so much work to do, I can scarcely stop to ask a patient how she is feeling, let alone converse. It is the monotony that drives me to insanity. Chores, rounds, paperwork, chores, rounds, paperwork. I find myself taking my meals in the house, rather than the dining hall. It is almost little difference carrying my plate from the kitchen to my room than to the hall in any case.

I helped to settle some of the new patients into their routines this morning. Two of them are most certainly beyond treatment at this point. We shall just have to make them comfortable. A third — Jane Hughes — is one of the strongest patients I've seen yet. I should say her prognosis is quite fine. She is what our Superintendent *would label 'a hopeful'. So it befuddles me why she should be placed in a bed beside the terminally ill. I find myself quite agreeing with our Dr Palmer. Remaining positive is crucial to recovery, and these terminals are quite often a death sentence for the hopefuls.*

And it wasn't just new patients who arrived yesterday. We finally have another doctor to assist us in the female wards. Dr Albert Hammond. He is just a few years my senior, and honestly quite the most dashing man I have ever met. He keeps his hair styled in the latest fashions, but there are several hairs that always seem to escape his attempts, which pop free to frame his sharp face. He seems to care quite deeply for his patients already, taking time to speak with each one, while us nurses frantically run around behind him. He is stoic and calm in the bustle of boredom. Perhaps Waterfall is not so dull now that he is here.

* * *

As Charlie finished reading this last entry, she heard the familiar rumble of the buggy returning. She closed the journal, standing to stretch before making her way to the front door. She could see them approaching now. A black speck in the grass, shrouded with a halo of white fumes. She waved at them with her full arm. As they came closer, she saw it wasn't Tess who was driving, but Raff. His long hair whipping back, Tess laughing with joy as the buggy bounced over the shallow dips faster than it really should have.

"*Ma chére!*" Tess yelled in breathy excitement as she stepped down from the buggy, her legs wobbling slightly from the adrenaline rush. "That was wonderful! We have the whole tiny village planned out, and Raff is going to build it for the cost of meals and materials, and a few hundred dollars for fuel. Isn't that wonderful?" Charlie took Raff's measure as he stepped more confidently from the buggy, running his hand back over his hair to try to tame it from its wind-swept tangle.

"That's great, Tess. I'm glad he can help."

"*And,*" Tess continued as she walked up the veranda steps and towards the front door. "He doesn't think the Grey is there anymore either. It's nice to have someone confirm what you already knew, *non?* Maybe his soul has finally moved on, now that Marie is free." It *was* good news, but Charlie found her dislike of Raff bubbling towards resentment, and so shrugged nonchalantly, keeping her eyes on their visitor. As Tess had said, she'd already theorised this anyway, so what had she needed Raff for?

"*Tess!*" Raff's voice was laced with concern and warning as he bellowed from the bottom of the veranda stairs, catching Charlie off-guard and making her wince and jump, every nerve pinching painfully. Charlie spun to look behind her, the way Raff's eyes were trained. "Look out!"

The Black was there. Looming over Tess, so tall that its back arched across the porch roof like a horrible black cat's, its face angled over the top of Tess's head. Those moon-eyes glinted with malice. Tess also turned, unable to see exactly what Raff and Charlie could, tensing and freezing on the threshold of the door. The moment's hesitation gave the creature the opportunity it wanted, and it rushed at Tess, sending her flying through the entryway and out of sight. The Black rebounded from the entryway violently as Tess sailed through it. The sound it made was not a howl or a scream, but something worse. It almost sounded like laughter, the way it broke and pitched, but the sound was far from joy. It was raw and rusted one moment, like sound pushed forcefully across a ragged throat, and the next high-pitched. Like the sound of a newborn baby, or terrified cat, but melded together in horrible synchronicity and pitched a full octave higher.

"Tess!" Charlie ran past the figure and through the door, gasping as she saw how far Tess had been flung into the living room. She was slumped against the coffee table, the rug beneath her snagged and rippled, but at least hopefully having slowed her momentum before she hit the table. She blinked groggily as Charlie knelt beside her. "Tess! Are you okay! Can you hear me?" Tess batted Charlie's hands away from her as she pulled herself upright.

"Uh, *salopard...*" Charlie sat back on her haunches, her hands tremoring close-by in case Tess needed her. "*Fils de pute!*" She struggled to sit upright, and Charlie slowly helped her to her feet. "I'm okay, I'm okay. Nothing broken. Just battered." Charlie, relieved her friend would be okay, turned to look back at the door. The Black was still there, bent over, its face looking down at them from the top of the door. Its gaze was almost like a creature itself, alive and wriggling, as it rested on her.

"Get out of here!" she yelled at it, as she would a Grey. "*Get out!!*" The Black didn't move at first, but then floated slowly around the edge of the deck. It wasn't gone. She knew that by the feeling of its two white-hot-poker eyes nestling on her. It was soon back, by the window, watching her through the glass. Its eyes filled the top half of its face, beaming on her like headlights. She felt like a deer trapped in their glow.

"I'm afraid that won't work," Raff said as he came to stand beside her. "Not with a Black. And certainly not with one this imbalanced. You can't send it away." He put a large, rough and callused hand on her shoulder. It felt as uncomfortable as the Black's gaze on her did. "The only way that one leaves this place, is if you do."

"Leave?" Charlie breathed, turning to look at Tess with her swollen, blackened eye. Her grazed and bruised elbow. She knew there would now be new bruises blemishing her back along with the older scratches. Her stomach tightened and sank into her guts.

"Until we know who your Black is, and how to free it — to keep Tess safe — you need to be apart. This isn't going to stop. But it will follow you wherever you go. Who knows when it'll figure out how to get into the house if you stay." The thought hit Charlie coldly.

"Where? Where would I go?"

"To Waterfall Sanatorium, of course."

16

Unpredictabilities

Charlie threw her duffle bag into the boot of Raff's Landcruiser. She tried not to look too closely at the mess of rubbish, boxes, and other junk strewn about his boot. She particularly tried not to think about the smell, which reminded her of his caravan. Musty, stale, and sharp.

Raff had explained his plan to her and, infuriatingly, it had made sense. He and Charlie would travel to the Sanatorium to see if that was where his Black was haunting. Unlike Charlie's Black, Raff's couldn't follow him. It would be just like how they'd checked out the former hospital in Newcastle. And, if Raff's Black was at the Sanatorium, perhaps they could figure out which sister it was, why she was imbalanced, and how Charlie's Black was connected. As Maryanne had said, it couldn't be a coincidence that two Black spirits were reaching out for help at the same time. Any information they could glean would help them.

It was a four- or five-hour drive to Waterfall, south of Sydney. She wasn't looking forward to having to breathe the musty car air for such a long period of time. Charlie slammed the boot closed and turned just in time for Tess to hug her front-on. She carefully put her own arms around her, mindful of the dark bruise on her back left shoulder, the scratches, and that horrible puffy eye.

"I'm sorry I can't come with you, *ma chére.*" She gave her a quick kiss on each cheek, Charlie's hair pressing to her face as she did so. "Keep me updated each step of the way. And if you can't get rid of it, just…just come home." Tess turned to Raff next, gave him a big grin, and a hug as well. Kissing him softly on just one cheek, near his ear. Although Tess whispered what she said next, Charlie caught it well enough. "Don't you let anything happen to her, or I'll be your worst nightmare." Charlie put a hand up to rub at her chin to hide her smile, made harder by Raff's bewildered and somewhat offended expression. Charlie slid into the passenger seat, grimacing as she swept dust off the ripped fabric. *"Je t'aimerai pour toujours,"* Tess said through Charlie's open window as Raff began driving slowly down the gravel driveway.

"Jat-ah-me-ray Par-too-jers," Raff butchered the French with his Australian accent as they approached the end of Charlie's long driveway, and the start of the even longer country roads. "What does that mean?"

Charlie cleared her throat uncomfortably, resting her elbow on the edge of the open window, and looking out at the gate, breathing deeply from the country air. Hoping it would take some of the car smells away with it. "It means 'I promise I'll love you forever'."

"Ah, mmhmm." He made the noises deep in his throat like he suddenly understood everything. "You two are…you know?"

"*No,*" Charlie replied firmly, understanding his insinuation. "Tess isn't gay. We're just very close friends. Sisters really."

"And tethered." He nodded to himself as he sped the car up to the 110km legal limit, and slightly beyond it. "I've never known a Keeper — any *spirit* Guide really — to evade death like that. To literally anchor their life to another living human. Devious. Good on you. Though it must take a toll, on both of you."

"I didn't do it on purpose." She glared at him, seeing nothing but genuine curiosity in his face. "I *did* surrender myself to the Dream. I thought I would die. But the next minute, there I am, crawling out of the creek, very much alive and breathing. And I did nearly die afterwards anyway. Dipping in-and-out of the Dream literally sapped my energy dry. That's before I learnt how to draw energy from the Dream."

"Huh. I didn't know you could do that."

"There seems to be a lot of things we don't know." She squirmed to get comfortable in her seat, edging closer to the car door, leaning on it as she watched the gum trees pass them by. The occasional falcon circled high above them, watching the grass. "You're sure Tess will be safe? That it'll come with us?"

Raff nodded. "One hundred per cent. See for yourself." He nodded to his rearview mirror. Charlie stole a glance and flinched as she saw the moon-eyes reflected there. She frantically turned to look behind her, seeing nothing, then back to the mirror, which was also now empty.

"Fucking aye! You're pretty jumpy for a Keeper!"

"I'm just not used to these Blacks. Not all spirits are so tortured and twisted you know. And I'm also not used to seeing them pop up in the mirror."

Raff's tone grew graver, and more serious, his face falling flat. "They're not that way for no reason, sheila. And they're not the tortured ones anymore, they're the torturers. It's only fair, isn't it? That they get to be on the other end of the stick for a little bit, before they move on to their happily-ever-after. Or whatever it is that comes next."

"Do you *really* believe that?"

He caught her eye briefly before turning back to look at the road. "I do. I wouldn't be a very good Black Guide if I didn't, would I? They just don't normally go to the extremes *he* is." Raff motioned over his shoulder with a thumb. "He needs our help. Just like one of those sisters needs our help. Then it will all be put to right. You'll see."

"*He?*" Charlie looked over her shoulder, but the Black still wasn't there. "Are you sure?"

"Most definitely. I've been around my fair share of Blacks. I was pretty certain when I saw him yesterday afternoon. Glimpsing him just now confirmed it for me. I can't explain how I know, but I do. Most of them are women, so the men tend to stick out a bit."

"Well... That's something..."

* * *

It took just over four hours for the two of them to reach Waterfall from Greenfields. They'd stopped only at a petrol station for fuel and for Raff to 'empty his own tank'. They'd discussed on the drive how the Sanatorium had been converted into a nursing home in 1957 — mostly for patients with advanced dementia. This had made Charlie think of her mother, and to thank God Elsa hadn't lived long enough to end up in a place like that. A facility where you had to traverse at least two or three doors just to enter the building, each locking behind you. The majority of the Sanatorium buildings, however, had been abandoned. Left to the whims of rot and vandals, and the unforgiving passage of time. Raff had made it abundantly clear he wouldn't go anywhere near the hospital during the day, to avoid unwelcome questions or interference by staff, visitors or patients. Charlie couldn't help but agree with the plan to evade unwelcome attention.

It was just after 4:00 p.m. when Charlie redirected them to the nearby town of Helensburgh, which she'd read about in Adelaide's journal. She'd tried, mostly unsuccessfully, to keep the smug tone from her voice while summarising for Raff the contents of the journal so far. The flirtations between the sisters and the male nurses and wardsmen. The triviality of life in the hospital, and how boredom drew them to Helensburgh and *other* distractions. She'd chuckled as she'd recalled the several entries that had mentioned the pranks the nurses played on each other, and some of the stories Addie had written about the patients she treated. The privileged women who couldn't get into a private care facility, and the wards of the state who had nowhere else to go. Addie documented the strictures the matron and superintendent had imposed on hospital staff, but also her enduring respect and awe for the superintendent and his 'new' methods for treating tuberculosis sufferers.

"Just this morning, I was reading about how the superintendent set up a pig farm on the property, enlisting the help of the groundskeepers and some of the wardsmen. Addie was a little mortified that the superintendent joined in 'the muck', as she called it, of rearing pigs." Charlie laughed at this, recalling the tone of Adelaide's words.

"I wonder if he was a pig fucker…" And there it was. Every time Charlie found herself slipping into familiarity with Raff, there'd be a comment like *that* to snap her out of it. She scoffed and rolled her eyes, looking out at Helensburgh as the satellite navigation told them they were approaching the pub: the Helensburgh Hotel. A park appeared just ahead of them and to their left, with plenty of street parking just off the main road.

"Pull in here," she directed, wondering to herself if this might have been the same park that Adelaide had mentioned in her journal entries, full of picnicking revellers from Sydney. As Raff pulled over, Charlie saw that they were right in front of the police station. Even though it had modern plastic signs with the blue checkers on white, this building was old. *Perhaps even the original police station*, Charlie thought to herself. "We'll walk the couple of minutes to the pub. It'll do us some good."

When Charlie jumped out of the car — eager to extricate herself from its dingy and pongy interior — she caught sight of the Black again in the side mirror. It filled the entire glass behind her own silhouette, this time almost billowing with black energy. Its eyes were even bigger this close; the 'objects in the mirror may be closer than they appear' warning sticker was jarring. As the adrenaline seized her muscles, she could swear she could feel her heart beating against her very skin, willing to push itself out. She felt a noise build in her chest, a combined gurgle, scream and groan, that stuck in her windpipe as her gaze stuck on the nightmarish vision. She finally let the noise go in a breathy "*fuck!*", dancing on her toes and flicking her fingers, trying to rid herself of some of the energy that had built up in her courtesy of the adrenaline.

"Our friend does seem to like you, Charlie," Raff laughed as he circled around to her side of the car.

"Urgh!" The word released yet more of the pent-up revulsion. "*Fucking mirrors!*"

"You know it's one of their favourite places, right?" Raff struck up conversationally as they looked both ways and crossed the road towards the park. "Mirrors, camera lenses, video screens, window panes, anything with a reflection. And it's not just the Blacks, it's all kinds of spirits. I never knew why, and Maryanne can't seem to tell me, but they seem to find those spaces comfortable. Or comforting. Perhaps because mirrors and the photos are merely a likeness of the real world. Just how the spirits are just a reflection — a manifestation — of their former selves."

The depth of Raff's thoughts stunned her. "You're just unpredictable, aren't you?" Charlie said before she could catch herself. "I never seem to know what's going to come out of your mouth."

Raff seemed to take this as a compliment as they made their way around the playground. Young children and their parents were making use of the final light of the day before having to return home to dinner and bed. The hotel itself was just like any other regional pub. Square, stone, and solid. It boasted the same rural menu, and the usual customers. Tradesmen, dirty from a day's work, sharing a beer. Families eating bucket-loads of chips, while their children screamed around the outside courtyard unsupervised. Pensioners enjoying an early discounted dinner. The local drunkards, dirty and dishevelled, slouched over the bar with their 'happy hour' drinks in hand. Nothing 'happy' about them.

Raff and Charlie joined the throng, sitting at a table by the door, pints of beer in hand, and their own early dinners before them. Chicken parmigianas, dripping with cheese, atop a mountain of chips, served with a too-well-dressed side-salad. Night would fall early, with Autumn well-and-truly settling in, so the early dinner was not such a bad plan. Raff sat in silence, observing the people around them, not interested in any of her attempts to make conversation. So Charlie fished out Addie's journal, taking the opportunity to continue reading.

17

You Shouldn't Be Here

Tuesday 25 February 1913

I tried not to let it happen. God damn me, but I tried. My physical attraction was not instantaneous, as it was with the other men. The boys who meant nothing to me but a distraction from tedium. Dr Albert is a handsome man, no doubt about that, but I simply did not think to look at him this way. No, it was his kind nature, gentleness with the patients, and good humour that first sparked my attraction. Only then did I notice the softness of his skin, the angles to his jaw, the breadth of his shoulders, and the depth of those eyes. My God, but I think I may have fallen for him. It is giddying.

These two weeks without Beryl have been lonelier than ever, so perhaps that is why the attraction built so strongly, and so quickly. I believe he feels it too. I wouldn't dare to hope, except I sometimes catch him watching me a little longer than he should. Or I see his eyes darting to watch my lips as we converse about the patients. In those moments, I've seen his tongue dart out to lick his own lips. Almost like he's hungry for mine. His daily rounds, where we can meet and talk, are a sacred time now. I wonder if he describes them the same way.

Oh, Beryl, I am sorry. I am the first to break our pledge. Our promise not to become attached to anyone but each other. Not to fall in love. Not to abandon the other.

Monday 15 April 1913

I had the most intriguing encounter these past few days. It almost has me questioning everything I know. I shall have to ponder longer, and I hope this diary entry will help me to do so.

An elderly Aboriginal woman and her granddaughter arrived at the Sanatorium late on Saturday night. They were the first indigenous people I had seen here. Both were malnourished and travel-worn. Their simple clothing was torn in places, mended-over several times, and covered in dust. It was hard to tell the woman's age. She may have been in her sixties, or older. She was lined and had grey in her hair, but could not tell me her age or the age of the child. I guessed the girl to be four years old.

The thing that most shocked me, was how articulate the woman was. There was no sign of booze on her breath. She spoke English well, and even seemed to have something of an education behind her. She was not hostile or ignorant. It went against everything I'd ever been told growing up. That I should walk on the other side of the road if I saw them coming. That they were uncivilised, uncouth, aggressive, thieves, and drunk at all hours of the day. This woman...well, she was none of those things.

The child she had with her was so unwell, she could scarcely speak. I made her comfortable in the ward, with the other women and children, but I just knew from the moment I saw her that she would not survive. Her grandmother told me the girl had only just succumbed to the disease a few days ago. How swiftly it took the poor little thing. I also cannot believe the grandmother herself has been sick less than a week. Though she refused treatment, she is little better off than the girl. And if she is to be believed, she came here from Salt Pan Creek on foot and by water in less than a day. A long way to travel when well, let alone when cursed with the White Plague.

The child died last night, as I suspected she would. The Aboriginal woman wanted to leave with her body straight away. We were all suspicious. What means could this woman possibly have to bury her safely? To avoid further spread of the contagion? But, when the woman picked up her kin, holding her over her shoulder, tears running down her lined face, how could we stand in her way? She took the girl's body and she left, back the way she had come. As I watched her walk into the bush, I wondered if she would even make it home.

Dr Albert told me this morning that it is quite common for the Aborigines to die quickly from consumption after the first sign of symptoms. And that the death rate is much higher. Though there are no statistics, so we cannot know exactly how many, or even begin to fathom why this is so.

Perhaps it is because they do not seek treatment? I asked the grandmother why they would not come to the Sanatorium. Her answer chilled me. Perhaps because, for us, it rings too true. "We do not come to the hospital, because the hospital is where you go to die." She had seemed almost guilty that she had thwarted this custom for the slimmest chance of saving her young granddaughter. "We would rather die with our family," she'd said.

So many patients who die here are forgotten by their families. Maybe that is the real tragedy.

Wednesday 18 June 1913

I cannot believe it has been so long since my last journal entry. In those early months, boredom had seen me confiding in these pages often. Now that I have settled so — and now that Dr Albert is here — the days seem to fly by.

The Doctor has settled into his own routine as well. He is quite besotted by the Superintendent, as I am. I admire his dedication to his profession above all else, even our affections. Most recently, the Superintendent decreed that we shall all stop using the term 'consumptives' or 'Consumption' and instead only refer to this scourge by its proper name. Tuberculosis. It is these small changes that may seem insignificant to most, including dear Beryl, but that I understand are so important to turning the tide of opinion and treatment. On this, Dr Albert and I are of one mind.

Beryl takes all this seriousness in her stride. Though she rarely joins our conversations, preferring to joke, to steal away for fun and pranks, or to barter cigarettes and alcohol. Dr Albert knows she is doing this, and still she has not gotten into trouble. It endears him to me even more, that he should protect my sister for me. And dear Beryl, she has also taken the doctor into our circle. She's never said a cross word to me over our broken bargain, or over the amount of time she now has to share me with him.

Thursday 4 December 1913

To think I have not picked up this journal in months, again. Perhaps it is because everything has become so similar. The days and weeks are blurring into each other. Everything is the same. Why should I document the constant?

But today, something was different. It was Beryl who noticed it first, but now the rest of us cannot help but wonder how we failed to see it before. Mrs Palmer, the Superintendent's wife, is most certainly with child again. Her stomach is quite rounded. I would not hesitate to guess at her being in her fourth month already. The hospital was abuzz, and so the superintendent of course confirmed it to the doctors, and Dr Albert confirmed it to me.

Children come and go all the time in these walls, but this feels different to me. Perhaps it is a sign? I wonder if Albert and I shall one day soon commit to a life, and to children, together as well?

* * *

On the road again, Charlie unexpectedly found herself in the Dream. She was back in Sandgate Cemetery, the Catholic church looming over her, casting more shadows in what was already a deep night. Any hint of moonlight was obscured by its towering frame. She thought back to how she ended up here, nervous that it was not her own intent that had brought her to the Dream. *The last thing I remember, was getting back in the car with Raff*, she thought to herself. *Leaving the hotel, and driving... Shit, I think I'm asleep.*

The last thing I remember... Charlie lurched as the message slammed into her, echoing her own thought. While there were no voices, as such, in the Dream, the tone of this communication was still strong. Masculine, as Raff had said. It was also deep, but not in a pleasant way. The words almost reverberated as she registered them, like how a sob catches in your throat, or a call might echo in a deep cave. She tried to spot him — the Black — amongst the tombs; the angels, crucifixes, and cherubs of Sandate. She couldn't see him anywhere and yet his voice continued, pounding at her desperately. *The last thing I remember...*

Show yourself. Charlie approached the door to the church unconsciously,

106

scanning its shadowed path, door and windows. *Tell me what keeps you here. What is the last thing you remember? Or are you copying me? Mocking me?*

The last thing I remember... I remember... I'm not supposed to be here. Charlie could not tell which direction the voice was coming from, but she continued to the base of the church, now standing before its huge, plain white doors. This was where he had appeared before. This was where she felt she'd find him.

Not supposed to be where? The energy built at Charlie's question, the reverberations his words had left inside her not dissipating but growing. She felt if she were to look down at her white, gleaming form, she would see herself coming apart. Spreading as mist-like tendrils, just how this spirit liked to show itself. Small pieces of herself breaking, fracturing, but hanging on as she spiralled into chaotic shapes.

The moon-eyes opened before her, invisible eyelids peeling back mere millimetres from her own. Each eye was large enough to cover her entire face, absorb her head and then some. Together, they blinded her. She felt apprehension paralyse her as he loomed up and over her. *YOU are not supposed to be HERE!!* The anger of the voice thrust her from the Dream, knocking her back into Raff's passenger seat with a loud intake of breath.

Charlie spluttered at the sensation of being ripped from the Dream, of feeling winded whilst holding a lungful of air tightly in her chest. She felt wildly at the ripped seat, the seat belt tight against her, the padded door of the car, the dusty dashboard, and even Raff's hairy, taut arm. As though touching these things would help ground herself back into this world. She released the air in her lungs forcefully, before sucking another gulp of breath greedily. "Welcome back." Raff pulled his forearm away from her, gripping the steering wheel with both hands. He rubbed at the hairs on his arms, which were standing on end.

"I-I was in the Dream," Charlie said as she massaged her forehead, finally feeling like she was back to reality.

"I *know.*"

Charlie turned to stare at him, seeing for the first time how dark it had become outside. His face was illuminated in yellow glare from the car's headlights. It made his stubble and spindly beard look even more ragged, and the pock mark scars in his cheeks seem deeper. "You know?"

"You really should spend more time around people like us, Charlie. Yes, you can always tell when someone is in the Dream if they're near to you. It's like…It's like part of the Dream seeps out, you know? Nah, you don't know." Charlie turned now to look out the windscreen at the gravel road illuminated in the night. The shadows of squat gum trees and thick scrub were evident on either side of the dark road. They were far from town.

"Where are we?" Charlie wound down her window, despite how chilly the air had gotten, smelling the wet, deep scents of the Australian bush at night. The sounds of crickets and tyres scraping gravel came through the open window along with the smells.

"I did some scouting while you were napping. Trying to find the best way in. And then I just *drove*. Nothing else to do until it got late enough." Charlie checked the dash clock: 10:49 p.m. She hadn't just 'dozed off'. She'd been in the Dream for hours. "It's weird."

"Hm?" Charlie prompted when Raff left the statement hanging, unfinished. Anxiety started to replace the shock, bubbling under her skin like little acid pustules. They would have to make it to Waterfall soon. She felt the pressure of time popping those abscesses beneath her skin, making her itch and tingle.

"It's *weird. You.* Getting sucked into the Dream when you're sleeping. I mean, that happened to me at first, *of course*. It's how the transition starts for all of us. Sometimes it happens when a spirit first reaches out to me. But as soon as I accepted my purpose, got control of it, it stopped. Being pulled in like *that,* being pulled in by a spirit I've already connected to, hasn't happened to me in years."

"Maybe it's different for Keepers?"

"Nah…" Raff drew out the word, tilting his chin up and widening his eyes as he said it. "Nah, I don't think so. Not going off the other Keepers I've met. I think it's because you're *not supposed to be here*. Not like this." It felt like an accusation again. Like Raff blamed her for staying alive, and she clenched her fists until her nails bit into her palms. It also terrifyingly reminded her of what the Black had said to her in the Dream. What was she supposed to say in response to a statement like that? She decided to ignore it and moved the conversation in a different direction.

"I saw my Black again, in the Newcastle cemetery." She paused for effect, and to let Raff know the previous conversation was done. "He was angry, copying me, mocking me almost. He didn't seem to want me there."

"Yeah, nah…" Raff trailed off, keeping his eyes on the road. His constant use of the contradictory euphemism annoyed her. "He needs you, and he knows it. He probably just doesn't like that we're *here*. Either because he feels ignored, or because there *is* a connection between him and those sisters." Raff took one hand off the steering wheel and motioned at the dark night around them. The streetlights were back now, illuminating a concrete bridge just ahead of them. They passed under it and he pulled to the side of the road, before doing a u-turn and heading back the way they'd come. Charlie tensed in her seat, her hands still balled into fists.

"Here where?" She couldn't see any buildings around her.

Just passed the bridge again, Raff pulled off the side of the road into a large shoulder, his tyres practically hugging the edge of the bush. "*Here.* Waterfall Sanatorium."

18

Breathed Into Existence

Charlie pushed her mobile phone into the hidden pocket of her tights, her text messages sent. At least Tess and Trent would know where they were and what they were trying. The felt lining of her tights helped keep her legs warm, but she still shivered. The shadows of the trees reminded her of the time Tess, Trent and she had snuck into the dig site of the convict's road. It had felt like the night was closing in around them, ready to swallow them. She pulled the cowl of her hoodie up, tightening it around her, and adjusted the straps of her backpack. A torch, hooked onto the strap for easy access, knocked into the bones of her wrist. She felt every sensation deeply, her nerves on overdrive.

"What are you doing?" Charlie asked, seeing Raff still bent inside the vehicle, one leg held aloft for balance. He pulled himself free, dusting his hands.

"Making sure no one tows or reports the car." He motioned to the paper he'd put in the window, but quoted aloud for her so she wouldn't have to squint in the dark. "*Car trouble. I've gone to organise a mechanic. Please don't tow the car. BRB.* There's a phone number too, but I've smudged out some of it with water so they won't be able to reach anyone."

"And if the cops check the rego?" Charlie asked suspiciously.

"It's registered to my sister. She has a record as clean as a whistle." They crossed the road to the edge of the bush, Raff leading the way up a dirt track dry but rutted by repeated heavy rains and poor maintenance.

"I didn't know you had a sister…"

"A lot you don't know." Charlie had the distinct impression Raff wasn't just referring to his own family history. As a retort built inside her, she reminded herself there was a lot *he* didn't know either.

A short way up the track — which was wide enough for a car despite the bush trying to reclaim it — they came to a metal fence. It was chained and padlocked, and a large, white and red sign sat prominently to its side. SPECIAL AREA. NO ENTRY. MAXIMUM PENALTY $44,000. THIS AREA IS UNDER SURVEILLANCE.

"I do *not* have that kind of money to waste," Charlie said, trembling.

"Who does?" Raff walked past the sign and swung one leg over the fence.

"Is-isn't there another way?"

Raff rolled his second leg over and landed heavily on the other side. "Nope." Those anxiety blisters beneath her skin were overflowing now. She felt lightheaded, as though she might pass out if she tried to climb this fence. This fence, that wasn't just a barrier to a 'special area,' but a divide between who she'd always been, and who she was becoming. She was a *lawyer*. Or at least, she had been. She didn't do this type of thing. "There's no other way, Charlie." She took a breath so deep she could imagine her rib cage expanding and pressing down on her guts. Forcing them to compress and quiet themselves. And she joined Raff on the other side of the fence.

As soon as she was through, it was as though something in her had broken. It snapped some of the anxiety loose, although the adrenaline continued to pump in waves. She'd done it. And now she had to keep going forward. She pulled at her hood again, ensuring it was tight around her face. "Here," Raff said, passing her a black baseball cap. "Put that on too. It'll obscure most of your face."

Charlie took it quickly, muttering "thanks" beneath her breath as she bowed her head to push the cap beneath her hoodie. They turned on their torches, red light only, as they made their way up and through the bush along the path. The ground seemed to hold water exceptionally well. Although there'd been no sign of rain for days, puddles still clustered between the larger rocks, and their feet sunk into the grassy dirt on more than one occasion. They picked up the pace, the briskness of their strides helping to absorb some of the adrenaline and calm her breathing. She fell into the rhythm of the exercise, something familiar, and focused on the red lights bobbing across the dark ground.

"She's definitely here," Raff breathed, not long after they'd begun their trek through the bush and to the abandoned Sanatorium. "I can feel that we're close. Wow, she's a powerful one."

"That's good," Charlie sighed, relieved. "Maybe we'll finally get some answers, then."

Raff had his phone with him. At first, he'd frequently checked it, occasionally steering them off the main path and through a wombat trail. Now, back on a main path, he simply kept his head forward. Walking even faster than before. "Can you *feel* it?" Raff whispered eagerly, passion and fervour breaking past his lips with each word.

Charlie tilted her head slightly as she allowed herself to reconnect with her emotions. At first, all she felt was the cool night air tingling her exposed skin. Then she felt the deeper cool, that exuded not just from the air, but some place deeper. She recognised it as the same chill that came with the Black now anchored to her, and tentatively gazed over her shoulder. He wasn't there. It wasn't just that she couldn't see him. She could *feel* he wasn't there. Perhaps so angry at her decision to proceed that, for a moment, he'd flitted back to Sandgate. "It does feel cold…"

"And?" Raff prompted.

"And like we're being watched." She shuddered at both sensations and bowed her head.

"Can you feel it tugging at you though?"

Charlie opened herself slightly again, wondering if Raff was now directing them not with satellite maps, but his own internal blackened compass. "No," she said. Raff didn't answer, but pushed on even faster. Charlie jogged a little to catch up with him, and then saw what he must have been feeling — if not seeing — ahead of them. Structures were looming out of the darkness, far blacker and more opaque than the trees. Much larger too. A huge, towering trunk was the first they passed. In the dark, its pale concrete walls appeared covered in mould. Dark fingers of it ran down its sides. Perhaps a water tank? To their left, a telephone tower rose higher than the trees. And then before them, and to their right, more towering boulders covered in scraggly scrub loomed. Except they weren't boulders. They were *houses.*

As they got closer, their red torches reflected off more metal fences, these hung with further warning signs. DANGER. NO UNAUTHORISED ENTRY. DANGER. ASBESTOS. DANGER. The shock of these buildings emerging out of not only the dark, but from the bush, kept some of her fear momentarily at bay. When reading about Waterfall Sanatorium, it had said the location of the hospital had been chosen for its remoteness. Not just to keep others safe from Consumption, but because fresh air was considered the best treatment. Even with those Wikipedia entries, she hadn't pictured *this.* It was like walking into a ghost town, swallowed up by the bush and forgotten.

Raff turned off his torch, and she did the same. The moonlight illuminated enough of their path now they were on the main road. The light glistened on the fences and the broken windows of the cottages. "I didn't expect there to be houses here as well," Charlie whispered. The sensation of being watched, of being followed, grew. She could imagine countless black eyes peering at them from those boarded up asbestos-filled rooms. When had they been abandoned? When had children and families last run along these streets? When had the doors last opened to the sounds of people laughing, crying, shouting, or doing *anything* inside. When had they been *forgotten?* Although it had been tarmacked, the narrow road beneath their feet was full of potholes, covered not just in dust but in thick layers of dirt from years. Decades.

The houses all looked the same. Dark red roofs. Pale walls, covered in those same black fingers of decay. They were all the same shape and size, squat and square, sitting amongst the dense grass. Most no longer had paths, though occasionally she saw a narrow dirt track meandering to their doors. Graffiti marred many of their surfaces. What had once been gardens were now overgrown, the imported palms and shrubs as eager to overtake what man had built as the bush was. In one, she saw an old swing set. So similar to the green and yellow set she'd had as a child. She counted the houses as she passed, to distract herself from the gaze of wisps gone by. One…two…three…four…five…six…seven…

Once the houses were behind them, they joined a very well-kept road. This one was not layered in the same dustings of time. It was used often. It was wider, too, and the carparks in front of them were well-marked with paint. This must be part of the hospital that was still in use. She tried to huddle into herself, make herself smaller, not wanting to be spotted by the surveillance that multiple signs now threatened. To their right, another narrow, though well-maintained, path snaked. "Which way?" Charlie whispered.

Raff nodded to their right with his head, to Charlie's relief. A couple of porch lights glowed dimly in the distance, and the dark narrow path seemed the safest option. They followed it, hugging the fence that bordered the abandoned cottages. As the trail looped around to the left, more mature trees sprouted before them. "Come on," Raff whispered, so softly that Charlie could barely hear him. The thought of patients and staff mere metres from them, through those brick walls, made panic start to rise in her again. It felt like every beat of her heart was pained and forced. She gratefully followed Raff away from them and to the cover of the trees.

As they approached, Charlie saw yet another fence. This one mostly obscured in the night and deep foliage. She laced her fingers through the metal, leaning forward to look into the distance at another abandoned building. This one not a small cottage, but much, much bigger. The building wasn't close to the fence, so it was hard to see, but she caught a glimpse of a railing, leading down and into the brush. "Is this it?"

Raff nodded his head. "I can feel it." He motioned to his right and they walked around the fence, their footsteps incredibly loud in the quiet. They drew closer to the large building, which seemed to breath itself into existence from the night.

19

Forgotten Eyes and Hands

Catwalks peeled from the building's top stories to be swallowed by the darkened gardens. As Charlie and Raff raced along its fence and around the corner, it emerged in its entirety. Two floors spreading so far in front of them it was impossible to tell how long it was in this gloom. It wasn't just the building itself that was imposing; it was the feeling that emanated from it. It struck in waves of roiling turmoil, misery, and fear. Confusion and desperation were its undercurrents. She paused at the corner of the fence, turning to look through its chain links. Here the bush was having more success overtaking the walls and windows. As was the decay.

"R-R-Raff…" It was more of a breath than a whisper. "I don't know if I can go in… I-I-I…" He pressed a hand to her mouth and nodded with his head further down the road. Flattened by the sheer depression of this place, she'd missed something. Something terribly important. Parked in front of the fence, about halfway down, was a white car. From this far, it was impossible to tell what was written on its sides, but the fact it had writing at all, as well as lights on its roof, indicated this was the 'surveillance' that had been threatened by so many signs.

Charlie brought her own hands to her mouth, allowing Raff to move his away. He began pushing on the fence, gently, as he slowly walked in the direction of the car. She heard a stone shift under his foot, and the fence whine gently, and grimaced. It hurt to hold her breath, but it hurt more to breathe. Finally, the fence gave way a little more in one spot and Raff motioned her forward. The fence had been pushed back here before. A small gap had opened between the criss-crossed wires and the pole. Barely wide enough for a person to squeeze through. Raff went first, agonisingly slowly, the wires grating and clinking. How she longed for a breeze, anything, to mask their sounds in the night.

Now through the other side, the brush crunching under his feet, Raff motioned frantically for Charlie to join him. She faltered, looking up at the Sanatorium. Its dark, broken windows loomed like gaping mouths. If she'd thought the ghost-houses had been full of eyes, *this* was something else. Not just a feeling of hundreds of watchers looking down at her, but a sense of their hands waiting in the dark to snare her. The faintness in her head was back, her limbs tingling while her vision tinged white. *"Charlie..."* he hissed. It wasn't just Raff she could hear now. The crunching of boots on rough tarmac and gravel was also beginning to echo towards her. Looking up she saw the palest flash of light far in the distance, bobbing and swerving. The guard was coming. And here she was, caught between natural and supernatural danger. It literally felt like she was tearing in two. *"Charlie!"*

Before she could think herself out of it, she bent her head low, refusing to look at those windows or walls, and instead focussing only on the fence. She pushed until the gap opened up and then snaked her leg inside, followed by her torso. It may have only been a chain link fence, but it seemed to separate entire worlds. While suspended there, the fence crushing down on her chest and stomach, she could feel the cold, the tangled grass, and the decay of that other world press against one leg. Her other leg, trapped in reality, was covered with goosebumps as the guard strode closer. She squirmed as her backpack caught and the footsteps continued. She didn't know whether it would be worse to be caught, or to succeed and to enter the abandoned hospital.

Raff didn't give her the chance to deliberate any further, reaching for her, pulling her free, and then roughly shoving her through the first doorless entry and into the Sanatorium.

* * *

Charlie tried to quiet her breathing as she and Raff made their way through the abandonment, decay, ruin and destruction. Her lips felt dry as each breath pushed out roughly. Each intake shuddered as it entered her lungs, as though even her windpipe was gasping and trembling. Everything had been vandalised. Broken glass crunched under foot in every room and hallway, and graffiti marred every wall. Smiling faces, obscene words and warnings, and several larger-than-life penises. Under the steps, an ominous "he waits here" made every hair on her neck prickle and vibrate. Pretty much anything that could be carried away easily had been. Most rooms didn't even have curtains anymore, and those that did were ripped, dirty, and stained. Their flower patterns were barely recognisable. While the beds were long gone, for some reason, it looked like every chair had been left behind. Plastic, metal, upholstered, wooden…red, blue, cream… Seeing them stacked in rough, crazed patterns was as unnerving as the emptiness.

It wasn't just glass that crackled underfoot, but plaster fallen from the walls and ceilings, as well as decades of dirt and the nature that had found its way inside. The dark mould she'd spotted outside had taken root inside as well, its tendrils wrapping around the ceiling as well as the walls. It reminded her of the Black spirit and his own branches reaching out to her, and she shuddered. The sensation wasn't helped by how much colder it was inside, and an intensified feeling of being observed, watched, followed. Inside, the doors had begun to rot, some of them hanging from their hinges. Even the internal glass panes had been smashed, evidently on purpose. Occasionally, a broken piece would glint in the moonlight, startling Charlie into thinking she was seeing those moon-eyes.

Neither Raff nor Charlie said anything to each other as they solemnly walked through this place. Charlie wondered how many of these emotions Raff was feeling. Could he only connect to the Blacks? Or could he feel the tragedy, the insanity, the pain, the loss as well? She could feel niggles of Purples, Blues and Greys here, and other types of spirit she'd never encountered before. The thought of connecting to all of them at once terrified her enough that she considered rushing to one of the open balconies and screaming at the guard for help. There was no end to the verandas; every level opened outside at some point, no doubt to let in the fresh air the patients so desperately needed. She could picture the patients in their beds and chairs, doing nothing but sitting, breathing, as the disease consumed them.

Mostly, the hospital was a series of open wards. There was the occasional enclosed room, and bathroom of course, and hallways. It began to feel like a maze. She lost count of the wards and archways, keeping track by whether the view out the window was of the security guard and his car, or of the entangled gardens and catwalks. Raff led them upstairs after only a brief exploration on the bottom floor, and the oppression deepened. Upstairs largely mirrored below in terms of layout, but the holes in the ceiling were wider, like mammoth maws eating away at the roof. The walls were full of holes, at times revealing wiring hanging loose. There was even more debris and mould; some walls were more black than yellow. In one room, a tree grew from its centre. Unfathomably. This was the *second* storey and yet there it was, reclaiming its place in this world.

Upstairs, there was the occasional rusted bedframe left behind. And she could see, through the gloom, that there were railings on the ceilings in the wards. For curtains, she guessed, to give the patience some semblance of privacy. Every step she took, every turn she made, she felt as though she were encountering *something*. The emotions were thick: loneliness, agony, sorrow. Wisps danced everywhere here; not just embodied emotions, but memories, replaying their last moments of life over-and-over. Mostly they were patients, ambling, coughing, laying in imaginary beds. She saw the occasional nurse or doctor as well. Worse than the wisps were the echoes and calls of spirits she had not connected with. That had not entangled her. *Dozens.* Whose responsibility were they? How long would they wait here for a Keeper or a Guide to show them the way? Most were balanced, she realised, as they moved deeper in. Simply experiencing what they needed to move on. It was the sheer gravity of them that overwhelmed her.

And those *eyes*. Those *hands*. All of them watching, waiting, *stalking*.

Finally, she fell to her knees. The plaster grated at her flesh through her leggings, and she could feel the burs from the grass and bush from their nighttime walk scratching at her from the pressure of her own body. "Raff," she whispered so softly she didn't think he'd hear her. But his echoing footsteps halted, debris grinding as he spun on his heels to look back at her. "Can you feel them? *All* of them? So many...so...so..." Raff returned and squatted beside her on his haunches, reaching down to lift her hands. He brushed the dirt and plaster from them before holding them gently. "Can you feel them?"

"Not like you can," Raff said compassionately as he shook his head. "They're barely echoes to me." The sound of their voices splitting the silence was both unsettling and comforting. Hearing a living voice snapped some of the tension, even though it risked them being overheard by the living outside. She wasn't sure if she even cared if they were apprehended.

"I don't know how I'm going to dig through all of this to find your Black," she said. Raff stood, gently encouraging Charlie to her feet by pushing on her elbows. He guided her back the way they'd come. Back past the tree growing in the floor, and through to a room that looked out and over the tangled walkways and overgrowth. He quietly brushed some of the plaster aside with his hands before encouraging her to sit.

"The others don't need you," Raff said softly, evenly, sitting opposite her and holding her hands again. "Don't focus on the noise, or the bustle, or the emotion. Focus only on the *need*." Charlie's breaths were shuddering on entry and exit now, and she closed her eyes, trying to calm them. The cold had sunk so deeply into her that even if she could quieten her anxiety, she doubted the shudders would cease. "You'll need to enter the Dream."

Charlie's eyes fluttered open, the cold stinging as it reconnected with her moist eyeballs. "Can't *you* do it? *Please?*"

Raff shook his head. "I could, but it wouldn't achieve much. I could find her, but I can't see what's imbalanced. I can't figure out what's wrong like you can. I can teach her, let her know she's a Black and what that means. But I can't help her find Balance, which she needs to do first. I need you to help me." Charlie squeezed her eyes shut again, and pressed her lips together until they folded inwards on themselves. She gave a brisk nod.

"Don't leave me here, please. Just watch. Please, just stand watch."

"Don't worry, Charlie. I won't leave you. I'll watch over you. You'll be safe."

20

Neglected, Rotted Memories

As Charlie entered the Dream, she held one intent firmly in her mind, *no new connections*. Maryanne's words of wisdom to maintain control were ringing in her ears. As was Raff's more recent advice to drown out the bustle of noise and emotion, focussing only on the *need*. She allowed herself to see, like opening her eyes, and found herself standing in the same room in which her mortal body sat. In the Dream, in this moment, the room was almost unrecognisable.

The walls were intact and smooth, the ceiling a bright white. No plaster or dirt crunched underfoot, and each window was intact. Interspersed along the ceiling were hanging candelabras in simple but elegant black metal. Two candles glowed brightly in each one, and a lantern sat on a small table in the middle of the room, glowing calmingly. There were twenty beds in here, ten on each wall. Each was positioned with an open window on either side of the bedhead, so not only natural light but also air could breeze through. The single beds were small, yet just as elegant as the candelabras with their black frames and slim, small, metal canopy above. Small oxygen tanks hung suspended from some of these canopies. Each bed was dressed in white sheets, with a white ruffle-edged blanket atop them.

Spots of greenery were also speckled about the room. On the centre and end tables and in vases on the bedsides. Some beds had chairs at their feet, too small, it seemed for an adult. Charlie took all of this in, in a single heartbeat. And then the wisps emerged. Breathing themselves to life from the very walls. Colourless imitations of their former selves, pulling their forms together from the colours around them. Most moved too fast, or were too blurred, for their features to stand out. And yet Charlie could identify the distinct nursing uniforms: The stiff blue dresses, the white smocks that fully enwrapped them, the white caps encompassing their well-kept hair, and the veils trailing either in front of the nurses' faces or behind them.

Other wisps must have been patients. If she stared long and hard enough, Charlie could make out their dressing gowns, their slippered feet, and their ankle-length nighties. Some of the wisps were small. It was then Charlie realised that young girls must have stayed in this hospital as well. She laughed to herself as one of the wisps, in a dark, long-sleeved gown chased after several of the smaller wisps. She could almost hear their echoed shouts of 'hurry! The mistress is after us!'

The normality of the Sanatorium in this layer of the Dream calmed her. It wasn't anything like the place she and Raff had come upon at night in the real world. Perhaps it was the decades of neglect, not just of the building, but of the memories and the very place, that had made it so dark and foreboding. The building hadn't just been left to rot. Its history had been left to be forgotten as well. That was the scariest, and the saddest, part of it all. No wonder those spirits left behind had become so frenzied.

Need, Charlie thought again, starting to make her way through the ward. She reached a balcony, in excellent repair. None of the wooden planks on the floor or ceiling had rotted. Black metal-framed beds, dressed in the same white linen, stood here as well. A white fabric frame encircled the head of each bed, and each had its own small, white wooden bedside table. These were adorned with flowers in vases. Such care had been made for the patients' wellbeing. Charlie smiled wryly to herself as she thought, seeing the beds pressed up between the windows, that if whoever was in each bed were to lean forward, they would be able to converse with those in the beds inside as well. They were all so close together. The view from here, looking out and over the bush, was excellent. Hammock-style chairs sat beside the balustrade. It was no wonder people believed this view, this country air, was healing.

On the balcony, one of the figures who moved amongst the beds solidified. She was not a wisp. Her short, boxy frame was instantly familiar. Even though her veil hung over her face, Charlie knew this was Adelaide. She reached out to her, attempting to connect. It was like reaching out to grasp hold of mist. Her attempts slid through, and off, Adelaide, who remained oblivious to Charlie's presence. Even if she was Raff's Black, Charlie couldn't reach her. He'd made the connection first. Another fully-formed person strode past her and towards Adelaide. This was a man, dressed in dark trousers and a dark tie, but with a white buttoned coat reaching down past his knees. His stiff, white collar stood erect around his throat, showing off the navy tie's band. A pair of round spectacles were balanced on the tip of his nose.

Dr Albert? Charlie thought to herself. Adelaide raised her head and confirmed this suspicion by addressing him. Charlie could understand how Addie had described Dr Albert as 'dashing' in her journals. He indeed had a firm jaw line, with prominent baby's-bottom-chin. His long, thin nose was perfectly proportioned for his equally long, thin face. There were no bags around his large eyes nor lines around his mouth. A pencil moustache clung to his upper lip like a manicured shadow. His dark blonde hair was side parted with strong wax, the fringe waving across his forehead. There were, as Addie had described, several hairs that had evaded his capture. His glasses only made him more dapper.

Charlie took a step towards the doctor and the Dream shifted, darkened, became somewhat closer to its present state. Dr Albert was still there, but bent over one of these hospital beds. The bed was pushed up against a corner and such bleakness surrounded it that she could hardly see if they were in one of the open wards or a smaller room. *"Please,"* Albert begged, his breaking voice drawing Charlie's full attention. The agony was enough to shatter her own heart. "Don't leave me, my love." She took another step forward, seeing now that Dr Albert's large hands encircled another hand so small, so frail, it was almost overwhelmed. The hand looked skeletal, withered, consumed.

Addie? Charlie sent. The vision continued uninterrupted.

"I cannot…I c-c-can—" Albert's sentence was left unfinished as he bowed his head over the wasted hand and his shoulders rumbled with unshed cries.

"Iiiit'sss…tiiiiiimmmme…" The voice that scraped from that woman was torturous. She could feel its rasping breath shuddering into her as it left the sick bed like an infectious breeze. It was impossible to tell whose voice it was. All tone, all character, all inflection had been stripped away by the disease. Charlie took another step forward and glimpsed more of the emaciated arm.

"I promise," Albert found his voice again. "I promise we'll be together again. I'll ensure it. Our bodies shall lie together in the ground for all eternity, so our souls will always be entwined. Even in death."

This patient, this withered woman, was Raff's Black spirit. It must be. She went to take another step forward, now almost close enough to peer around Albert and see the woman's face. As she went to move, the Dream blurred. She felt the tug of that invisible string in her back and was pulled, floundering, into a different layer of the Dream.

No! Charlie sent the word without thinking, disappointment and frustration spewing from her. She'd been so close to finding the identity of the Black, to confirming if it was Adelaide.

Instead, Charlie was back where she'd started. In that same room, that same ward. Except this time, she was not alone. A large, black figure loomed menacingly in the corner. The black of its features was so dark and deep, they glistened. It was *not* her Black spirit. She was certain it wasn't Raff's Black either; this was undoubtedly a man. His shoulders were broad, and a cape cascaded around his entire body. Like the feathers of a raven. His white eyes glistened brightly, mischievously. His limbs were human-like, although each finger ended in a sharp and curled talon.

Even though she'd never seen this spirit before, it felt familiar. *Very* familiar. *Raff?* It didn't look anything like Raff in the real world, but somehow, she knew. She could feel him, his soul, his character. His appearance startled her. She knew that she manifested in a different way in the Dream too. She'd seen glimpses of her shining white arms. Of course Raff would look different; she just hadn't put much thought to it until now.

What are you doing here?! I asked you to keep watch.

You were taking too long. Raff's disembodied voice entered her mind like a whisper. Despite the unpleasantness of the experience, the tone of the words was distinctly Raff.

That's not the point. You promised *you'd keep watch.*

What can I say? Raff took a step towards her, his black feather cape moving like water behind him. *I'm a Guide for Blacks for a reason. Betrayal is part of my nature. It's what I know best.*

I was so close... Charlie resisted fleeing the Dream in rage. What would be the point? They hadn't found what they needed. *I almost knew which sister it was, until you pulled me back.*

We're both here now. I can help you. You need me. We need each other. I can feel her *now. She's here. It's why I entered the Dream.* Raff held out one of his taloned hands to her. His watery feathers swirled up and around each finger as he moved. Charlie felt herself sigh in resignation, and she reached for his hand.

21

Midnight

As Charlie grasped Raff's hand, they were pulled to yet another layer of the Dream. It was Beryl they were watching now. Her honey hair was only just visible beneath her white nurse's cap, but even so, it was evident she'd perfectly coifed the fringe, rolling each side into beautiful scrolls. "Come now, Jane!" Beryl was saying, knocking at a closed door. "You've been in there quite a while now. Honestly, it's no bother if you need some help. There is nothing I haven't seen." She pressed her ear to the door, her cap and fringe flattening as she did so. "Jane?" Beryl stood back and flipped her veil over her face. "I'm coming in now." Beryl twisted the door handle, but it wouldn't open. She pushed her shoulder into the door and still it wouldn't budge. "Jane!" Beryl yelled more frantically now, drawing the attention of the nearby wisps of nurses and other patients.

"Sister Agnes, get Dr Albert!" Beryl whispered fervently, returning to the door to knock and repeat Jane's name over-and-over. "And bring some of the wardsmen or groundsmen!" She yelled over her shoulder, turning back to the door to mumble. "We'll need to get through this door... Jane!"

It wasn't long before Dr Albert was running towards the scene, his coat, Addie and several excited wisps trailing behind him. "Mrs Hughes!" he said forcefully as neared the door, rapping at the wood. "Mrs Hughes, are you quite alright?!" He turned to Beryl. "What happened, Nurse Morgan?"

"Sh-she said she needed to-to go to the bathroom, doctor."

"And you didn't accompany her? Friend or no, you should know better."

"No! She wanted privacy. And she was fine, she was getting better. She should have been fine."

"Mrs Hughes, please stand back from the door." Dr Albert took a step back and motioned at the wardsmen who'd followed him to push against the door. They charged at it, repeatedly with their shoulders. The wood started to crack, and there was a sound behind the door of squeaking as something rubbed against the floor. With a final shove the door came free, before rebounding back at them, forcing them away with echoing exclamations. Beryl was back at the door first, pushing it open to find the tie of a robe securing it like a bungee. She quickly removed a pair of scissors from her apron and cut it free, pushing the door wide to reveal a horrid scene.

A broken chair had fallen to the side, obviously used to brace the door along with the gown's tie. Beryl, who hurried straight through, stepped into a large, darkened puddle of blood. It had oozed over almost the entire bathroom floor, already starting to congeal and stick. The lighter tones of red swirled in the darker in beautiful, yet dreadful, patterns. The mirror above the vanity had been broken, shards of glass speckling the sink. A patient lay in the middle of the room, and the blood, her white nightgown so covered in gore it appeared black. A ragged gouge split her throat in two, revealing sinew and muscle. Streams of blood still trickled down the angry cut, although it appeared to have ceased pumping in earnest.

The woman — Jane — had wrapped a hand towel around her knuckles and was loosely clutching a large shard of broken glass in her right hand. Charlie wondered only for a moment why she'd save her knuckles from the cuts of breaking the mirror when she had done *that* to her throat, only to realise it was the sound not that pain Jane had been avoiding. Her open eyes, already glazing, stared at the ceiling, and a small tug of a smile was frozen on one side of her mouth.

Beryl screamed. Every ounce of her breath was expelled from deep in her stomach, bellowing from her as she brought her hands to her face. She spun, directly into Dr Albert's chest, and began to sob inconsolably. "Out!" Dr Albert commanded in a firm but even tone to the wardsmen and gaggle of

127

observers. "Nick, alert the superintendent. Nurse Adelaide, keep the patients back if you please. Sister Agnes, alert the Matron if you will." As Albert relayed his calm instructions, Charlie could not tear her gaze from Jane. This wasn't just a memory replaying. There was something else, something tugging beneath the surface of this woman.

Charlie? Raff sent, after silently observing the scene. As she spun, she saw Beryl walking towards them again. Confused, she looked back to the now closed door.

"Come now, Jane!" Beryl said as she rapped on the door.

It's a loop, Raff sent to Charlie. *Come on, let's keep moving.*

No. Charlie pulled back from Raff, not allowing him to touch her and perhaps drag her away again. *It's not just a loop. There's another spirit here. Someone else needs my help.*

Jane?

Yes, Jane. There's something...tugging, pulling, beneath her. Her spirit is stuck here.

Replaying the loop?

Charlie turned back to the door as Beryl began shoving at it with her shoulder. *She must be... I can't leave her...* As much as Charlie hadn't wanted to connect with any of the other spirits in this place, she was glad for the chance to help this one. What torment it must have been to relive the moment of your suicide over-and-over for more than a hundred years. Raff merely nodded at her and stepped back.

Charlie didn't stay to watch as the scene replayed, instead she willed herself into the white-tiled bathroom. Blood gushed from Jane's open throat and from the corner of her mouth as she gulped for air. The muscles contracting through the gash forced more life fluid from her body. Jane's eyes were open, imploring. Even if her mind and spirit had willed her existence ended, her body still valiantly fought for life. *Jane...* Charlie knelt by her, the blood unable to touch her. She could see, this close to the body, that the blood still rippled and pooled, whereas the edges had started to congeal. It happened so quickly. *I'm here to help you...*

The woman's final breath gurgled through her open wound. Her eyes turned slightly to focus on Charlie before going vacant. The writhing inside her began in earnest then. As though her spirit were fighting to break free from her own death. Charlie reached a hand towards Mrs Hughes, gently touching her arm, and bracing herself for the woman's life to rush through her.

Jane had been born in Sydney to a banker and his wife, the eldest of four children, and she the only girl. Her mother had passed away following the birth of her youngest brother, from 'complications'. Charlie couldn't see what complications because Jane herself did not understand. All Jane could understand was that the doctors and her father had chosen to save the baby, and not her mother. Charlie saw a twelve-year-old girl step up to fill her mother's shoes, looking after the brothers who were so highly valued. At least, that was, until she'd been married-off herself, to yet another banker. Aged just seventeen, and unwillingly sentenced to begin a family of her own. Because this was what was expected of the women in her family.

Charlie felt a deep and dark sadness in Jane's life, throughout her teenage years, and into adulthood,. A constant companion — a depression — that never abated. Not even with the birth of her daughters. Only daughters. Then, it simply deepened. Not only a postnatal depression, but a fear that her children would end up *just. like. her.* It was only when she was diagnosed with Consumption in her early thirties, and sent to Waterfall, that some of this depression lifted. She was outcast, yes. But she was *outcast*, finally. Free to be not just a daughter and a wife to a banker, but to be herself. She'd revelled in the fresh air, in the bush, and in her conversations with the nurses and other women. Especially with the young and vibrant Beryl. Jane had come into herself. And she had recovered. She had recovered too well. And so, her life in Sydney had awaited her again.

Oh, Jane... Charlie tightened her grip on the woman's arm, on her spirit, and felt the writhing lessen as her ghost emerged from her body and into the room. She was a blue spirit, but not like Marie. Not light and playful. She was a deep, dark, roiling blue spirit. And a deep, dark, midnight blue.

A Midnight. The term came to her unbidden. A Midnight spirit. And just as the term had come to her unbidden, so too did the purpose of a Midnight.

This was a person who had suffered such deep sorrow in life that they had ended it too soon. This was a spirit that needed time to fully process this suffering before they could move on; there was no escaping despair, even in death.

If Charlie could have cried in the Dream, she would have. It wasn't fair. *It isn't fair*, she felt Maryanne's wise words repeat at her. *Who are you to judge?* Certainly not Charlie. If she were to judge, she would not sentence a woman who had experience such sorrow to yet more misery, just because she'd tried to escape it early.

Release her, Charlie... the unbidden voice instructed and before she could think to resist, she did as commanded. Giving Jane the nudge she needed to leave the memory of her own demise, and to accept her fate. As she did, the Midnight spirit loomed closer to her, whispering her pain over and over in tortured words.

So much betrayal, Charlie finally heard the message from Jane amongst her whispered cries. *Grief makes it hard to see...* With that, Jane pulled Charlie through more memories of the Sanatorium, each glimpsed through Jane's eyes. The sisters, Addie and Beryl, together as often as they could be. The doctor, Albert, following them like a third wheel or a lost puppy. There were multiple memories of another place too, that Charlie didn't recognise, deep within the bush. A hut, it seemed, crudely constructed, and buried secretly within the gum trees. She saw Jane there, with Beryl, on more than one occasion. Talking, laughing, feeling anything but this deep melancholy. *Grief makes it hard to see*, Jane repeated, and then she was gone.

The bathroom shuddered and began to rot around her. The tiles cracking, and some chipping from the walls. Dust and plaster settled on the floor. The mirror faded in and out, but broken glass shards were always underfoot. And then the dark mould appeared, spreading its fingers across the grout, tiles and tapware. Charlie and Raff were in the present, yet still in the Dream. She turned to him. He was watching her, his head cocked to one side. *It's time to go, Raff*, Charlie sent, tiredly. She could continue to draw on the energy of the Dream, but it wouldn't lessen the ache inside her.

Raff took a step towards her, his head tilting to his other side as he observed her. He leant his black face closer, his glowing white eyes watching her. *No.* He grabbed her hand again, unexpectedly, and dragged her further into the Dream.

22

Straying Too Deep

Charlie ripped her hand free of Raff's as soon as the Dream stopped spinning. She'd experienced going too deep into the Dream before, when she'd helped Ru's mother let go of her son's spirit. Charlie had almost been trapped there, as that deep layer had disintegrated around her. She wasn't willing to experience that again so soon. Or, if she could help it, ever again. *Enough*! she sent angrily to Raff. *No further. No deeper.* He just continued to watch her, remaining silent. *You can't force this. It will happen or it won't!*

Taking a moment to compose herself, Charlie looked around the room where they now stood. It was an office. A dark walnut desk, with green leather on top of it, sat by the open window. In a matching chair was a man Charlie hadn't seen before. He was slightly shorter than her, his skin olive, and his features dark: dark bushy eyebrows, a dark thick moustache, and short dark hair slicked to one side. His nose was prominent, his most striking feature. He wore a dark woollen suit, complete with vest. His white collar stuck up, just as Albert's had, to reveal the entirety of his black tie. He looked *tired*. Deeply so, and his puffy eyes gazed before him with concern and regret.

A much older Beryl sat in a wooden chair opposite his desk. Instead of the stiff long blue dress, she now wore a stiff, short-sleeve and knee-length blue dress, with white cuffs and collars. Her white apron wasn't as large and only wrapped her front, bulging out slightly at her breasts. She looked slimmer than she had before, and the years had not been kind. Greys peaked out of her honey hair, which had been cut short, and had frizzed slightly. More startling than her age, were the cuts and bruises on her face. One cheekbone was so swollen and raised that it pushed at her eye. Both cheeks were a deep shade of blue and purple. She gingerly held onto a wrist that was bandaged and limp.

"Tell me again, Nurse Morgan," the man said in an even-tempered and gentle tone. "How did you break your wrist? How did you get those bruises on your face?"

"Superintendent," Beryl began. Her voice was much slower and monotonous than Charlie had heard it before. She sounded much older than she should, like her vocal cords had stretched and widened. "I merely fell on the stairs. I slipped. I was careless. Forgive me."

"Beryl, *please*," the superintendent leaned forward, bracing himself on his elbows. His tone was serious and grave, yet the compassion still seeped through. "Anything you say to me within the confines of my office will be kept confidential. To a point, at least. The safety of my wards — my patients and staff — is my utmost responsibility and priority. I don't know how they did things in Egypt, but you've been here long enough. You know me. Please, Beryl, let me help you."

"I-I-I slipped, sir. It was my own fault. I-I deserved it."

Charlie... She turned to see Raff shimmer and fade out of the Dream. Taking one more look at Beryl, who refused to meet the Superintendent's eyes, Charlie did the same, pulling herself away and back to reality.

* * *

Charlie blinked groggily. It took her a moment to orient herself. Something lay over her face, coarse and thick. She could just make out specks of light through the weaves of the fabric. She coughed as she breathed, and the smell of decay, damp and stagnation filled her lungs. She floundered with her arms, pushing the fabric off her, and sat up, breathing deeply. She was in the Sanatorium, of course, but the night had long since passed. Bright daylight spilled through the windows, illuminating the hospital in far more detail than she'd seen it the previous day. She could see every hole, every word of profane graffiti, and just how much this place had rotted away. Wasting just like the tuberculosis patients within its walls had wasted so many years ago.

She pushed the fabric off her completely, noticing that it was one of the old curtains. Chairs had been stacked around her too, fencing her off from the rest of the ward in a protective barrier. A second curtain twitched and groaned beside her before Raff sat up, looking more dishevelled than ever. If the guard were to have found them, he would easily have mistaken Raff for a homeless man seeking shelter. Raff didn't seem to mind the decaying curtain blanket as much as Charlie did. "Morning," he yawned, still speaking quietly, allowing the curtain to drape his legs.

With that one word, Charlie felt herself explode. The burden of sending a traumatised spirit to an existence even more torturous ached in her. The way Raff had pushed and pulled at her like some sort of tool. The constant sensation of being watched and measured. *"Fuck you,* Raff," she spat, standing and dusting some of the plaster and corrosion from her pants. She walked quietly to the window, carefully peering out to see just how bright it was outside. The day had settled fully. The hospital would no doubt be crawling with staff and visitors now. She puffed out an angry and resigned sigh.

"We'll have to wait until night to leave again," Raff said calmly, ignoring her curse. "Might as well settle in, have some breakfast, get some rest."

Charlie looked around her. More plaster cracked and fell from the ceiling, leaving a trail of sparkling dust motes in its wake. She'd hoped the daylight would lessen the call of wisps and spirits around her, but it hadn't. It felt crowded, like she was on a peak-hour train with bodies of commuters pressed against her on all sides. It was claustrophobic, suffocating. She squeezed her eyes shut, her lips trembling, and willed the white shield around her once more. *No connections. No connections. No connections.* "We're trapped," she whispered, pulling one of the chairs towards her and collapsing into it. It groaned slightly under her weight, and more dust shook loose to settle to the ground.

"Never can tell how long we'll be in the Dream, can we?" Raff said conversationally, dragging his pack towards him, kicking his legs out, and rummaging inside for some food.

"Maybe if you'd left when I *told you to*," Charlie said through grated teeth. "We *would* have been back in time and miles away by now!"

"Did you even get what you needed, though? I saw a lot of history, but not a lot of clues as to why she's stuck here. Beryl, that is." A sound in the next room over drew both of their attention. Plaster and stones being kicked as feet moved over them, boots clicking. "Ignore her," Raff said. "Focus on me."

Charlie turned her attention back from the door. "It's Beryl?" She'd meant to ask if Raff's Black was Beryl, but instead he affirmed that the sound in the next room was her. "Are you certain she is your Black?"

Raff nodded. "Even if I hadn't seen her all bruised and cut up like that, yeah, I'd know. She was the first one we saw after I entered the Dream with you. I'm connected to her; I can feel it."

Charlie exhaled again as she pulled her own backpack to her and drew her water bottle free. The footsteps continued their circling trudge in the next room. "But *who* did that to her? That's what we still don't know. And why is she imbalanced?"

"You'll figure it out." He bit into a muesli bar, crunching loudly. He'd rearranged his curtain behind him into a makeshift pillow and lay back. "It's almost always the husband or boyfriend," he said around a mouthful. "It's not her parents, because they're not here. That narrows it down for us."

"But who was she seeing is the question..." Charlie mused aloud, reaching for Adelaide's journal next. "Addie was seeing Dr Albert, but she hasn't mentioned anyone for Beryl. Well, anyone serious. It sounds like there was a slew of wardsmen and groundskeepers keeping her busy." She pulled her phone out to check the time, seeing it was only just past 10:00 a.m., with plenty of day left. She wanted to groan. Instead, a low moan echoed from the room where the footsteps continued circling, making Charlie shudder. Another alert popped up on her screen, from Trent, wishing her a 'Happy Easter'. Of course, it was Easter Sunday. "Happy frigging Easter," she muttered.

* * *

Tuesday 11 August 1914

I didn't expect she would ever do it. Of course, word of what is happening in Europe is all anyone can speak of, Beryl included. But with her, it was something more. It was all she could ever think of. Such a morbid fascination in the subject. Dr Albert and I thought a trip to Helensburgh would shake her out of this despondence. How wrong we were, and how poorly timed our visit.

The Illawarra recruiting march, with servicemen in full regalia, came through town. They spoke of Germany's invasion of Belgium, our duty to the crown, and the glory our near-certain victory would bring. They already had dozens of young men from the towns further south trailing behind them. All on their way to Sydney to enlist. The march grew in size as it passed through Helensburgh. And it wasn't just the young listless town boys who followed them. Several male nurses and groundskeepers marched right along to Sydney with them. And not just them, but dear Beryl!

I can understand the young men with their heads stuffed full of glory. But how could Beryl succumb to such propaganda? Our place is here, in Waterfall. We already have our calling, to help the sick and dying fight the scourge of the White Plague. I thought Beryl and I were of one mind in this view, in this calling. I thought she would never leave me. Why, dear Beryl? Why did you do this to me?!

23

It Had To Stop

Charlie tiptoed to the window of the Sanatorium again, peering out the now-curtainless frame. In the distance, she could see the bush that so many patients would have stared at for the last time. Either because they had recovered, or because they hadn't. The early-afternoon sun was deceptive. It glowed brightly, but its warmth struggled to touch the cool Autumn day. It struggled more to reach the abandoned halls of Waterfall Sanatorium. She shivered and pushed her hands into her armpits in an attempt to warm them. The longer they stayed, the deeper she could feel the cold seeping into her.

A clang sounded from the other room again. The footsteps had ceased after about an hour, but the silence hadn't lasted long. At first, it sounded like someone was banging themselves into the rotting walls. Now it sounded as though they were throwing debris about the room.

"You're sure its Beryl?" Charlie whispered, again. Raff, whose eyes were closed, merely nodded. He leaned against the exterior wall with that filthy curtain blanket around him. "She's going to draw attention from outside," Charlie fretted. Raff just shrugged and wiggled his shoulders, as though trying to get comfortable and return to sleep.

Charlie had considered returning to the Dream to seek more of the answers they'd come to Waterfall to find, but she couldn't bring herself to do it. There were too many wisps, too many other spirits trapped here.

She was worried she wouldn't just connect with Beryl, but with more like Jane. She and Raff might not know why Raff's Black was imbalanced, or who Charlie's Black was, but the trip hadn't been in vain. They knew Waterfall Sanatorium was where Raff's Black haunted; that the place must have been important to her betrayal, or her death, for her soul to linger there. And, if Raff was right, they knew she was Beryl. So, instead of re-entering the Dream, Charlie re-entered Addie's journal.

* * *

Wednesday 23 December 1914

The Sanatorium is preparing itself for Christmas. A lean Christmas, albeit, but the best we can do. As Superintendent Palmer continues to remind us, cheering the spirit is as important to our patients' recovery as the fresh air and high altitude, of Waterfall. I wish the decorations we'd made with the patients and sisters could cheer me. I wish the promise of a hearty meal could cheer me. Nothing seems to cheer me anymore.

I heard from Beryl for the first time today. Her letter was dated 10 October 1914, so it has taken more than two months to reach me. I guess that her other letters are lost. Or still on their way, for this seems not to be the first she has written me. It is agonising not knowing whether these words I read reflect her actual circumstances, now, on this day. Where is she? Is she well? What more has she seen? Will she ever return?

Of course, the letter is addressed not just to myself, but to dear Dr Albert. The three of us have become quite inseparable. Or at least, we had been. So I write my own journal entry knowing I must now pass the letter on to him. We shall be able to share our concern together, but how can I do this to him? Knowing that one day, these letters will inevitably stop. For surely, she cannot survive this.

10 October 1914

My Dearest Addie and Dear Doctor,

Last I wrote to you, I was sitting by the window of the auxiliary hospital in Antwerp, Belgium. I'd just arrived, one of only five

138

Australian nurses seconded to the British army. Sent away with barely any training, with the Allied Powers' desperation high for trained nurses on the front.

Today, I am not quite sure where I am. A British bus picked us up late yesterday and spirited us away to the coast. Somewhere. We were sitting there in that bus, jostled in-between loads of ammunition. I knew it wouldn't happen this way, but I could not help but picture the bullets setting themselves off and riddling me with holes. Worse, I had the image replay over-and-over in my mind of the bus rolling and tearing us to pieces. I am so very sorry to share such thoughts with you, but you are the two I trust most in the world. I feel better knowing you are with me in thought, spirit and in prayer.

You would think it would be the bullets that cause the most damage to the body here at the front. I certainly came to Europe with those thoughts. But no, dear sister and dear doctor. It is the shrapnel that is the bane of the front. It tears through flesh and limbs without prejudice. It is all too dreadful. Not a day goes by that we do not receive news of someone we knew never returning. I don't weep at the news now. I don't know if I can ever weep again.

By the time my letter reaches you, you may have already heard of what happened in Antwerp. The Press seems to fly much faster than any of us can. But let me recount it to you in my own words. It began at night, I'm told only two days past, though it feels so much longer. It sounded, at first, like the rumble of thunder. Not distant, but above us, below us, trembling through our very chests. We knew, of course, that this was an artillery strike. We knew to stay away from the windows, and immediately we began preparing our patients to move. Just as we tend to work on automatic at the Sanatorium, I find we do the same here. At the end of the day, we humans are simple routine and reactions.

The first blast near the windows did not rattle them. You would expect that, would you not? It was more like a giant hand had lifted up the house and dropped it. The curtains in the window did not so much flutter as bounce. As I helped prepare one of the patients, the smoke and

139

ash already filling the room, he looked up at me with wide and frightful eyes. I'll never forget how he looked at me, or what he said to me. 'Hell has come to earth. I want to go home.' I felt the same. Please do not judge me. I have already agreed to go back to the front to see out my secondment. But in that moment, though it shames me to write this, I wanted to go home too. I wanted to drop and hide under my patients' beds. I wanted to run. All that spurred me on was knowing we must all run together.

We carried those patients to the basement of the Burchmen Concert Hall. We cowered with them in those dirty caves beneath the kitchen. And then we ensured they were evacuated to safety. All 130 of them made it out. They will no doubt say that honour drove us. Our passion and heart for our countries. I am ashamed to admit, only to you both, that it was more so embarrassment and fear of dishonour. A duty not to our country, but to see them safe before we could do the same for ourselves. Yes, I feel for these men, and I want to protect them. Without the rain of Hell falling upon me, now I can look back with clarity and say that. But in those terrible moments, it is as though another part of you takes over. We humans are nothing but reactions.

Think kindly of me sister, doctor. Keep these letters hidden. And do write to me, to bring me news of home, to keep me from my melancholy. Tell me of Papa, Nick, Connor, Finn, Liam, Mary, Emily, Cormac, Ava and Ciaran. And of how Newcastle is faring. Tell me of Superintendent Palmer, Mrs Palmer, Henry, Muriel and Marjory. Tell me of the patients, of the sisters, of them all. Please write me.

With my deepest respects, and fondest regards,
Your Beryl

* * *

Charlie looked up from Beryl's carefully folded letter as another noise sounded from the other room. She wondered if Beryl knew what Charlie was doing and resented her for reading something that was never meant for her eyes. *I understand*, Charlie tried to send. *I don't judge you.* The sound of fingers scratching against the peeling paint and plaster screeched from behind the wall and tingled up her spine. She flicked a look at Raff, who was now snoring softly, despising him in that moment for not doing anything to help Beryl. It was irrational, just like Beryl's own shame was, but she couldn't help it. Raff *couldn't* do anything while Beryl's soul was so provoked.

* * *

Tuesday 1 June 1915

Beryl's letters are still arriving every week now, more or less. There are still months between her written date and the time we received them, but she is writing so regularly we never want for news. Sometimes, there is a gap between letters and my chest will clench, my heart will flutter. Is it that time? Has she succumbed to something, finally? And then we will receive bundles of them all at once. It is agony. Not just for me, but for dear Dr Albert. He has lost weight. We both have. Neither of us can turn our thoughts to marriage with such dread hanging above us.

Beryl is no longer in Belgium. In fact, she is no longer in Europe, but in Egypt. She explained in great detail her journey there, so I shall not recount it in my pages. What I fear as I scour every letter is that I have already lost her. The tone of her letters has shifted. She writes in brief and jarring sentences. Has she lost some of her emotion as she claims? Has she lost some of her light? Some of what makes Beryl, Beryl?

Her handwriting, too, is changing. It is scratched, scrawled. She speaks of good experiences too. Of the friendships she has made. Of the sights she has seen.

It has to stop soon... I brace myself for it. The letters will no doubt stop soon...

* * *

Charlie knew it was midafternoon by the glare from the sun coming through the window. She'd had to take a break, stretching her legs, and carefully walking small circles, away from the window. She wanted to explore more of the hospital in the day, but fear of the security guards, of someone hearing her, and of Beryl kept her rooted. She would need to walk past Beryl eventually, if her spirit wouldn't leave that room, because it was the only way out.

The hostility in the air had only grown throughout the day. It was more than just feeling unwelcome. She felt threatened, despised, as though Beryl saw her as tainting the very ground she sat on. Like Charlie was worse than the rotten fingers of mould. Raff had finally woken and gone for a walk himself. Charlie regretted her choice not to go with him, expecting Beryl would have followed him. Instead, Charlie was left trapped in this small decaying room, with the angry Black spirit scratching at the walls. Each time she heard her, she revitalised her shield of light around her.

* * *

Thursday 27 January 1916
This will be a short entry for I cannot hold my pen straight. And I fear I shall blot the pages with my tears. The letters have stopped. They've stopped. I feel my heart tearing, but they had to stop eventually, didn't they? Didn't they? They had to stop?

* * *

Despite the heaviness of each journal entry, and each letter that Adelaide had saved from Beryl hidden in the pages, Charlie could not stop reading. *So this is how you died...* Charlie startled and shuffled back against the wall as she saw a blackened face peering at her from around the doorframe. It was emaciated, withered, twisted in on itself like a rotting corpse. Black mud drowned it, running from its crushed scalp like hair, over its bony shoulders and along each-and-every exposed rib. It ran from its eyes, from its nose and ears, and even pooled from its open mouth. Every tooth was black and stuck with mud. *Beryl...* the thought shuddered out of her. Was she appearing fully now because Charlie had discovered how she'd died?

The gaze from those eyes was as penetrating as the bullets and shrapnel she'd so eloquently described in her letters. *But why...? How...? Why are you a Black? How were you betrayed?* The creature made its inhuman noise then. Its mouth opening in a shallow tremble, more blackened liquid dirt spewing from it and blending with the mud running down its chest. The noise was both pitiful and terrifying. It sounded like a gasp, a cry, and a screech in one. She reached a hand towards Charlie, and then she was gone.

Charlie squealed and ducked as more plaster fell from the ceiling directly above her, smacking her on the back of the head, the dust tickling her as it settled on her skin and inside her clothes.

* * *

Monday 6 November 1916

I have not had the spirit to write in this journal since Beryl's letters stopped. For months these pages have sat empty and waiting. At first, it was despair that kept me from writing. Then, it was something worse. Like the despair became a living thing, latching on to me, draining me.

I have more empathy for our patients now. While those like Superintendent Palmer and Dr Albert had succumbed to the White Plague in childhood, I had not. And I'd begun to believe, after all my time here at the Sanatorium, that perhaps I was immune from its scourge. Despite what happened to dear Mama, Sophie and Grace. Yet all it took was grief to pull me down within reach of its clutches. It truly feels as though this disease is a death sentence for the women of our family. I so narrowly escaped its clutches.

Tiredness does not begin to describe it. Nor does fatigue. This disease sucked the very life from my bones. I could not eat. I could not sleep, for the chills and sweats. I could not breathe. Each breath and cough was agony in my chest. I thought surely I would die. It had to stop, did it not? Perhaps this is what I deserved?

But no, dear Dr Albert would not lose me. He persevered, and then so did I. It was like he called me back from the upper layers of Hell himself.

24

What Now?

Night had finally fallen on the Sanatorium, and it had been hours since Charlie had heard Beryl. Ever since she'd caught sight of her, and that plaster had rained down on her, everything had been agonisingly silent. She'd heard Raff approaching minutes before he returned to the room. Even her breathing seemed to echo in the walls. What hadn't stopped, though, was the sensation of being watched, observed, by dozens of spirits.

"Okay, it's time to go," Raff breathed, stepping back from the window. "Keep quiet, don't say anything, and step lightly. She might follow us as we leave, do things to you, but try not to scream. Try not to react. Okay? Keep your shield up." Charlie merely nodded as she put the cap on under her hood and pulled the strings tight to hold it in place. The dread *was* worse at night. Or perhaps it was because they'd been there so long. She just wanted, *needed*, to get out. Messages to-and-from Tess and Trent throughout the day had been barely a distraction. And her phone battery was dangerously low, even with her battery-pack charger. She hadn't wanted to drain her torch with its red light, so had used her phone torch during the day. That certainly drained the battery fast.

Charlie let Raff lead the way, holding her breath as she passed through the door to Beryl's room. She braced herself, but nothing happened. It was empty, aside from that plant growing through the floorboards. She peered at the doorframe as they passed, noticing several new long, thin scratches in the peeling paint and plaster. As they left the room, feeling their way across the walls and via the moonlight, something shifted. The room grew even colder. The sensation of being watched pushed on her like an unseen mountain. She peered over her shoulder and saw her. Not peeping around a corner this time, but full bodied. Though Beryl wasn't as tall as Charlie's own Black spirit, she held as much of an air of intimidation and power.

She may have been wasted from her eyes to her toes, appearing like the roots of one of those fig trees, all sinew and bone. But she didn't limp or falter. She moved like a Queen. The mud pooled at her feet, wrapping around her like her nurse's apron. Charlie's voice caught at the sight and she whimpered. "She'll follow us," Raff whispered, reaching back to squeeze Charlie's hand. Charlie still couldn't tear her gaze away. "Try not to watch her. Just look at me. Look at my back. Look forward." Raff's abrasive palm gently cupped under her chin, pulling her away. It broke some sort of spell as she looked up at him, shivering uncontrollably now, and simply nodded.

Charlie felt like Orpheus from Greek legend, walking out of Hell and forbidden by the Lord of the Underworld from looking back. Unlike the myth, though, she felt like if she looked back to see Beryl, it wouldn't be Beryl who would be sucked back to Hell, but Charlie. She kept her gaze focussed on the small of Raff's back, between his shoulder blades, staring so fixedly that the edges of her vision blurred. Beryl's footsteps started coming louder now, as though she knew what Charlie was thinking, and was doing everything in her power to tempt her to look behind.

Finally, they were back down the stairs and heading towards the opening through which they'd entered this place so recently, but which felt like so long ago. As they reached the open, un-boarded outside door, Raff turned back to Charlie and froze. She flinched at the look in his eyes, bracing every muscle in her body to prevent herself from turning around. She clenched her muscles painfully, the ice in the air taking her immobility as an opportunity to tickle her skin. To whisper through her hair. "*Charlie,*" Raff whispered. "Focus on me. We're nearly out. Just focus on me."

She started to hyperventilate. She could feel herself doing it, hear her breaths coming faster, but she had no control. She felt bubbles in her windpipe. Even though she stared fixedly forward, something started to blur in her periphery vision. Something slowly poking itself forward and over her shoulder. Something dark, something muddy. A hand colder than ice fell on her shoulder, burning her even through her layers of clothing. She whimpered, grit her teeth, and stared even harder at Raff. Her eyes swam. The face — because that's what it was — continued to jut over her shoulder. This close, she couldn't help herself. Her gaze flicked to her right, and looked straight into one of Beryl's black, swimming eyes. Rivulets ran down her twisted blackened skin. Her teeth, with mud oozing around them, jutted forward in a threatening scowl.

"Charlie," Raff whispered, taking a slow step backwards and beckoning for her to follow him slowly. She clenched her eyes shut, a tear not of sadness but of fear, squeezing itself out. But she gave her head a small nod. She could feel Beryl's mud dripping onto her shoulders now, running down her front and her back like frightfully cold lava. She took a step forward, and the claw on her shoulder tightened, digging into her. It wasn't going to let her go.

"Raff…?" She wasn't sure what to do in this circumstance. She couldn't send Beryl away like she would a Grey. And here, on *her* turf, where would she send her anyway? A deafening crack sounded above Charlie's head and she *knew* it was more than just plaster about to rain down on her head this time.

"Charlie!" The next moments happened in a blur. The hand ripped free of her shoulder, something thrust into the centre of her back, and she fell forward as the ceiling rained down where she'd been standing. Not just plaster, but rotten wooden beams, floorboards, and chunks of concrete and metal. Part of the ceiling grazed the back of her calf as she fell. It was hard to tell which sounds were the roof collapsing, and which were Beryl's screams. Both grated and thrummed on the inside of her eardrums.

The next thing she knew, Raff was pulling her to her feet and into the night. The air outside was chill but felt positively balmy compared to the inside of the hospital. She gasped at it greedily, glad to be free. "Not out of the woods yet!" Raff said, perhaps a little louder than he should have, pulling at her as they both stumbled the few feet to the fence, through the overgrown grass. Raff pushed her through the hole in the fence first. She didn't care when the wire scratched at her or pulled at her clothes. Raff was soon to follow, Beryl now screaming again behind them.

"Hey!" called a startled, gruff voice. Charlie looked up toward it. The security guard was back, obviously having heard the crashing roof. He was older than them, his mostly grey hair as frazzled as his nerves seemed to be. He was overweight as well, the buttons of his white uniform straining and revealing a sad belly button surrounded by white hairs. "Hey!" he yelled more certainly now, pointing his flashlight in their eyes, and momentarily blinding them.

"Run!" Raff shouted. Charlie hadn't needed to wait for his instruction to turn tail and flee back the way they'd come the other night. Sprinting for the tree line. She could hear the guard puffing behind them, but his plodding feet were falling further-and-further behind. With adrenaline and fear spurring her on, along with the taste of freedom, there was no way this man would catch her.

"*FUCKING VANDALS!*" the guard's voice screeched at them from a far distance. They'd made it to the ghost houses now, being careful as they ran down the potholed road not to trip.

"Keep going!" Raff pulled at Charlie's elbow. "We're not safe yet." Charlie took just a moment to look over her shoulder. The guard's torchlight was far behind them now, but they were still being followed. It looked like Beryl was walking as calmly as if she were taking a casual stroll along the hospital gardens. Yet her speed defied her movements. As Charlie breathed in another lungful of air, readying herself to sprint again, her chest squeaked.

Not safe yet.

* * *

Charlie fell against Raff's car, gasping. Her legs were poorly-set jelly, wobbling and barely keeping her upright. Raff fumbled with his key — the batteries long since dead — until he got it in the lock and let them inside.

She ripped the handle back and fell into the seat, almost catching her own ankle as she slammed the door behind her. Beryl had followed them into the bush, at least halfway back to the car. Even though Charlie hadn't seen her for some time now, she still couldn't shake the ice from her veins.

"Drive!" Charlie tried to shout, but croaked instead, as Raff sat beside her and rested his head on the steering wheel. "Drive! Please!"

He flopped his head backwards against his head rest now, raising two fingers of his left hand to pause her. After a few steadying breaths, during which Charlie felt the light-headedness return, he finally said, "It's okay. She can't follow us here."

"But…"

"She can't follow any further." Despite having slept practically all afternoon, he looked exhausted, drained. *Did he have the same problems that Charlie had last year?* "She's tethered to me, not you, remember? She can't follow us past the place she's haunting. Only you — only a Keeper — can drag spirits away from their place."

Charlie let her own head flop onto the head rest, the relief shaking her almost as badly as the adrenaline had. She felt it leaving her, replaced by trembling exhaustion too. She closed her eyes and the memory of Beryl's face pushing past her shoulder flashed to mind. Breathing out deeply, she snapped her eyes open, and ran both hands down her legs towards her knees. "She can't follow us…" Saying the words out loud helped make them feel more real. "Do you think the guard saw our faces? Do you think the security cameras got us?"

"No." He turned the ignition on slowly, the headlights illuminating the dark around them. The gravel shoulder, the tarmac road, and the shadowy trees. He pulled his sign asking people not to tow the car down from the windscreen. "The cameras won't have been able to catch our features in the dark, not with these hoods and caps. And it's not like we're being idiots and uploading urban exploration videos to YouTube. We'll be okay." He turned the steering wheel and drove onto the road, heading back towards the bridge. He yawned as he accelerated the car, rubbing at his eyes.

Charlie sighed, "Where now?"

"I don't see we have any choice but to go back to your place, right?"

"But Tess?"

"She said it herself," Raff murmured. "She told you to come home."

"I'm not doing that," Charlie said stubbornly. "That thing could have killed her with that bird bath. *Your* Black nearly killed me by collapsing the roof."

"We'll work it out," Raff said, trying and failing to comfort her. He pulled his phone out of his pocket and drove with it in one hand, scrolling through the contacts, and swerving on the road in his distraction. Charlie hated it, but was too tired to object. The phone began to ring, and Charlie realised he was making a call and had put it on loudspeaker.

"Bonjour?" Tess's voice came through the line, faded and distant from the loudspeaker. "Raff? How'd it go? Did you get out? How's Charlie?"

"It's okay," Raff said quickly, cutting off Tess's frantic questions. "We got out, Charlie is right here next to me, we've just left."

"Good. How long until you get home?"

"Tess, no—" Charlie started.

"I *told* you, come home. If you can't get rid of it, *come home!* This place isn't home without you. *A chaque oiseau, son nid est beau.*"

Charlie sighed, rubbing at her dirty face with her hands. Tess could be as obstinate as Charlie; worse! *And I would love a shower, and my own bed. Can my shield keep her safe...?*

As Charlie pondered, Raff spoke up, "We can be back in four hours. We found out the Black is Beryl, and she's *definitely* haunting Waterfall Sanatorium. That place is important. Whatever happened to throw off Beryl's balance, Waterfall is connected. And she came after Charlie, tried to pull the roof down on her head."

"Nom de dieu de merde! Come home, *ma chére.*"

"I'm not doing tha—"

"Ta gueule! Raff, just come back here."

"Will do." He shrugged at Charlie in fake apology. "Now we have more information to go on, hopefully we can get this sorted quickly. If Tess stays inside the house, inside your shield, things should be okay. What do you normally do next?"

Charlie gave up. Outnumbered, exhausted, and with no other option but to grab for the wheel, she resigned herself to it. "The three of us — me, Tess, and Trent — research using whatever information I've been able to glean from the Dream. I keep on trying to connect..." She shuddered at that thought. Beryl most certainly wanted nothing to do with her.

"Don't recommend that approach."

"No," Charlie agreed. "So we research. We try to figure out *why* she's imbalanced. Who betrayed her. Why she's still here, but not accepting her fate. And we try to fix it. *And*," Charlie added, "we find out what my Black follower has to do with all this, and how to move him on as well. So he can't hurt Tess anymore."

"He?" Tess asked, reminding them she was still on the line.

"Yeah, sorry," Charlie mumbled. "That's something else we discovered. Raff's Black is a woman — maybe Beryl."

"*Definitely* Beryl," Raff cut in.

"—and my Black is a man."

"See, you made plenty of progress, *ma chére*." The line began to crackle as they headed out of town. "I'll let you go. Focus on driving. Get back safe. *Je t'aimerai pour toujours.*"

"I love you forever too, Tess," Charlie whispered, as Raff hung up.

"Don't worry. She seemed safe enough *inside* your house," Raff bobbed his head. "We'll take precautions, but the clock is ticking now. It'll only get worse from here." Charlie nodded, agreeing.

"Did you know," she said after a pause. "that you look like a Black in the Dream? You look more human. I mean, you're not withered or alien-like in your proportions. In fact, your shoulders are huge. And you have a cape of raven feathers swirling around you, and the brightest white eyes. Like a raven too."

"Sounds pretty dashing."

"Wh-what do I look like?" Raff flicked her a quick glance before looking back to the road. She hoped he'd take her seriously, and not treat this as another opportunity for his crude, basic humour.

"Stunning." He let the single word settle before continuing. "Pure light.

Like a fucking angel."

25

The Scent of Gossip

Charlie was the one who flicked the indicator on and moved the Landcruiser through her gate and down her driveway. Raff snored in the passenger seat, his mouth limp, his nostrils and Adam's apple flaring with each chainsaw breath. Tess was waiting for them under the light of the veranda, despite the fact it was well past midnight. With the midge bugs circling her head, it was Tess who looked like the angel in this moment. Raff snorted awake as Charlie pulled the handbrake up and cut the engine. "Back already?" he asked through a mouth thick with sleep.

"Back already."

* * *

It had taken hours, a good sleep, and multiple cups of tea for Charlie to rid herself of the chill that had settled into her at Waterfall Sanatorium. She'd caught Tess up on what had happened, messaging the key details through to Trent, who asked her to meet him at the library the next day, when he was back in Greenfields and back to work. She tapped her message reply out to him:

Beryl Morgan is the Black spirit tied to Raff. She died in WWI, according to Adelaide's diary. But we need to find out how she was betrayed in life

152

before I can help her. She was abused at Waterfall Sanatorium at some point. She looked a lot older when it happened. Beryl did fool around with a lot of the wardsmen apparently. We also know that Addie and Dr Albert Hammond were an item and were even considering marriage. And that Addie, Beryl and Albert were inseparable when they were together. It's all a bit of a mess! Anything you can find will help. Still no idea who my Black is, but it is a man.

In the light of day, Charlie could see that Tess had been busy working on her Tiny House while they'd been away. The entire exterior had been stripped of paint and sanded down, and the materials for her deck had also been delivered over the weekend. The bruises around her eye were starting to turn yellow and the swelling had gone down. The scratches on her chest and back had also scabbed over and lost their angry redness. Charlie had compared her own scratches to Tess's, those deep on her shoulder where Beryl had grabbed her, and found them very similar.

"I don't think you should come with me to see Trent tomorrow," Charlie said, blowing on her tea as she lent on the kitchen bench. "I want you to stay inside, where it's safe. My Black can follow me anywhere I go." It was well-and-truly mid-morning, but Raff was still sleeping in their guest room. Charlie had relented and allowed him to sleep inside after everything they'd just been through.

"Of course, *ma chére*. I'm hoping to take advantage of Raff being here anyway, and get started on those decks. Who knows how long it is until you two sort this out and he leaves. I'm not sure if I'll be much help anyway." Charlie felt her stomach clench. It was a reasonable enough response, but she couldn't shake her desire to keep those two apart.

"I think he's *dangerous*, Tess. I don't know if we can fully trust him." She paused to let her whispered words sink in. "While we were away, he told me that betrayal is in his nature. He promised me he'd keep watch when I entered the Dream, and then he just left me and joined the Dream too."

"But he got you out of the Sanatorium when things got bad too, and he didn't leave you. It would have been easy enough for him to do that. It sounds like Beryl wanted you, not him."

"Because he *needs* me."

"And we need him, *ma chére.*" Tess took a calm sip of her coffee, refusing to let Charlie's jealousy shake her rationalism. "I don't think he's too bad." She shrugged, moving around the kitchen bench to join Charlie on the stool beside her.

"Who's not too bad?" Raff said coyly, and a little haughtily, as he emerged from the hallway, running his hand through his untameable long hair. Charlie shuddered internally at the thought of those greasy locks on her good pillowcases. He'd obviously heard what Tess had said, going by his eager smirk. He winked at her as he went to the kitchen and began opening every cupboard in search of a glass. He was still wearing the clothes he'd worn yesterday and didn't seem to have any intention of changing.

Maybe I should just replace all the sheets, Charlie thought to herself as Raff finally found what he was after and filled his cup, drinking so quickly it slopped down his chin. Wet droplets shone in his beard.

"Did Charlie tell you what I look like in the Dream?" Raff jiggled his eyebrows suggestively. "*Dashing,* wasn't it?"

"I never said that word—" Charlie started.

"Yeah, that was it. A dashing dark figure cloaked in raven feathers." Tess burst out laughing.

"You know, I've been thinking," Raff grabbed a banana from their fruit bowl and began peeling it, leaning against the sink as he did so. "What if this Dr Albert is the Black that's following you around, Charlie?"

She seized on the idea. It was like a light had gone on in her head. She hadn't considered this possibility. Maryanne was certain the two must be connected. He was always prominent in the Dream. It made sense.

"It could be," she exhaled strongly, forgiving Raff momentarily as she lent on her hands, distracted by the idea. "He didn't want me at the Sanatorium for some reason. Maybe it's because he'd been there before? Or because he knew Beryl would be there… And she did come after me."

Raff was nodding as he shoved the banana into his gob, chewing loudly with his mouth half open. He sucked the remaining remnants of banana from each of his fingers before saying, "And you told me you saw him in the Dream at first. Before I joined in."

"That's right, by someone's death bed. Someone he loved."

"Addie?" Tess asked, sipping her coffee. "Perhaps they did get married after all."

"Does that happen?" Charlie asked Raff as he reached for another piece of fruit. "Two Blacks being born from the same moment in time?"

"Not often," he said around a mouthful of apple. "But yeah, it can. Kids who were all abused by the same parent sometimes group together, for example. It didn't happen to me, but I once heard about half a dozen Blacks being born from a mass suicide at a cult somewhere in America. And from what the Midnight spirit showed you — Jane Hughes — those three were connected at the hips. Like running a three-legged race through life." Charlie reached for her notebook, which she'd continued to fill in that morning, planning to make a few more notes. Raff playfully pulled the book away from her.

"Hey!" He went to give it back to her, then pulled it out of reach again, smirking and chuckling as he did so. "That's not funny. Stop being so *childish!*"

"Ah, come on, Charlie." He took another bite of apple. "Enough work for now. You'll pick that brainiac's head tomorrow and then we'll make a plan for next steps. Why dwell now? It won't fix anything. Give yourself a break." He threw the journal back to her. She scowled at him as she opened it back up to her page and took up her pen again.

"Perhaps he has a point, darling?" Tess put a gentle hand on Charlie's shoulder. "You've always been a bit of a workaholic. And what happened... it sounds like quite an ordeal. Why not take a small rest, hm? I wouldn't mind some help today. I'm not allowed outside, after all."

Charlie smiled up at her. "Oh, so I should take a break with some hard labour building decks and sanding tiny houses, should I?"

"Something like that."

* * *

155

The next day Charlie was on her way to Greenfields, on her own. Her arms ached. Tess had put her and Raff to work the day before, moving the decking materials down to the stockmen's ruins in Raff's truck of a car. Charlie had felt more than useless at the trade side of things, usually directed by Raff to 'hold it straight' as he pulled the frame of the deck together. They'd measured the planks for the decking next, Raff digging power tools and a battery pack out from under the mess of his boot to cut them to length. He and Tess were down there again now, putting those planks into place. Raff might be a slob in many ways, but his carpentry was certainly anything but sloppy. It was certainly good enough to earn himself some new clothes and burn those rags he wore.

Charlie stopped in at Dot's café first, deciding caffeine was the least she could offer Trent in return for his help. Just seeing Dot bustling in and around the tables through the café window was enough to bring Charlie's heartache back, thinking about what the woman would endure in the coming years. She wore her respirator mask (for her allergies), in case she'd needed to go inside to order the coffees, and was glad it could hide the downturned corners of her mouth. Dot caught her looking through the window and held up a hand to indicate she'd seen her and it would just be a few minutes. Charlie nodded and sat at 'her' table, loosening the mask on her face.

"Hi, darl." Dot smiled at her after a few minutes, flopping into the seat opposite her, her bulk spilling over the sides. "How you been? Don't mind me. I've been run off my feet all morning! Just need a teensy break."

The normality unwound some of Charlie's tension and she chuckled a little. "You can always take a load off with me, Dot! I've been good. Busy! We have someone staying with us, and he's a bit of a handful."

"Oh?" Dot inflected, leaning forward, suddenly not tired at all. The scent of gossip enlivened her. "A man, hey? Who....?" She drew out the last word.

"Oh, no one you know. Just a…a…distant cousin."

"Well good for you. Family is a balm for the soul."

"Speaking of family, how's Taylor?"

"Wonderful." Dot squeezed Charlie's hand and leant back in her chair. "I took your advice. And you know what? Taking some of the pressure off has been good for *both* of us. You know, I think she's even enjoying this pregnancy now the morning sickness has quietened down."

"That's *wonderful*, Dot."

"Now!" Dot pushed herself to her feet, the table creaking as she leant her weight on it. Evidently a few minutes off her feet and some good gossip had been all she needed to keep going. "What can I get you?"

26

Abso-fucking-lutely

Trent welcomed Charlie into his office, drinking the coffee with a groan of pleasure. This was the office where she'd first cried her eyes out to Trent on that horrible sofa, before she became a Keeper, and before they'd even become friends. She sat on it again now, her own coffee close to her lips. "No cake?" he asked in feigned casualness. She could hear the hope in his voice and decided to tease him just a little longer.

"I thought Brent was complaining you were getting podgy?" She poked at his small belly, which barely hung over the top of his belt. Trent's movie-star-esque boyfriend had high standards. Trent's face fell and Charlie laughed as she pulled two paper bags from her handbag, shaking them at him. "Dot wouldn't let me leave without them. She's trying another peanut-free recipe. Lemon and coconut."

"You tease!" Trent smiled as he grabbed one of the bags from her and flopped onto the couch besides her, rather than in his office chair.

"Good Easter?" Charlie asked, putting her own cake back in her bag for later.

"You bet!" Trent said around a small mouthful, groaning in delight as the delicacy crumbled in his mouth. For some reason, Charlie didn't mind when Trent talked around his food. With him, it seemed because he was too eager to talk to finish chewing. With Raff, the person with whom she detested the same behaviour, it seemed more because he just didn't care. "Brent's whole family got together. He has a sister and a brother, both with two kids each. It was great to see the nieces and nephews. Yours? Good?"

"If you think being trapped in an abandoned rotting building with a bogan and his psycho Black spirit is good... yeah." She leant back in the couch with her head on his shoulder. "I can't stand him!"

"I'm looking forward to meeting him properly for myself then." Trent pushed her playfully with his shoulder before settling back and laying his head atop of hers. "It won't be long until he's out of your life, honey. You always crack these problems sooner or later."

"*We* always crack them. Forget the Famous Five or the Secret Seven. We're the Tremendous Three." *Tremendous Two*, she thought glumly as she thought of Tess off working on her deck with Raff while she sat here with Trent.

"And on that note..." Trent sat forward, forcing Charlie to sit upright as well. He reached to his desk and for his familiar satchel, pulling it back to him. Even in his office, he seemed to prefer packing his notes into his bag. It was like his safe, or his repository for spooky history. "I found Beryl's full service records. Everything they had on her, anywhere they might have it. And she did *not* die in the war."

"Wha—?"

"She was transferred from active duty at the end of 1918, when the Great War ended. She came home. You know, only around twenty-five female Australian nurses died during the war. And that's out of the 3,000 civilian female nurses who signed up. So I was surprised when I got your message."

"But..." Charlie pondered back to the journal entries. "Her letters stopped coming... In 1916. Addie and Albert thought she was dead."

"But she *wasn't*," Trent stated firmly. Thoughts raced through Charlie's head, and she pulled her own notebook from her bag.

"Okay. So, Beryl returns from the war and goes back to Waterfall Sanatorium presumably. It's so confusing when the snippets of the Dream don't happen in order. When I saw her beaten, sitting in the Superintendent's office, she looked old. That must have been after she came back then?"

"I wish I could confirm for you," Trent sighed, throwing his satchel down by his feet and taking up his coffee again. "I did keep digging into the history of Waterfall Sanatorium, but we don't have — and we'll never have — the full story. The Wollongong City Council didn't even know it had responsibility for the cemetery at the hospital until the 1990s. According to what I could find, before then, only a handful of people even knew the cemetery still existed. It looks like a lot of the original paper records were lost when the hospital changed hands." He coughed. "Or were destroyed…"

"Why would they do that?"

"The more I looked, the more I found complaints. In 1926 there was even a petition to the Health Minister about it. It complained about poor segregation, not just between men and women but between children and adults. Especially the girls. Food quality was poor, there wasn't enough equipment, sanitation was substandard, and the place was understaffed and overcrowded. They put patients *on the balcony* when all the beds were full."

"I saw that!" Charlie chimed in. "But it didn't look all that bad. I suppose if it was particularly hot or cold it wouldn't have been pleasant, but the staff obviously took care to make it as comfortable as they could."

"I'm sure some did. But that doesn't change the fact that they never had the resources they needed. I found a scathing article in *The Sunday Times* from October 1927. It reported 'scandalous activities', 'misconduct', and said the whole hospital was an 'antiquated institution'. Hang on…" Trent pulled a black-and-white print of the newspaper from his satchel. "They didn't have hot running water, they didn't have enough toilets, and they used elderly people from a nearby *mental asylum* to do their gardening and laundry, and to dig some of the graves." Charlie skimmed the newspaper article as Trent kept talking. "Male patients were allowed to roam wherever they wanted, including to the nearby town pub to bet on the horses, but the women were confined to the grounds. Apparently, the staff were kept busy trying to prevent 'abuses' of the women and at least two babies were born there between 1910 and 1920 from 'misconduct'. A Committee which was set up to investigate the hospital recommended all the women be moved to another institution for their safety and 'freedom'."

"So there was a lot of abuse there," Charlie said thoughtfully. "I expect not just of the patients either, right? We know there was *some* abuse of the nurses. Otherwise we wouldn't be dealing with Black spirits."

"And it's not just what's in this article either. There were more complaints. People often got sick from contaminated milk, the food was very poor quality, there was rape — including of the children — and a lot of illegal gambling. The staff and the patients frequently had sex together. Which was even more taboo back then."

"My God," Charlie breathed, putting the newspaper article to the side. "Okay, I can see why some people would think the records were deliberately destroyed."

"The Illawarra Historical Society did a lot of research and managed to pull together a pretty good record of people who were interred in Waterfall Cemetery. But it was a tough job. The records were incomplete and inconsistent, so we can't be sure they got everything right. But they found over 2,000 records of people buried there. And that's just *half* of the number of people who actually died there."

"Wow... I didn't even see the cemetery."

"You wouldn't have. It has almost been lost entirely. It's been completely overrun by the bush, it was damaged in a large bush fire, and there's no public access. It's completely off limits. Another failure of history and the Government. Of all of us, really. That so many thousands of people were forgotten."

"Some of the staff *did* care, though." Charlie fought to defend what she'd seen of Beryl, Albert, and Addie so far. "They really did worry for the patients."

"Oh, of course... I didn't mean to insinuate that systemic failure was the fault of the staff. Or at least, of all the staff. The Sanatorium's first Medical Superintendent, Dr Wilfred Palmer, was called a 'constant and energetic crusader'. He was constantly fighting for better facilities for the hospital, and for better treatment of his patients. I wouldn't be surprised if many of the complaints that made their way to the Health Minister came from Dr Palmer himself. It was *he* who finally got electricity connected in the early 1920s, and the laundry facilities upgraded. I found something he'd written in 1922 as well... It'll be in the notes somewhere." Trent waved his hand at his bag but didn't reach for it.

"Essentially," Trent continued. "Dr Palmer complained that *fifteen per cent* of deaths in Australia were caused by tuberculosis, but the Government had made no progress towards controlling or preventing it. He was frustrated that more attention was given to the flu than TB and described his hospital not as a sanatorium, but 'merely a home for consumptives'. Apparently, it was only the sickest who even stayed, because the rest of them couldn't stand to see so much death around them. If they were well enough, they got themselves out of there."

"No wonder that place felt so depressing," Charlie murmured. Trent settled back, letting Charlie lean her head on his shoulder again. "It was *awful* in there."

"Honestly, honey, I'm surprised you're being haunted by the nurses and not the patients."

"Oh, trust me, the patients *tried*. There were so many of them… I couldn't let them all in or they'd break me. I did help one woman, who committed suicide, but that was all I could manage."

"Why'd she do it? She couldn't stand the facilities?"

"No! On the contrary, she didn't want to leave. She was getting better and couldn't stand the thought of going back to her life in Sydney. Even if she was confined to the grounds, she still had more freedom in Waterfall than she ever did back home."

"Yeah… depressing…"

"I think I've figured out my next step, though." Charlie yawned and snuggled deeper into Trent, relishing this friendship and the contact she'd been craving since all of this started.

"Mmm?"

"I want to go back to the Dream with Raff again, but *on purpose* this time. And with *me* driving the intent, rather than him pulling me around everywhere."

"I'll come with you to the property when you try." Charlie sat up and turned to look Trent front on.

"Are you sure?"

"Abso-frigging-lutely. If you don't trust Raff, then I don't trust him. I want to be there too. Can you wait for me to finish up at work? I should be able to wrap up around 3:00 p.m. today. And you can give me a lift?"

"Yes! Abso-*fucking*-lutely!"

27

The Best and the Worst Year

Charlie left Trent's office to let him work in peace, and found a quiet corner of the library, where light was streaming through the window. She set herself up at a table with bench seat, legs spread, and journal in hand. Charlie noticed as she found her place in the journal how little she had left to read. Perhaps these final pages would have the answers she needed.

* * *

Thursday 19 July 1917

Tonight is my last night not only as a nurse, but as an unmarried woman. I took off my cap and veil for the last time this afternoon, after an afternoon tea put on by the female staff and patients. It was a subdued affair, with tea, butter and flour still hard to come by. Thankfully, the Superintendent's pigs are doing well, and we are able to barter with the nearby Asylum for vegetables and milk. So we cannot complain. And the effort truly touched me.

I don't know how to feel. I have been a nurse six years. Nearly ten if you count my time in training. I always so strongly believed that supporting recovery from the White Plague was my calling. It shall remain so, from tomorrow, as I support my husband to continue this endeavour for the both of us. My husband. My hands tingle as I write these words down.

We shall have a small ceremony at Holy Cross Parish in Helensburgh, under the patronage of St Joseph. I actually cannot think of a more fitting Saint to bless and watch over our marriage. The husband of Mary, mother of Jesus. The patron saint of workers and the sick, and protector of the Catholic Church. I shall have to share these musings with my soon-to-be-husband on our wedding night.

With all that is going on, we shall not honeymoon just yet. It would not be right. It was enough work to convince Dr Albert not to wait at all. Who knows when this war shall end? It seems to drag beyond any hope. At least we shall have this union to celebrate and cherish in dark times. And when we honeymoon, after the war, we shall travel to Newcastle, to celebrate our matrimony with our families, who cannot be with us tomorrow.

I know it is not what every girl dreams of, being such a subdued affair. But for me, it shall be perfection excepting one thing. The absence of my dear Beryl.

Wednesday 24 October 1917

My hand trembles as I write these words. While married life has kept me busy, running our home at Waterfall, tending our garden, and cheering the other married patients and former staff with weekly clubs... I had felt something missing. And now, we shall be complete. Shall be whole. I am pregnant!

The nausea keeps me abed most of the day, and whoever called this morning sickness has never been with child. Yet even this sickness cannot dampen my spirits. I lay here, knitting small boots, and dreaming of what he or she shall look like. Shall be like. Shall they have my brown eyes? Or the doctor's blue? I've never felt so close to him as I do now, with his child growing within me.

And this shall be good for him too. Something to cheer all of us. And just the start, I feel. Soon enough we shall have gaggles of children running at our feet and filling this cottage.

Thursday 30 May 1918

Sarah. That is her name. Our baby girl. Sarah Amelia Hammond. She is absolutely dear. Born one week ago, a little early, her head the size of an orange. I've never seen such a precious thing. And I've never seen such love as I saw in Albert's eyes, the first time he held her. He cooed to her with sounds more gentle than a dove's. The picture of her little finger holding his perfect hand shall be forever ingrained in my memory.

I must write what he said here as well. I cannot believe I will ever forget what he said, but I shall like to look back on this journal and read the words. "She looks just like you, dear Addie."

Saturday 24 May 1919

I didn't think I would ever write in this journal again. But it was Sarah's birthday yesterday. How that first year flew... At first, I did not write because of those agonising sleepless nights and days. A colicky babe robs you of both time and sanity. And then...

But I want this for her, if she ever wishes to know. I do not know what the future may hold, but at least the past shall be known. I need Sarah to know the truth.

The year 1918 was both the happiest and the worst year of my life. Happy for many reasons. The birth of my darling Sarah. The end of the Great War. And... the return of Beryl. That was both my great happiness and my greatest despair.

Sunday 25 May 1919

I had to take a break from my writings yesterday. The pain of this is still too great to tell. The betrayal too deep and unfathomable. Not just the betrayal of that most sacred sacrament of marriage. But of the bounds between sisters. For I am quite certain now that my Albert and my Beryl have struck up an affair. To be betrayed by my husband has broken me. I am tired all the time, but sleep viciously eludes me. And yet, to be betrayed by my sister in the same act... I am lost. I am adrift.

My Albert has never been the most attentive husband, I'll admit. He has been distracted by his work, which keeps him longer and longer hours. And we have not been intimate since before I found myself pregnant (forgive me these details, Sarah). I was recovering at first, but even later, he seemed to have lost his interest. Ever since she returned.

I did not see it at first. I was used to his long hours at the Sanatorium. And her, I was not used to at all anymore. I gave her such grace, knowing she must have seen such things during the war. And of course it was normal for the three of us —

now four of us — to spend time together at every opportunity. Revelling in her return, sharing news. And she was the most attentive Aunt.

But then my Albert stopped coming home at all. He claimed he spent the nights at the Sanatorium, but when I eventually thought to question it, the staff refuted this. Beryl, too, would spend nights away from the nurses' quarters. How she got away with this, I will never know. Perhaps everyone was too tired to notice. Perhaps her friends helped her hide it. She is more devious than I knew.

The gossip! Oh, the shame of that burns brightest of all. Not just the staff, but the patients, talk of it. Thank Goodness I am now a mother. I could not stand to work amongst them. I spend all my time indoors now. I cannot remember the last day I did not cry...

* * *

Trent had been ready to leave precisely at 3:00 p.m., with just a handful of pages left to read in Adelaide's diary. At first, Charlie had been reticent to leave, hoping to finish scouring the pages, but then she'd scarcely been able to stop talking during the thirty minutes' drive to her house. As Trent set himself up in the kitchen to begin cooking — his usual routine — Charlie excitedly pulled Tess and Raff away from Tess's tiny house to share all she'd learnt.

Huddled around her dining table, red wine in hand, and delicious smells of homemade pizza sauce already wafting over them, Charlie repeated her theories. "I know you said the Black is Beryl," Charlie said. "But is it *possible* you mistook her for Addie? They were sisters after all. Practically twins, and very close. Addie was betrayed not just by her husband but by her sister as well."

"It's certainly been enough to turn spirits Black in the past, if they can't let go," Raff mused, sucking down half of his wine in one gulp. "That smells bloody fantastic, mate!" he called to Trent. "No wonder these two keep you around." Trent smiled and raised his spoon at him in salute, but didn't join in the conversation. Charlie could see Trent's mistrusting gaze as he watched them and loved him all the more for it.

167

"So it could be Addie then?" Tess asked, twirling her wine more than sipping it.

Raff rolled his eyes, shook his head and raised his chin all in one combined motion, before shrugging. "I mean, I've never dealt with an imbalanced Black before. So I guess so. Anything's possible. I was just so sure she was Beryl." He topped up his wine glass, emptying the bottle in the process.

"We did see Beryl abused as well I suppose," Charlie sighed in exasperation, running her hands across her face.

"Perhaps by the doctor?" Tess reached over and picked a pistachio nut from the bag Trent had brought, flicking the edge of the shell rather than peeling it. "If he could cheat on his wife, he could probably do more as well."

"Either way, we need to go back to the Dream," Charlie directed the statement at Raff, staring him down. He just shrugged at her, reached for his own handful of pistachio nuts, and lay back in the chair. "And *this time*, I'll set the intent, you make the connection. You'll follow my lead."

28

Beryl Was Right

Charlie and Raff sat next to each other on the couch, with Tess and Trent both looking on from the matching armchairs. Charlie couldn't stomach the idea of lying next to Raff in her — or any other — bed. The smell of delicious pizza wafted through the air, reminding her of how painfully full her stomach was. Raff had ensured there were no leftovers. His appetite rivalled even Trent's. Charlie had a nice low buzz from the red wine that had accompanied the food, like a hum under her skin. She focussed on that as she prepared herself to enter the Dream. *Bring Raff*, she willed. *Follow my intent. How is his Black imbalanced?*

She could feel Raff slipping into the Dream just before her and marvelled at the sensation. Raff had been right; it would be impossible not to notice when someone else like them had entered the Dream close by. It was like Raff was no longer just an indentation on the couch beside her, breathing his soft garlic breath. His weight seemed to have doubled, tripled, dragging the edges of the couch into his centre. And her along with it. As she herself stood on the cusp of the Dream, she didn't reach out to Raff, lest she fall into his vortex. Instead, she pulled gently at him. She felt his centre sliding towards her own, like a blob of oil on the surface of the water pulled reluctantly towards a draining sink.

When Charlie opened her eyes, she was in *her* Waiting Place. What she described as a dreamscape of not-quite-white, not-quite-grey, platforms, arches and doors. It moved hypnotically, flashes of colour at the edges revealing that her world wasn't just white. It was a culmination of every possible colour. Raff stood before her, in his Black form, looking around him in what she could only describe as awe. His bright white eyes were glinting and wide, his head twitching on his neck as it flicked to take in every angle of her world. *It's different,* was all he sent to her. *So much colour. So much potential...*

How different? Charlie thought before she could catch herself. Her curiosity, as always, too strong.

There's no structure or platforms in my Waiting Place. Just constantly shifting sands and skylines. I don't have doors or archways to open. I follow footprints in chaotic deserts.

Charlie nodded, remembering what Tess had said to her. In fact, what Maryanne and Raff had also said to her, each in their own way. *'There are things you don't know. Give him some patience.'*

Come on, she sent, holding her glowing white hand out to him. *I set the intent, you set the direction. We're going to find out why your Black is so upset, so broken and kept from her purpose. Focus on her, and I'll do the rest.* As Raff reached out, she repeated her intent in her mind, over-and-over, and together they shifted. This time, standing not before a staircase or an archway or door, but before a long tunnel. She nodded to Raff, who towered over her this close, and they stepped through.

They found themselves inside a small, yellow-panelled room. Charlie couldn't quite tell its purpose, although there was a desk, several bookcases, and two comfortable armchairs. The fabric was a deep cream, almost yellow, and the wood was deliciously dark and shiny. A magnificent mirror hung on one wall, and sketches in matching gilded frames on another. The whole room had a feel of elegance and glamour to it, despite its small size. Perhaps a study, perhaps a library, perhaps a sitting or entertaining room — or perhaps all three.

The illusion of peace and luxury was quickly broken as a loud thud echoed beside the mirror, shaking the walls. The glass in the mirror flexed, and the frames on the walls tilted, almost falling. Two figures came into focus then.

Dr Albert, his shirt dishevelled and wrinkled, his dirty face poorly shaved, and streams of sweat running down his neck. He held Adelaide firmly by the shoulders, pushing her into the wall. She was squirming in fear, her face pinched and pale in terror. Her mouth gaped as if she couldn't believe what was happening to her. Her loose, navy dress was immaculate, except for a tear at the collar. Her dark hair, now grown to a bob, was tousled unevenly, her part no long sitting just to the side but in crazed loops.

"H-how... c-could you?" Adelaide stammered. Tears spilled from her eyes. Her tone was one of anger, not fear. "How could you choose her?" Albert let her go then and she sagged only slightly before bringing herself erect and taking a step towards him defiantly. "I am your *wife*! The mother of your *child*!"

"How could *I*?" Albert scoffed and chuckled wryly, no humour in his voice. He turned away from her, removing his glasses with one hand, and running his hand through his hair with the other. His hair, thick with grease, stuck up crazily. It was shorter than Charlie had last seen it and greying. He began laughing again; a terrifying sound that held no mirth and seemed to shake the walls as much as his earlier anger had. He spun back toward his wife, a single finger held aloft so tensely his whole body quavered behind it. "If I could divorce you, *God knows* I wouldn't wait another second. Another moment. I'd be *rid of you!*"

Shock and despair contorted Adelaide's face, her mouth hanging open and quivering as much as Albert's finger. She gritted her teeth, stepping forward with her hand held aloft to slap him, but Albert caught her hand roughly, squeezing her wrist so hard that Charlie could swear she heard the joints popping. "You're *hurting* me!" Addie's cries indicated the pain was not just physical, although there was certainly plenty of that, but so much deeper. She was a broken woman. He released her arm with such a forceful motion that Adelaide fell to the ground at his feet, the rug in the centre of the room crumpling inwards with the force. "I gave up everything for you," Addie sobbed, her anguish now overtaking her rage.

Albert walked to the door of the room, resting his forehead and right arm against the door frame, breathing deeply. Charlie wondered for a moment if he would turn back to Adelaide or continue on. It felt like a pivotal moment. Finally, he smashed his fist into the wall, breaking the plaster into white chunks that fell from a red brick beneath. And he was gone. Adelaide crouched where she'd fallen, staring after Albert, still quivering and sobbing, before fading away herself.

There's more, Raff sent. Charlie merely nodded, reached for Raff's hand, and pulled forward along the memory. At first, Charlie was disoriented as they stopped, standing in the deep bush she recognised from her own time trudging through it with Raff. It was the bush that surrounded the Sanatorium in Waterfall. Night had fallen, and the trees creaked as their branches rubbed together. Charlie also recognised the crudely constructed hut they now stood before, from an earlier encounter in the Dream. It was in even worse disrepair now, missing its door and with part of its roof collapsed. This was Jane Hughes's hut, the patient who had killed herself, and who Charlie had seen sharing this special, hidden place with Beryl.

As she and Raff watched, Albert strode quickly through the bush, his feet crashing as he rushed to the hut. Raff and Charlie followed, seeing Beryl waiting for him on a mound of old hospital blankets. A kerosene lantern glowed weakly beside her, casting dancing shadows on her face. "I didn't think you'd come," she whispered, slowly getting to her feet. The intensity burning in Albert's eyes was brighter than the lights dancing dimly around them. "I thought you were sorting things with Adelaide..."

"I was." Albert rushed to Beryl and took her hands in his gently, almost pleadingly. "But you were right." He let out a loud sigh, letting his head fall to rest on the top of Beryl's hair. The energy in the room started to build, tingling. Beryl let out a soft whine, bringing one hand to her mouth as if to silence herself, squeezing her eyes closed. She shook her head so little it was as though she weren't moving at all. "You were right," Albert breathed again, lifting his head slightly and using one finger to tilt Beryl's chin towards him. "You and I belong together. We always did."

The energy in the air was taut now, as though it was a rubber band stretched to its breaking point. Shivering, either ready to spring back or split in two. Albert's lips pressed against Beryl's, and she melted into him, the rubber band releasing in a burst of passion. Charlie could practically feel the momentum of their kiss, sweeping her and Raff backwards. Albert pawed clumsily at Beryl's dress, kissing at her exposed shoulder. "I'd do *anything* for you, Beryl. I'd kill her for you, if it meant we could be together..."

Beryl took a step backwards, tears at the corner of her eyes. Her hands didn't stop moving across Albert's chest, though, despite her disapproval. She pawed at him hungrily, like a starving woman seeing a forbidden meal. "I love her, Mersey. She's my sister. How could I ever stop loving her?"

* * *

Raff and Charlie both came to at the same time, sitting up in their seats and rubbing at their faces, hands and legs. Charlie felt a moment of satisfaction, realising it wasn't just her who needed to check she was in fact physical again on exiting the Dream. The living room was dark; several hours must have passed. And yet, they sat alone in the dim cottage. For some reason, the lights hadn't been turned on as darkness fell. "Where is Tess and Trent...?" Charlie started to say as she stood, gulping air, her stomach contracting with sour trepidation. Time was fickle in the dream. It could have been minutes, hours or even days — although she wasn't hungry or thirsty enough for the latter.

The limited light in the living room danced across the walls, flickering and casting shadows. She realised then that she could hear something outside. Trent was shouting, and something else was crackling, popping, roaring. She turned and saw, fully illuminated through the window, a bonfire burning brightly at her doorstep. The flames licked at the sky in a frenzy, turning her living room a deep orange. The smoke that billowed around Tess's tiny house was *black,* not grey or white. As soon as Charlie saw it, she could smell it, burning the inside of her lungs like acidic fumes. Trent ran to-and-fro before it, screaming a single word over-and-over. "Tess! Tess! *Tess!*"

29

The Catholic Problem

The heat wafting from the roof of the tiny house was unlike anything Charlie had felt before. This wasn't just the strong burn of a good bonfire. It felt like the air had turned to scorching metal and was scolding every part of her as she tried to breathe. Raff had raced out of the house right behind her, the three of them yelling Tess's name in demented chorus. Charlie pushed at the door, immediately bringing her singed hands back, screaming in both frustration and the pain of her burn. "Tess! Unlock the door!" Charlie was frightened by her own voice. It wasn't just fear that laced it. Her voice crackled with horror and panic. Pitching and breaking as though she were too distraught to form the words properly. She screamed again, sobbing as she beat her hands on the blazing wood only to draw back in pain.

She could hear Tess in there, coughing, calling weakly. It maddened Charlie, knowing Tess was so close and yet so unreachable. How long until that roof of molten fire collapsed on top of her? She lost feeling then, becoming a mass of broken atoms and screams, barely held together with terror. "Charlie!" Trent wrapped his hands around her, pulling her back, both of them stumbling as Charlie's legs kicked up in the dirt. Her eyes were streaming with tears from the black smoke that continued to flood her lungs, seemingly blistering her from the inside. What must Tess be feeling, beneath the weight of it all.

From the corner of her stinging eyes, Charlie saw a flash of movement as

Raff ran at the tiny house, something large and grey thrust before him. The whole tiny house shook, the roof blazing dangerously. The crackling noise grew in tempo, and Charlie screamed as Raff again thrust his grey object at the door, which burst open in a shower of hot splinters. More black fog bellowed out like an animated beast, desperate to reach the sky as fast as it could. A single blackened, slim arm flopped at the top of the steps. Trent let Charlie go then, and all three of them were soon fumbling at the door, pulling at Tess, pulling her free from the ruins. Just as Tess's feet were free of the door, the ceiling lost its integrity and fell in on itself, shooting sparks, ash and more smoke bellowing upwards.

Charlie fell down the steps with Tess on top of her, anxiously patting at her friend. She barely registered Trent — or was it Raff — pulling her and Tess back across the grass and away from the fire. Tess's skin and hair felt almost unbearably hot to touch. Her whole body — skin and clothes — was blackened with soot. "What do I do?!" Charlie screamed as she cradled her friend in her lap. "*HELP!*" She knew it was pointless screaming, but she couldn't stop. Though her eyes still stung, everything suddenly sharpened. The state of her friend. The popping noises from the fire. Trent's hands on her shoulder. Raff disappearing from view as he ran back to the house. The corner of the broken, grey bird bath that Raff had used as a battering ram. And above it, above the fire, wrapped in the smoke as if wearing it like a cape, was the Black. *Charlie's* Black. Glaring down at her with its moon-eyes.

* * *

Charlie jumped as the hospital light above her burst. Not only throwing Tess's emergency bed into darkness, but showering them both with glass. The nurse exclaimed as she raced to them, spewing apologies, and telling them to be careful while she went to find someone to help clean up the shards. Little unexplained 'accidents' like this had been happening repeatedly ever since the four of them had arrived at the hospital. Charlie was willing that shield of light with all her being, but it wasn't enough anymore. The Black was getting stronger. The only good luck seemed to be that Tess was okay.

Relatively speaking. She had first degree burns to most of her body, and the exposed parts of her ankles, neck and hands were edging towards second degree. Small blisters were already starting to appear below the skin. Once Tess had regained some semblance of consciousness, woozy from so much smoke inhalation, the agony she'd been in had been difficult to watch. It was much better seeing her sleep in her drug-induced haze, even if dusted in shards of glass.

Everything had happened in such a blur back at the house. Raff had run inside to phone 000 emergency services from Charlie's landline phone, grabbing his car keys in the process. The four of them had limped into his 4WD, Trent in the front passenger seat, although constantly bent backwards to look at them. Tess had lain sideways across the back seats, with her head in Charlie's lap, coughing with every breath. The ambulance had met them halfway to Greenfields, transferring Tess to a stretcher and hooking her straight onto a supply of pure oxygen. A fire truck had sped by them not long after, sirens blazing, as it headed for the property. With the paramedics' hands tied as to what pain relief they could offer, Tess had been moaning and crying loudly by the time they'd arrived at the hospital. The sounds tore at Charlie, who sobbed alongside her. *Thank God for morphine.*

Raff and Trent appeared just as the wardsman came by with a brush, broom and small vacuum to clean the mess away. "Again?" Raff said, as he passed her an instant coffee in a Styrofoam cup. He'd over-sweetened it in an attempt to tackle the bitterness, and she tried not to purse her lips as she swallowed, ignoring the question. "You *know* it's the Black, Charlie." Raff whispered now, bending down to her, as the wardsman got to work on the floor. "You can't stay here. It's dangerous. What if the whole hospital goes up next?!" The last word came out as a hiss, spittle flaying her across her mouth. She wiped it away with the back of her hand angrily. She knew Raff was right, but that just made it worse. All she wanted was to be with Tess.

"You can stay with me and Brent," Trent said gently, squeezing her shoulder. "The guest room is small and stuffed with crap, but you're more than welcome."

"I'll stick to my caravan for sleeping," Raff promised, implored desperately.

"And I'll stay with Tess during the day. Then, when she's discharged, she can go *home*. I'll look after her. I promise. I'm sorry, you were right. We never should have gone back. I've never encountered a spirit so strong. One who could almost kill someone even with a Guide and a Keeper working against him."

Charlie sniffled as she answered, rubbing her hand across her nose now. "If anything happens to her…"

"It won't, I—"

"If *anything* happens to her, you can forget about me helping you with your own Black. She can haunt you forever. I don't care how many Shadows come after me, or how many ripples it makes in the bloody Dream. Do you hear me?" Raff just nodded as Trent helped her to her feet, anxiously coaxing her away from their friend. It hurt so deeply to think that she was the reason any of this had happened. The guilt threatened to drown her, and she sniffled again.

"She'll be alright, honey." Trent wrapped her in a tight hug as soon as they were out the front of the hospital. The hug was so tight, so warm, it felt like he was enveloping her not just from the front, but from behind as well. She bowed her head, hoping she wouldn't leave snot trails across his jumper.

* * *

Brent was fully understanding of Charlie staying with them, even though the reasoning had been a bit fuzzier than reality. Trent had neatly slipped in that Tess might be in the hospital for a couple of days, and Charlie wanted to stay close. Charlie had been impressed with his white lie; it was normally so obvious when he wasn't being truthful. Trent's version of support and care for Charlie was endless hugs and shoulders to cry on. Brent's was less physical but still incredibly effective. He pulled some of his best whiskey from their liquor cabinet, and then got to work on a carb and fat-loaded array of comfort foods. The smells coming from the kitchen made her mouth water unbidden.

"Why was Tess even in the tiny house?" Charlie asked, as Trent handed her a very full tumbler of whiskey. She and Trent were both wrapped in warm blankets and sitting on a porch seat out the back of Trent's place, while Brent cooked. She hadn't been in the backyard before, and it was nothing like the front. The front was perfectly manicured. The back was a tangle of fruit trees, herbs and a large veggie garden. It made her feel like they were completely secluded from the world in the leafy oasis.

Trent shook his head in disbelief as he answered her question. "She went to measure something inside. We'd been sitting watching you two for hours, and she'd been planning what she wanted to do with her renovations. She was supposed to only be gone a *minute*. I guess the Black just took its opportunity when she was alone. I didn't even know anything was wrong until the flames lit up the room."

"I *need* to find out who the Blacks are, how they're connected to each other, and how to get rid of them," Charlie practically panted over the top of her whiskey glass.

"We know at least one of them is Beryl or Addie." Trent's breath, this close, was sharp. It smelled of garlic and whiskey fumes. Charlie ignored it and snuggled into him again.

"And it's possible my Black is Albert. We *suspect* it anyway. I've been so focussed on Raff I haven't given this one the time I should. And now…" Her voice broke, and she lifted the whiskey to her lips to try to mask it. "It's all my fault…"

"Not in the slightest!" Trent chastised, squeezing her with one arm. "It's all just a shit show, that's what it is. Did you learn anything with Raff at least?" Charlie shrugged as she recounted what had happened in the Dream, still not fully sure herself how this was all piecing together.

Charlie said, "it sounds like he at least thought about killing Addie. *Horrible.* According to Addie's diaries, they'd been so happy. I don't understand what went so wrong."

"You said they were married in a Catholic church?" Charlie affirmed that they were. "Then that's why they couldn't get divorced. You think the church is strict today… It was even worse back then. No divorce. *Ever.* Otherwise it's Hell and brimstone, and a swift eviction from the church for you."

"But *murder*? *Infidelity*? Those can't be better options than divorce."

"The Catholic church doesn't exactly have a rosy history when it comes to what's right and wrong." Charlie couldn't help but agree with Trent on that one. "I think I might know what that hut was that you saw too." Charlie sat up so she could hear him better, adjusting her blanket as she did so. "I found one or two online references to it. Apparently, because of how strict and boring life could be at the Sanatorium, some of the long-term patients built secret huts out in the bush. They used to go there for illegal gambling, enjoying contraband, sex, anything they couldn't get away with in the wards. They used to use them as, like, safe havens. They kept them secret so their stashes of alcohol and whatnot couldn't be stolen, and so their freedom wouldn't be curtailed."

"But Beryl knew where Jane's hut was, because of how close they were. It's the perfect spot for an affair. Hidden in the bush, hidden from everyone else. That must be where they stayed when Albert never came home, and Beryl never went back to the nurses' quarters." Raff nodded, sipping his whiskey slowly. "But *even still...!*" Charlie felt irritation in her, like a headache pounding through her entire body, pushing at and trying to escape her skin. "How does this help me find *my* Black? Please, Trent. Please help me. I need to know who they are. I *need* to end this!"

30

Back-and-Forth, Back-and-Forth

Trent had gone to bed early that night, pleading exhaustion. He'd been the one to talk with Tess's son, Leon, and let him know what had happened. It had been a long conversation, ending with Leon passing instructions that he'd be down with Ella the next day. Brent followed Trent to bed straight away, apologising to Charlie, but she waved him off. She watched contentedly as she saw Brent follow after his partner with such care and attention. He put a hand on Trent's elbow as they turned the corner into their hallway, and Charlie wondered just for a moment what she might have missed out on in life. She had Tess — her best friend, her sister. Never more, though. Was it enough? It would have to be, she supposed. If not Tess, then no-one. She'd be more content alone.

Charlie tried to go to bed early herself, in the spare room crammed with boxes and dusty knick-knacks. She ended up tossing and turning, and then standing and pacing. Her mind kept racing with everything they'd learnt so far, and everything that was still so opaque. Most of all, her mind turned to Tess, laying in that hospital, with Raff watching over her. *It should be* me *watching over her...*

Frustrated, Charlie lay back on the bed, atop the covers, and placed both hands over her sternum. She let out a deep sigh as she watched the dark ceiling, deciding to enter the Dream and seek out some answers. To focus on *her* Black, and on getting back to Tess. On getting Tess back. She knew

Trent would never forgive her if she ended up stuck in the Dream through the morning and Brent demanded explanations for her comatose state, but she couldn't sit still any longer. She exhaled deeply, feeling her hands settle down into her stomach as she did so. *I need to know more about my Black. I need to move him on...*

The feeling of her hands settling down continued well past where they physically should, and she felt herself sucked into the Dream. Charlie found herself back at Sandgate Cemetery, rather than in her Waiting Place, and she knew that this was where her Black was stalking again. There was no doubt in her mind now, whoever he was, he was buried here. If he hadn't been connected to Charlie, this would have been where he endlessly haunted. She felt a sense of small relief to know he wasn't always following her. That sometimes she was alone. Once again, she found herself in deep night in this place, the tombstones merely blacker shadows against an inky backdrop. Deep silence as well. A silence so complete she could almost feel it pushing on her stilled eardrums.

I'm here to help you, Charlie sent, steeling her intent as she did so. With all the shadows here, he could be anywhere, ready to suddenly loom out, catching her in the grips of his bright and overly large eyes. *Please, tell me who you are. You're Albert, aren't you? Tell me. I* will *help you.* She took a step forward and found herself back at the Catholic church at the far end of the cemetery and looking at the Black pacing in his familiar corner. He was smaller in stature than she'd seen him before, his legs almost visible shapes instead of one giant mass. He still towered over her, but at least he didn't loom impossibly higher than the church. His eyes gleamed ever bright, not just reflecting the moonlight and starlight, but beaming as though they were each their own source of light. Standing here, watching him walking back-and-forth, back-and-forth, she viewed the Black in a slightly different light. Not just terrifying — though that emotion battled for breath and attention — but forlorn. Almost pitiful.

I can't trust any promises, she heard the Black almost muttering, though his tone was still torrid. Like the aftershocks of a large ringing church bell that vibrated through her. *Always broken... broken promises... Mine, hers, all of ours.*

Can't trust promises...

I won't break my promise to you. Charlie approached now, using a tactic she often did with troubled spirits. She drew that light from the Dream and willed it towards him. Willed him some peace, some steadiness. *I can't break my promise. It's my purpose, so I must help you.* The unspoken part of her need reverberated through her even stronger. She couldn't let anything happen to Tess. The desperation leached off her, but there was nothing she could do to temper it. *Show me...?*

She took another step and was now almost able to reach out and touch him. She barely reached up to his elbow, despite his form having shrunken in on itself. She reached out, her fingers caressing the very edge of his arm. And then, those moon-eyes fell on her with such force. She winced and jolted as the two of them were pulled into one of his memories. A memory she had seen before, but which he was not yet ready to face.

They stood in a small room. It was barely two metres squared inside; its roof was almost taller than the room was wide. Ceiling beams were exposed, and a lantern hung from one, although it was unlit. It was night, and unnaturally cold. She saw the Black enter the room, shrinking even further until it was the same height as Charlie. She couldn't tell if it was Albert, though the height was right. He dragged a small step stool with him, and a large rope. *It's my fault*, the Black spirit muttered. *It's all my fault...* He brought the rope up to the ceiling beams, standing on tiptoes as he looped it over the lowest beam and secured it. The Black shimmered and almost took its human form. Trousers became visible, light beige. Scuffed boots, too. And a crumpled, unbuttoned shirt. It faded in-and-out of his black, wispy spirit.

Sobs caught in his throat as he pulled a noose roughly over his head and around his neck, pulling it tight. "Forgive me my love... Forgive me... I'm sorry..." He kicked the stool away from him and jerked as the rope snapped taut. The rope bit tight but didn't snap; the fall was not enough to break his neck. His death was quieter than Charlie expected. His legs kicked and thrashed, the fabric of his trousers swishing and his boot heels occasionally clicking. His fingernails scraped at the rope, a scratching chorus with his whispering pants. Barely any sound escaped his lips, excepting gurgled half-gasps that never quite fully formed. Each rough and murmured croak that choked from him was quieter than the last, as he was unable to draw breath. Finally, his body went completely still. His swollen tongue pushed passed his puffed lips. Even so distorted, she recognised this face. Finally. *It is you, Albert...* He didn't respond.

Charlie wasn't sure how many hours passed as she stood there, watching the shadows of changing light dance over his bloated features and increasingly grey skin. She willed time to move faster. The single door to the room creaked as it was sluggishly pushed open. The movement was slow and staccato not because someone was creeping and sneaking, but because the person behind the door lacked the strength to move it faster. Chubby hands were visible first, and then a round, bright face, with Addie's dark hair and Albert's light eyes. A girl — all of three years old — took a tentative step into the room. As the door opened, a wave of heat attempted to push into the room. Judging by her thin white dress, the full heat of an Australian summer was burning beyond this freezing tomb. The cold, which seemed to have settled its icy grip onto Albert, refused to let up. "Found d-you Papa!" The girl's voice was forcefully bright, but even this young, Charlie knew the child understood something wasn't right. Her father was too still. "Founded d'you!" she yelled louder, confusion and fear bolstering her little voice. It demanded him to stop his foolishness, to come down. *"Papa!"*

Charlie closed herself off from the sight. When she allowed herself to see again, she was back in the cemetery with her Black. With Albert. Just as Charlie's own guilt about Tess had leeched from her like a thick odour, shame spilled from Albert. She saw, now, that those moon-eyes weren't moons at all. They were glasses, his spectacles, somehow tethered to him, if greatly distorted. *It's not your fault, Albert,* Charlie willed to him. Willed, because she wasn't sure that was true. He'd killed himself. He'd left his dangling, swelling body for his daughter to find. And what had driven him to it? What had he done?

I lost everything, he replied instead, resuming his pacing in the cemetery, his figure growing slightly taller with each step. *I lost my love... my child... What must I have done to deserve this?* Amidst the guilt, she felt anger, and a fight in him, too. Like he would — and could — keep pushing Charlie away, refusing to let her see what great betrayal had befallen him. The thing he was so ashamed of.

Albert?

It's Mersey, he whispered instead. *My name is Mersey.*

31

Acts of Reactance

Charlie had thankfully woken from a normal dreamless sleep as daylight had peeked around the edges of the navy curtains in the boys' guest room. No need to explain anything to Brent, then. She'd woken from the Dream in time. Her head felt heavy and full, like her skull had thickened at the top of her cranium and along her cheekbones. She'd barely had three hours' sleep, she guessed, as she pushed the old blankets and flannel sheets off her. She wondered which of the boys had brought these obviously vintage bedspreads with him from his childhood home. Just after she'd pulled her jeans back on and *tried* to tame her hair with her fingers, there was a gentle knock at her door.

"Charlie?" Brent's voice whispered through the plywood. "Did I hear you up-and-about?"

"Yup!" she called, picking her knitted jumper up from where she'd thrown it the night before just as the door fully popped open. Brent proffered a hairbrush, toothbrush and small bottle of 'Mum' deodorant.

"It's not much, but I have a few things here in case of emergencies..."

"Oh God, you're a *lifesaver*!" Charlie gratefully bundled them up, and then Brent was proffering a towel through the door with his other hand. She smiled and chuckled internally to herself at Brent's awkward politeness, wanting to put as little of his own body into the guest room as possible.

"Shower's all yours."

* * *

After a quick stop at the local grocer for supplies — a packet of too-big granny panties and Bonds long-sleeve singlets — Trent and Charlie were climbing the stairs to the library. She'd felt uncomfortable staying at their house during the day, and instead opted to sit and read the last of Addie's diary at Trent's work. Brent, who Charlie had only just discovered was an accountant, had disappeared into a home office shortly after breakfast. That had made the prospect of lingering in their house even more awkward. "You know what?" Charlie paused partway up the stairs, looking up at Trent who was a few steps in front of her "I think I'm going to walk to the hospital first and check in on Tess."

"You sure, honey?" Trent asked slowly.

"I've got my mask in my handbag, and the fresh air will do me good. The chances of coming across someone with peanut butter toast on the footpaths should be pretty slim." She had deliberately misconstrued his concern, which she knew was more for Tess, not her.

"But not zero chance. You got your Epipen?" Charlie nodded and patted the side of her handbag. She never went anywhere without at least one, even in emergency situations such as last night. "And…" Trent trailed off, leaving the second half of his fears unsaid. But Charlie knew; it's what she'd tried to ignore. But she also felt that terror in the very depths of her soul.

"I won't stay long. Just a quick visit to make sure she's really okay. Not long enough for the Black to do anything to her. I promise, I—"

"Okay, Charlie. It's okay. Say hi for me. Let me know how she is. I'll see you soon, honey."

The twenty-minute walk shook some of the sleep fog from her, lightening her head, as she took brisk strides and breathed the fresh air. She was soon riding the elevator to the small hospital's second (and top) floor, walking to one of only half a dozen ward rooms. She couldn't help but peek in the open doors she passed, seeing mostly elderly women or men shuffling their feet into their slippers, or watching their corner TVs while blowing on lukewarm tea in plastic mugs. While not religious, she found herself praying to whatever waited on the other side that her Black — that Alfred, or Mersey, or whatever he wanted to call himself — would give her just a few moments' peace with her friend. That Tess would remain safe.

"Tess?" she whispered as she knocked on the door. She was laying on her side, facing the curtained windows, so Charlie couldn't see if she was awake. Tess stirred and tentatively rolled over to face the door. Her chapped and cracked lips broke into a smile as soon as she saw her. Relief that Tess wasn't frightened of her made Charlie feel nauseous with relief. Tess's face was still bright red, as though she'd spent all day in direct sun. Small oxygen tubes pushed up at her nostrils. Tess winced as she finished turning. Raff was nowhere to be seen.

"*Bonjour, ma chére,*" Tess croaked in a soft, hoarse voice. It sounded like she'd chain smoked a whole packet of cigarettes in one go. Perhaps that was similar to what had actually happened to her lungs. "*Je t'aimerai pour tou—*" Before Tess could finish, Charlie was kneeling at her bedside, a hand placed on the edge of her face as softly as she could. She wanted to squeeze every part of Tess and never let go, but the bright red burns, and her bandaged hands, begged caution. Charlie felt as though she were internally squeezing tightly to her own heart instead. The pressure through her whole being begged to burst free.

"I am *so* sorry." Charlie's bottom lip trembled and she hated herself even more for this momentary weakness. She didn't deserve to cry. She wasn't the one who'd nearly burnt to death in that God-awful tiny house. She wasn't the one who'd had a powerful, vengeful, malicious spirit unleashed on her by her supposed best friend. She shouldn't have even come. Charlie sniffled instead, wiping her nose on the edge of her shoulder. The tears seemed to have found a different passage through which to escape. "It's all my fault. And look at me?! I just can't stay away... I-I just had to know you were okay..."

"*Ma chére...*" Tess's voice was a whispered scratching, and Charlie hated herself again for making Tess talk when it was so obviously uncomfortable. Charlie unwillingly let out a whimper instead of a sigh. "*Tais-toi, balai de chiotte...*It is *not* your fault."

187

THE CORNER OF HER EYE

"That's a new one," Charlie laughed, referring to Tess's obvious French insult. Tess gingerly raised her bandaged hand, placing it very tenderly over Charlie's own, which still rested on her face. Charlie could only just feel the slightest tickle and pressure from the bandage, which felt too rough for Tess's normally smooth skin.

"This is *not* your fault," Tess repeated firmly, if still quietly.

"I wish I could be the one here with you. I wish none of this was fucking happening. Where even is Raff?" Charlie could feel her sense of helplessness and guilt twisting into anger, but felt little remorse at it being directed towards the absent bogan. "He'd better be looking after you."

"He *is,* darling. He's off meeting Leon and Ella. You should go easier on Raff. I like him. There's a lot you don't know. He—" The door to Tess's room suddenly slammed, shaking a plastic cup full of water on her side table. They both watched the ripples trembling in the cup and gasped as the cup shot across the room, crumpling against the wall and spraying water into a dark mass on the paint. Tess flinched, shrinking in on herself, and shrinking Charlie's heart along with her.

"I need to go." The tremble in Charlie's voice rose, in anger and fear. "I'm so sorry. Tell Raff to keep me updated. I promise I'll love you forever."

"*Je t'aimerai pour toujours,*" Tess croaked, nodding a little. Charlie fled from the room, mask secured to her face, and tears once again threatening at the corners of her eyes.

* * *

Monday 29 November 1920

This shall be my last entry. It has been so long since I even thought about these pages. Such agony my life has been that I could not think to prolong it by writing it down. To make it more real by preserving it here. The only happiness in my life now is my dear Sarah, who is growing more and more inquisitive every day.

I found this journal while looking for one of Mama's pins. I wanted Beryl to have it. To be buried with something that s— ——- r-mb—by. My God, but I need to stop sobbing so I won't ruin my letters any more than my trembling hand has already.

It was always Beryl and I. Right from the start. Though we were born a year apart, she has always been there. I remember no part of my life without her. And she was my whole world for so long. We were in it all together, always. And at the end, it was just the two of us once more. The Administrative Assistant Superintendent took pity on me, the dear old man. Charles helped me to arrange for Beryl's body to be taken to the Waterfall Cemetery without fuss, without fanfare, and — God, most of all —without the gossip. It had to be this way, burying her in secret. For the sake of my daughter, for the sake of Sarah. I can't have more of a spectacle with Albert.

But, God help me, it was awful. We had an unseasonably wet November, the rain falling in sheets as if mourning everything that had happened to Beryl and I in our lives. How it had finally come to this. The ground swelled so much with these unearthly tears, that her grave filled with water. It was like we were burying Beryl not in the ground, but in a watery tomb. The two wardsmen who dear Charles had found to help us had to drill holes in her coffin. To flood it. To help sink her down. I couldn't help but picture her in there, all withered away, and then floating inside her box as the water filled her up.

Worst of all, with only two wardsmen, I had to climb atop the coffin with them, to weight it down, to push her into her grave. The three of us balancing on this unholy boat, while Charles said last rites over a storm so loud I could scarcely hear the words. I stood there, atop her body, atop her grave, slowly being sucked down in there with her. Thinking how that very water that lapped at my ankles was also lapping at her carcase.

Oh Beryl, I—

* * *

Charlie squinted at the final lines of Addie's diary, the whole entry of which had been splattered with tears, making some parts almost indistinguishable. That final sentence, scrawled in spidery handwriting was totally illegible. Not just because it was so poorly written, but because it was smudged.

"I wonder how she died," Charlie later said to Trent in his office. "I guess

Beryl is Raff's Black after all. She died first. And Albert Mersey Hammond is *my* Black. Can you find them now, Trent? Can you find where they were buried?"

32

The Heart Can Bleed

Charlie, Trent and Brent sat in the boys' living room, a pile of letters that had been tucked in the back of Addie's journal in front of them. Brent had prepared a tray of assorted teas and set a warm fire, which crackled in their freestanding fireplace. Charlie had wanted to dive into the letters as soon as she'd seen them, but had needed to see Leon before he and Ella left to return to Sydney. She'd promised him dinner, and it had been nice to catch up and discuss 'normal' things, like his impending nuptials.

Brent, who had changed into his slippers and tartan dressing gown, was positively brimming with excitement as he carefully lifted the bundle of letters. It had been carefully tied with string. There'd been no harm in Charlie telling Brent she'd been reading an old journal she'd been given by a friend, which had sparked an interest — in both her and Trent — in Waterfall Sanatorium and Newcastle's Sandgate Cemetery.

"Now I know why Trent *really* likes spending so much time with you, Charlie," Brent joked, carefully placing the bundle back down. "Finally, someone who enjoys personal Australian histories as maniacally as he does." He smiled fondly at his partner, while scratching behind the ear of their black-and-white cat. The cat had appeared to bathe in the warmth of the fire. "It *is* cold, isn't it Mr Kent."

"*Kent?*" Charlie laughed, as the cat started purring and rubbing its head against Brent's hand. "Oh, come on!" But she thought it was brilliant. Trent,

Brent and Kent. An unlikely rhyming trio.

"So!" Trent clapped his hands together and leaned over to pick up the bundle and a pair of scissors he'd retrieved from the kitchen. "You don't mind me snipping these free?" Charlie nodded at him to proceed. The knot was too old now to come undone, melding together tightly from its long decades of disuse. "Oh, and before I forget. I did look into Waterfall Cemetery before I finished work. I couldn't find any record of someone called Beryl Morgan being buried there. *But* that doesn't mean she wasn't. The records aren't complete, remember? There were many records lost, so if the journal says that's where she is, I think we can trust it more than we can our local records." Half a dozen letters fell free, and Trent passed one to each of them, letting his hand linger on Brent's for a moment.

Charlie's letter — which was the first atop the pile — was a single page, neatly folded in two. It was yellowed and spotted with age, and much thicker than any paper in common use today. She could see and feel the bumps and indentations where the paper had initially been pressed together. Her hands shook slightly as she opened it, hoping it wouldn't tear along the indentation. The handwriting was careful and looped, and nothing at all like Adelaide's petite cursive.

> *When the love-burst came, like an English Spring,*
>> *In days when I moved from town,*
>> *And the hem of your skirt was a sacred thing*
>> *And your hair like an angel's crown.*
>> *The shock when another man touched your arm,*
>> *When the wardsmen sat in a row;*
>> *The hope and despair, and the false alarm*
>> *When I had yet to say hello.*
>
> *By the arbour lights on the southern wards,*
>> *I remember the question put,*
>> *While I watched like a boy on the misericords,*
>> *And you trembled from head to foot.*

The electric shock from your fingertips,
And the murmuring answer low,
The soft, shy yielding of warm red lips
When you claimed that I must know.

Dear Beryl, leave me not in misery put,
*   In the harried grips of unknowing,*
If in every stolen glance or hidden look,
*   An embered warmth comes glowing.*
Please leave a message for me to read,
*   Where the red carnations grow;*
Do you know how the heart of a man can bleed
*   If left where he cannot know?*

"It's a love poem," Charlie said, gently holding the page in the slightest pinch she could manage. "To Beryl."

"Mine is a love letter to Beryl too," Brent piped up.

"And mine..." Trent reached out for Charlie's piece of paper, leaving his own to the side for the moment. Brent, who was sitting on the lounge beside him, leant across to read over his shoulder.

"That's a Henry Lawson, isn't it?" Brent asked, watching Trent's lips as he silently muttered the poem, perhaps moved by the words on the page. Trent seemed oblivious to the affection as his mind raced.

"I think so..." Trent handed the letter to Brent to continue reading, while he pulled his phone from his pocket and started tapping at the screen. Kent took the momentary distraction as an opportunity to jump onto Brent's lap, pawing at his dressing gown, before curling up and falling to sleep. "It's *sort of* a Henry Lawson... 'Do You Think That I Do Not Know?', at least parts of it. But the verses are changed, and the last one is pretty much completely new. Obviously changed up for Beryl."

Trent carefully leafed to the last page of his letter and picked it up for everyone to see the signature. "Mersey," he read aloud, although they could all clearly see the poetically scrawled hand. The name by which Beryl had called Albert in the Dream. And the name by which Charlie's Black had called himself.

"So these letters are from their affair…" Charlie thought aloud, taking the papers from Trent

"No," Trent shook his head, reaching for another letter. "That letter is dated May 1913. Albert was sending Beryl love letters within a year, likely within months, of arriving at the Sanatorium."

"But… Adelaide…" Charlie's mind raced back to the journal entries she'd read, trying to remember if there'd been any hints or clues as to Beryl's feelings. Or Albert's. She came up wanting. "He loved Adelaide."

"According to Adelaide's journals." Brent lay back in his seat then, sipping his tea while he scratched a purring Kent's ears. "Both sisters must have loved him. And either Addie didn't see it, or she didn't want to. Didn't you say the sisters were inseparable? And of course, Albert spent a lot of time with both of them. How scandalous. How romantic! Maybe I can get into these histories after all, love."

"And even though relationships between staff were pretty common," Trent jumped in. "It wasn't exactly encouraged. It was even frowned upon. Though, I think the Superintendent ended up marrying one of the nurses after his first wife died…" Charlie started reading this letter as Trent droned on about the history he'd uncovered of Waterfall Sanatorium. Trent's words faded as Albert's — as Mersey's — own words loudly recited themselves in her head.

11 May 1913

My Dearest Beryl,

Your letter filled my heart with such joy I could scarcely continue my duties. If my words were art to you, it is because you are my muse when I write. Your angelic figure and grace inspire such better and higher form in me, in everything I do. I dream of the day I will kiss your eyes, your lips, your cheeks, your haloed hair. If I develop into a doctor of any consideration, it will be because of your love and trust.

I respect your desire for me to establish my reputation here before we proceed any further. It makes me yearn for you even more. But my dearest Beryl, the longer I am here at Waterfall, the more I realise that to make you happy has become my sole ambition.

For now, let us continue to profess our love, our deepest desires and ambitions to one another through the mighty pen, and beneath the hearty red carnations. Every day I shall stroll past them, for hope of a word from you. Just the prospect of your letters shall buoy me each and every day.

...

* * *

The three of them — four if you included Kent — sat by the fire well into the evening, reading professions of love from Dr Albert to Beryl, under the name of Mersey. They found themselves wondering what had happened to Beryl's letters back to the doctor, where he may have hidden them, and if they had now been completely destroyed or were merely lost somewhere, waiting to be found. Perhaps they'd been buried with Albert or burnt by the scorned Adelaide. Trent and Brent made plans to travel together to Newcastle the next day — a public holiday — to track down Albert's grave in Sandgate. A morbid, though somewhat romantic, date.

After they'd both retired to bed, Kent following along behind them, Charlie phoned Raff. She hoped he was with Tess at the hospital this time. She hadn't wanted to phone Tess and have her fumble with her bandaged hands at her mobile phone. "G'day Charlie," Raff's thickly accented voice shouted loudly down the phone. "Hey, Tess, it's Charlie!" There was the sound of clumsy fingers and the pitch of the call changed as Raff switched it to speaker phone.

"*Bonjour la nuit, ma chére.*"

"Oh, you sound so much better!" Charlie breathed in relief as Tess's sweet voice carried through the line with less croakiness than it had that morning.

"*Oui, ma chére.* I think they'll let me come home tomorrow. And I'm off the oxygen now." A deep sigh forced its way out of Charlie as utter relief shattered some of the tension she'd been holding in her chest.

"Thank God… I am *so* glad. I also have some news. I think we may be closer to solving this whole thing and getting you safe again." The line went quiet, and she could picture both Raff and Tess leaning in. "Albert and Beryl didn't just start an affair when she got back from the war. They'd been sending love letters and poetry to each other since at least May 1913, maybe even a bit earlier. They were keeping it quiet while Albert settled into the Sanatorium, so he could build his reputation as a respected doctor. Either Adelaide didn't know, or she refused to acknowledge it."

"A bit of a psycho," Raff interjected, making Charlie's neck prickle with agitation.

"We *don't* know that. I finished reading Addie's journal and Beryl died in November 1920, a couple of years after she got back. A couple of years into the affair. I assume the 'affair' kept going in-between journal entries. Beryl is definitely your Black, Raff."

"Well, yeah, no shit…" The arrogance in his voice made the hairs on Charlie's neck practically vibrate.

"I wonder…" Tess whispered. "You said the war-time letters from Beryl to Adelaide and Albert stopped in, what was it, 1916?" Charlie mumbled an affirmation. "I wonder if they didn't stop at all, but Addie just stopped delivering them to Albert. Beryl always addressed them to Addie and asked her to pass them on to the doctor, correct? And how was it you said she worded it…"

"*The letters had to stop…*" Charlie breathed, in sudden realisation. It all clicked together in such a way that she couldn't believe she hadn't realised before. "Beryl never stopped sending letters! Addie just stopped delivering them. She let Albert believe Beryl was dead, and then she married him! When her sister loved him!"

"*Salope! Ça me fait chier…* How could she do that to her own sister?"

"At least we have a good idea how Beryl was betrayed," Raff jumped in.

"And don't forget she was abused as well." Charlie tapped the back of her mobile phone as she thought, closing the door to the guest bedroom so she

196

wouldn't disturb Trent or Brent. "I wonder if he even knew what Adelaide did. Maybe Albert felt guilty about the affair and took it out on Beryl? Fuck me… Poor thing."

"But we don't know why her spirit is so imbalanced," Raff added. "Worse things than this happen all the time, and the spirits accept it and get on with things with just a nudge. And how was your Albert betrayed, other than by Addie tricking him? Why is he so crazed too?"

"Tess, would you be okay if Raff came to Trent's house tomorrow morning, just for a couple of hours? So we can enter the Dream together again and try to get some of these answers."

"Of course, *ma chére*. Let's get these two out of our lives for good."

These three, Charlie thought quietly to herself, as Raff started making plans for the next morning.

33

Remembrance

Charlie had set an alarm to ensure she was up with the dawn and was pleased to see Brent shuffling quietly in the kitchen when she tiptoed out. He'd already pulled a candle out from some unknown drawer or cupboard and was just striking a match as she whispered a good morning to him.

"Morning to you as well, Charlie." Brent cupped one hand around the candle as he reverently lit it. "You know Trent isn't a morning person," he chuckled. "He'll commemorate ANZAC Day by eating too many biscuits later." Charlie cherished the one-on-one time with Brent that morning, rugged up with spare blankets, sitting on the front porch bench with the candle flickering between them on the ground. Completely silent; nothing but the early morning parrots and insects retiring for the day greeted their ears. Though Charlie imagined she could hear bugles playing somewhere in the distance.

ANZAC Day — which stood for Australian and New Zealand Army Corps — fell on the 25th of April every year. Although it officially commemorated Australia and New Zealand's part in the Gallipoli expedition of World War I, the holiday had evolved to mark all Australian and New Zealand military service in every war since. Charlie knew that all around Australia, New Zealand, and the world, Aussies and Kiwis would be gathering together to remember their countries' military service at the dawn. She thought of Beryl as she sat there, watching the candle flame dance. Of what she must have seen and endured in her own military service, perhaps without ever knowing she was being betrayed by the person she most loved and trusted in the world. It was heartbreaking.

* * *

Raff arrived just as Trent and Brent were preparing to depart for Newcastle, a Tupperware container of ANZAC biscuits held tightly in Trent's hands. "G'day fellas! Oi, are those biccies?" Raff started reaching for the container before Trent could even offer him one. Charlie had already enjoyed a couple of the delicious, gooey, crunchy ANZAC biscuits with her tea that morning. Brent had mastered the consistency. Just enough crunch, just enough chew, and a delicious balance of golden syrup and butter. Trent's face fell slightly as Raff pulled four large biscuits out.

"You know, these were the biscuits sent by wives and women's groups to the ANZACs in World War I..." he started saying, but Raff waved him off.

"Whatever, they're bloody delicious. Thanks, fellas." Raff pushed past Charlie and into the house without looking back. Charlie grimaced and shrugged slightly in apology for his brisk behaviour.

"How do you know him again?" Brent asked suspiciously, peering over her shoulder, no doubt worrying what he might come home to. Or what might be missing.

"A cousin... a *distant* one," Charlie muttered. "He knows a bit about Adelaide, Beryl and Albert. I promise, I'll keep an eye on him."

After friendly hugs, and waving them off, Charlie returned to the house to find Raff sitting at the dining table, only two cookies left, though the crumbs of the others were scattered across the table's surface. She muttered under her breath as she went to the sink to get a cloth, noticing on the kitchen clock the time was creeping closer to 10:00 a.m.

"You know..." she said as she roughly pushed in front of him to wipe the crumbs away like a disapproving mother, putting the remaining cookies on a plate she'd found in the dishwasher. "I have my call with Maryanne. Sorry, I should have thought of it last night. Why don't you walk down to

Dot's and get us a couple of coffees?" Raff stared at her for a moment, and she sighed loudly, walking to her purse to fish out a twenty-dollar bill. He snatched it from her hand.

"Easy-peasy," he smiled as he jumped up. "Tell the old bird hallo from me. And tell her sorry for missing our last session. You know how it is."

Actually, Charlie didn't know. She rarely missed an appointment, and always felt awful when she did. She grimaced at him, breathing in relief as she pushed the door closed behind him and rested her back against it. The end of this ordeal couldn't come fast enough. Maryanne, as always, promptly called her at 10:00 a.m. on the dot. "Good morning, Charlotte."

"Hey, Maryanne." Not only was Maryanne wearing a turtleneck under her tunic today, but a large felt coat that hung off her. In fact, Maryanne did seem to have lost a little weight. She looked much better today — her eyes weren't so sallow and darkened — but her skin was still quite pale. "How are you feeling?"

Maryanne shrugged off the question. "Well, thank you." It was a well-rehearsed response. "How have you been? Any further along with those two Blacks?" Charlie relayed everything that had happened since their last call. That they'd at least identified who the Blacks were, how they were connected, and some of the betrayal and abuse they'd suffered. There were still questions to answer, but Charlie felt like they were finally close.

"And there was one other thing," Charlie added as she finished recapping their time at the Sanatorium. "I encountered a new kind of spirit. A Midnight. Have you heard of those yet?"

"Yes," Maryanne answered slowly, tilting her head to the side. "If we're thinking of the same spirit. A deep blue. Someone who committed suicide, usually, but has to face the grief or pain of their life fully before they can move on. An incredibly depressed soul, who tried to escape that depression early, but needs to process it fully before purgatory will let them go. Is that what you mean?"

Charlie nodded. "Are they a common spirit too? I know suicides are, unfortunately, not that rare.

"Thankfully not so common," Maryanne continued. "Not everyone who commits suicide will become a Midnight, just like not every child who dies will become a Blue. The depression, the emotion, needs to be incredibly strong to ground them so. Strange though... How did you know they were called Midnights?"

"It just...came to me. I can't explain it." Maryanne nodded and continued writing in her notebook. "I helped her to move on. She only required a nudge. No thanks to Raff, though. I was worried he'd pull me away and keep following the two Blacks. I don't think I'll ever be so grateful to get people out of my life." While Charlie had included Raff in her round-up of Albert and Beryl, she hadn't intended for Maryanne to pick up on this.

"You should go easy on Rafael, Charlotte. He's been through a lot."

"Everyone keeps saying that!" Agitation always seemed to bristle just below the surface with Charlie lately. Perhaps she was picking up on the Black spirits' guilt, grief and anger. Perhaps it was her concern for Tess making her snappy. Or maybe it was just that Raff rubbed her the wrong way. She didn't like how close Raff and Tess were getting.

"But have you actually listened? Have you asked him?" Charlie paused before answering. She again found herself in the position of wanting to be the one to abruptly end the call on Maryanne. "Do you even know his last name?" Charlie shrugged at her, not liking the insinuation that she was in the wrong here. At least partly. "It's *Morgan*. How else do you think he got Adelaide's journal? She was a great-aunt of his. His grandfather's sister. This is personal for him."

"He never mentioned..." It wasn't all on Charlie to ask the questions, she tried to reason to herself. Communication worked both ways. "He should have told me. Did he know?"

"Know what? That his Great-Aunt Beryl was an imbalanced Black? No, he didn't. He inherited Adelaide's journal when his grandfather passed recently, and that sparked the connection for him. That's what sparked all of this for him."

"And he's not related to Albert, at least by blood, so he only connected with Beryl..." Charlie pondered aloud.

"Everything is connected, Charlotte. Those ripples I spoke of at our last

201

THE CORNER OF HER EYE

session, they don't just extend out on their own. They can cause other ripples. The fact that *you* connected with Albert before Raff even found you… Just think about it."

Charlie nodded, more because she wanted the call to end than anything else. Raff wouldn't be too long with those coffees. The last thing she wanted was for any of this awkward conversation to be had with him listening in.

"And think about *why* Raff is a Black Guide, Charlotte. Think about that."

* * *

Raff got back with the coffee, and a bag of some sort of pastry (no change), not long after Charlie had disconnected the call. She'd been sitting at the dining table, trying *not* to think through everything Maryanne had said. Or everything Tess had said at the hospital the other day. But it couldn't be helped. Was she actually the one in the wrong here? Her curiosity piqued as the two of them drank their coffees in near-silence, Raff merely shrugging when she mentioned that Adelaide and Beryl had been his great-aunts. As though it wasn't an important factor at all, and his own personal connection bared no importance. "Which one was your Grandpa?"

"Ciaran, the youngest."

"I wish you'd told me…" Raff ignored her and her anger and frustration bubbled even closer to the surface. *Asking does nothing anyway!*

"Ready to get this over with then, chook?" he asked, dusting the crumbs off his hands and straight onto the table and floor. "You want to lead on the intent again, and I'll just hone in on Beryl?" Charlie nodded, standing to make her way to the sofa. She'd only half-registered what it was he'd said. "Okay then, you lead the way."

As they sat, Charlie's mind was still focussed on her recent session with Maryanne. Everything was connected. Even though it was Raff who'd formed the bond with Beryl, she could still reach out to her, *through* him. She wondered… As her hand touched Raff's arm, she sucked them both into the Dream violently, as though spinning down through a sudden and angry current of a fast-flowing river.

202

They surfaced from the swirling stream momentarily to view a lightly tanned young boy with dark hair and bright green eyes. He would have been about five years old, and he was cowering in the corner of a dark bathroom. The memory was distorted, dark and blurred, as though nervous energy was shaking and skewing it. This was Raff's memory, she knew, shown how he remembered it. A huge, fat man towered over him. His belt hanging in one hand, the other gripping the edge of his trousers. "What, don't choo want candy, no mores?" The voice was supposed to be sickeningly sweet, Charlie thought, but it was too deep. Too *monstrous*, she thought, realising that was how Raff viewed this horrible beast of a man. Larger and rounder than any man could be in reality. This was Raff's monster.

"No…" the boy whimpered, softly but with his own edge of defiance. Likely as tough as he could make it, with the amount of fear making his stomach boil with nausea.

"Watcha say?" The man, the monster, growled now. All pretence of sweetness was gone from his voice, which echoed so loudly all around her. Abnormally loud, each resonance growing in intensity rather than dimming. Her head pounded, the words seeming to come from *inside* her own skull. He whipped the belt with one hand, making a large crack that echoed the same way, and let his trousers fall.

Charlie gratefully let the rushing river of the Dream suck them both back down, wondering how to extricate herself from this nightmare inside of Raff's head. The current was moving too quickly though, and she found herself in another horrid memory. This time with a slightly older Raff; a scrawnier, though taller, boy. He was panicking as he sat up in a large bed, the darkness pressing around him so that only the edges of the sheets were visible. Not even the edge of the bed. Like he was adrift in a sea of linen. His breath came more ragged, his chest heaving in panic. *How did I get here!* she could hear the boy freaking in his mind. *How did I get here?!* A mass beside the boy suddenly grew from the edge of the sheets, again abnormally large and round. It was a bloated bulk with a pin for a head. It was the monster, Raff's monster, his bald and wrinkled skull much too small for a body this size. The young Raff screamed and Charlie pulled herself back into the flowing Dream.

"Ma…" This time Charlie found herself in daylight in Raff's memories. An almost emaciated woman sat across from a young teenage boy, a dirty and badly scratched table between them. She had a deck of cards in front of her and was taking long drags from a cigarette. By the look of her yellowed fingertips and teeth, the cigarette was likely as much a part of her hand as any of her fingers. Her hair was dark like Raff's, but wiry, and patchy. It wasn't clear how much of this memory was distorted too. "He *touches* me. Please, believe me. He… does things to me when you're not here. He…"

"*Rafael!*" the woman screeched, throwing her cards down and spraying the boy with grey ash from her cigarette and spittle from between her yellow teeth. Charlie could feel the boy's longing for a hug from his mother, for a word of comfort. Instead, her face twisted into one of utter distaste and disgust. Not at what her son had told her, but at the son himself. "Shut your fucking dirty mouth." Charlie could feel this memory writhing, like a filthy worm, burrowing out of Raff's dark subconscious mind. She tried to pull away from it, but it wouldn't let her.

"C-c-can I at least go live with Grandpa, *please*?" Charlie realised Raff must be even older than she'd guessed, seeing as he was probably at least as badly malnourished as his mother. "You always telling me I'm a fucking waste of space anyway. It'll be better for both a' us."

The woman burst into a horrible cackling laugh. Charlie imagined this was what a real witch would sound like. Not the fairy tales of the Wizard of Oz, or the heroines of Harry Potter. But the pure evil demons that ate children and worshipped the devil. "That old fag! He can barely look after himself, you dumb shit. And why would he want you anyway? Fucking worthless prick." She laughed again. "If it wasn't for your dumb ass father, that faggot would be long out of our lives anyway, Rafael."

"Don't talk about Dad like that!" Charlie wasn't sure if it was this young Raff, or the adult Raff she'd unwittingly taken with her, that screamed back at the woman.

"Even ya Dad didn't want you, Rafael. Even he *died* to get away from you."

⁎⁎

Charlie gasped as the Dream was broken, and she fell off the couch, landing heavily on the carpeted floor. Raff was on his feet, glaring down at her not just with anger but *hurt* in his eyes. That was what hit Charlie worst; the sadness and pain. The anger was hot, but the rest of him was molten. *"What the fuck, Charlie!!"* he screamed at her, taking two steps back and holding his hands to his head.

"I-I-I'm sorry...I d-didn't mean t—"

"That was fucking messed up. You *fucking bitch!"* He took a few steps towards the kitchen, his hands still massaging his temple or pulling at his hair, unable to stay still. "I fucking trusted you."

"I didn't mean to!" Charlie found her voice now, getting to her feet. "Maryanne told me that you had a history and the thought was in my head when we tried to enter the Dream. And it *just fucking happened.* Why would I *want* to see that?!" Shame burnt brightly in Charlie with those words and she flopped back onto the couch. She shouldn't be personalising something that was such a deep and private trauma for Raff, but she couldn't help it. She bristled at his words. *I didn't mean to!* No wonder he hated being called Rafael. "I'm so sorry Maryanne calls you Rafael..." The words slipped out before she could stop them.

Raff turned back to her, some of the anger and shame releasing from his flushed face and tensed shoulders. He still clenched his hands into tight fists as he took a couple of steps towards her. "That was *my business."*

"I know..."

"How would you feel if I went digging around in *your* head?"

"I know!" The memory of Raff dragging her around in the Dream that first time, in the Waterfall Sanatorium, came back to her unbidden. A fresh flush of anger clipped off some of her guilt. "Look, I didn't *mean* to."

"Whatever..." Raff sat on the couch again, but at the very edge of the cushion, and as far away from her as he could. "Let's just fucking get this over with. But if you *ever* do that to me again, you'll be the one *I* leave behind. And we'll see how well you deal with your own fucking Black without me."

34

To Know

Raff resisted as Charlie attempted to enter the Dream with him, this time void of physical contact. She kept her intent very clear in her mind; *what happened to Beryl and Albert?* She sent this intent to Raff as well, in appeasement and reassurance as he continued to fight her. She couldn't blame him for closing off from her, but her own tangled web of emotions was also battling for precedence. Her worry, her guilt, her frustration, her jealousy — and she tested the full power of her Keeper status, grabbing hold of Raff and pulling him through into the Dream with her.

Standing opposite Raff in her Waiting Place, she saw the physical changes in his appearance. He seemed blacker, taller. While these details were starker, the rest of him was not. He almost vibrated, causing the edges of his figure to blur. As though electricity were running through him, disturbing the very fibres that held him together. *I'm sorry*, she sent again, truly meaning it. *I'm still learning. I didn't mean to.* Raff just stood there, literally bristling. *Let's just get this over with.* Focussing again on why they were there, Charlie felt pulled towards an archway close by. Raff wasn't drawn with her this time, and she looked back to see him standing in the distance in *her* Waiting Place.

She was momentarily afraid, wondering what he might be able to do to her now that she'd brought him here. He knew more than she did about how all of this worked. Could he poke around in her head, like he threatened?

Could he actually cause damage? Was this Waiting Place actually a part of her mind, her soul, or was it something else? Her fears diminished slightly as Raff appeared beside her, facing the archway. She tried to force herself to relax and together they stepped through the archway and into the past.

Beryl was pacing in a small, modestly furnished room with two beds in opposite corners. The first bed was slightly dishevelled, as though someone had been sitting or laying atop the covers. The second was pristine; untouched for so long that it held a light layer of shimmering dust. She rubbed her sweaty palms together, intermittently holding a hand to her mouth or cheek, or lightly pressing on her breasts or stomach. Raff and Charlie took opposing corners, encircling her as they watched. Beryl suddenly sat on the dishevelled bed, both hands now clasped over her stomach, her shoulders so tight they arched close to her jaw. All in a rush, she burst into tears, sobbing as she bent low over herself.

She's pregnant, Raff sent, although whether it was purposefully to Charlie or not, she wasn't sure. She merely nodded in reply, feeling those waves of emotions from Beryl that so closely matched many of her own warring emotions. Guilt, fear, anxiety — but amidst it all, a small drop of joy and hope. She wondered how much more strongly Raff was feeling this through his connection. *Did Albert know?* he sent.

Charlie nodded again at Raff's question, honing her intent further, and pulling them both through another layer of the Dream. They were back in Adelaide and Albert's cottage, in that same room they'd been before. The small, yellow-panelled room with a desk, bookcases, armchairs and that magnificent mirror. But they hadn't just been to this room before; they'd been to this *time*. Or at least, they'd seen part of this memory. *I told you there was more*, Raff whispered to her, as the scene of Adelaide and Albert fighting again materialised before them. *There's more*, Charlie agreed and willed the moment to rewind itself, to show them how it all started.

After a blurred moment, Albert was alone at the desk, sitting in his chair, bent over a paper of some kind. He was still as dishevelled as he'd been that first time. The door to the room opened forcefully, but controlled. A gust of wind puffed into the room along with Adelaide, who held the handle firmly. "Albert." Her voice was measured, regulated, firm. She closed the door behind her, letting it slam at the last moment. Albert jerked but didn't raise his head. "Albert." Her voice didn't change pitch, and she folded her hands in front of her, waiting, patient. "*Albert.*"

"Blast it, woman!" Albert slammed his thick oak pen onto the desk, ink spraying from the nib as he did so. "Confound it all! Can I not at least have a little peace in my own house?!"

"I *know*, Albert." Adelaide's voice remained firm as she took two steps to stand behind him. Her voice broke just slightly, edging towards a sob, as she repeated, "I *know*."

Albert stood, turning to face Addie. All the energy drained from his face in that moment, his brows slacking and his face dropping. As though he were giving up. "Beryl told you then?"

"No, Albert. She kept your *horrid* little secret. But I *know*. I'm a nurse, I'm a mother, I'm her *sister*. Did you think you could hide it from me? It won't be long before everyone knows, and then—" Her voice fully cracked then, and she spun away from him, holding a hand to her mouth. "You *have* to send her away..." Her words were so breathy they were hard to understand.

"No." The word blasted like ice, and the room instantly felt cooler.

"No?" Adelaide spun to face him again, her voice dangerously close to a whine as her eyes opened in shock and anger. "*No?!*"

"No!" He took a step towards her, his face rigid once again, sweat now popping out at his greasy hairline. "I will *not* send her away. Never."

"You must, you utter fool! What about your *daughter*? What about me?!"

"I know too, Addie," he whispered in a voice so hard the very air in the room seemed to still. The dust motes were held captivated, or perhaps in fear, not daring to move. Addie's lips pursed and her eyes widened as if in defiance. Her twitching fingers gave her away.

"Know what, dear husband?" She said the words calmly, though venom laced the word 'dear'. She squeezed her hands into fists to still her tremors.

"*About the letters...*" His whisper broke the stillness in the air with a sharp bite. Everything seemed to swirl and move in flurries then. Like an emotional tempest that blew harder and harder with Albert's every word.

"Beryl said she *never* stopped writing. At first, I thought they must have gotten lost. I know that's what Beryl *wanted* to believe. But no...oh, no. You know your sister? Well, she knows *you too, dear* wife." Adelaide's sour expression melted, replaced with desperation and fear. She ran to her husband's side, lifting a hand to try to hold onto his stubbled cheek.

All poison was gone from her voice, only sickly sweet tenderness in its place. He tried to turn his face away from her but she would not relent. "Albert, *darling,* you can't possibly believe that..."

"Adelaide!" He pulled her hand from his face forcefully. She stood so close to him that his hand caught in the collar of her navy dress, tearing it slightly from the force of his movements. "Enough! *Enough.* Do not try to deny it."

"Fine. I do not!" Albert began pacing the small room now, his hands constantly moving as though desperate to lash out, energy building behind his fists. "She was *always* getting in the way. But *I* loved you first! And I didn't think she'd ever come back! I was doing it for us. To get the suspense over and done with. She should have died. It was selfish of her, putting us through what she did." Albert let out a loud yell, which groaned from his throat as he threw his head back and his hands wide. It turned into a horrid laugh of disbelief and madness. "It doesn't matter now. You are *my* husband. Not hers! You *must* choose me, send her away, and get this over with."

With a determined step, Albert approached Adelaide. "I. Choose. *Her.*" The air cracked as Adelaide slapped Albert's cheek, knocking his glasses askew. Her lip trembled, and tears threatened at the edge of her eyes. In an instant, Albert had Adelaide by the shoulders, thumping her into the wall, the mirror shaking, its glass flexing. This was the scene that Charlie and Raff had first witnessed. Adelaide squirmed in fear, her face pinched and pale in terror.

"H-how... c-could you?" she stammered, tears spilling from her eyes. "How could you choose her?" Albert let her go then and she sagged only slightly before bringing herself erect and taking a step towards him defiantly. "I am your *wife*! The mother of your *child*!"

"How could *I?*" Albert scoffed and chuckled wryly, no humour in his voice. He turned away from her, removing his glasses with one hand, and running his hand through his hair with the other. He began laughing again and spun to his wife, a single finger held aloft so tensely his whole body quavered behind it. "If I could divorce you, *God knows* I wouldn't wait another second. Another moment. I'd be *rid of you!*"

Adelaide stepped forward with her hand held aloft to slap him again, but he caught her roughly, squeezing her wrist. "You're *hurting* me!" Albert released Adelaide with such a forceful motion that she fell to the ground at his feet. "I gave up everything for you."

As Albert had the first time Raff and Charlie saw this memory, he walked to the door, hesitating slightly, before he smashed his fist into the wall. Then he was gone.

***

Raff and Charlie sat across from each other at Trent and Brent's square kitchen table. Some of the rawness of Raff's earlier emotions had dissipated, blunted by the memories the two of them had just shared. "I know you didn't mean to do what you did," Raff finally said, still looking down at his hands and avoiding eye contact. "It was still unforgiveable, but I know it was an accident." Charlie didn't say anything either, just stared at Raff's fidgeting hands. "I don't talk about it — what happened. It defines my life enough as it is, without me needing to rehash it with every Tom, Dick and Harry."

"I know…" Charlie realised only as she said the words how they mirrored Albert and Adelaide's own words to each other.

"And I know about what happened to Tess. She told me in the hospital all about that shithead ex of hers. How he used to beat her, force himself on her, stop her from having any friends. How he kept her on a tight allowance, even a diet. He controlled what she did, what she saw, so she couldn't get any perspective. Couldn't get any help. She—"

"I *know*," Charlie emphasised, finally making eye contact with Raff to drive the point home. "I was the one who took them in when they finally escaped him." She could understand how Raff didn't like reliving his trauma, because it was hard enough reliving her friend's.

"Maybe that's why me and her get on so well… She would have made a *beautiful* Black spirit."

35

Catechism 2280

Charlie was still bristling at Raff's comment about Tess and Black spirits, long after he'd left to meet Tess at the hospital. It had turned out Tess wouldn't be discharged until the next day after all, so Raff was spending one final night sleeping on the cot in her room. What must the nurses think? They probably thought he was Tess's boyfriend, and in this small town, gossip would spread like wildfire. There'd been enough gossip when Tess had moved in with her in the first place. She'd almost enjoyed that speculation, though. *This* turned her stomach.

Charlie was finishing washing a small stack of dishes in the kitchen when Trent and Brent arrived back home from their field trip to the cemetery, bags heaving with goodies from Newcastle knocking in each hand. "Is that everything?" Charlie laughed, moving to take a couple of bags from an overladen Brent.

"Couple more in the boot." Trent grinned his huge smile at her over the top of Brent's head.

"Ha! Did you leave anything in Newcastle for the rest of them?" She pushed her feet roughly into her sandshoes and went to the car to grab the last two bags, both of which looked to be brimming with fancy cheese, crackers and other assortments of deliciousness.

"We thought we might have a cheese plate and wine for dinner tonight," Brent said as she re-entered the room, nodding to the bags she was carrying.

Trent had already opened the fridge and was unloading selections of seemingly anything available from the deli section.

"Good trip then." Charlie deposited her two bags on the kitchen bench and stood back to watch the boys fluster about each other.

"*So* good," Trent turned with a half-eaten piece of chocolate hanging from his mouth.

"No room in the fridge for that piece, dear?" Brent jibed, poking him in the ribs so quickly it made Trent jerk and bend double, chuckling around his piece of sneaky chocolate. "You two head to the living room and debrief. I've got the rest of this."

"You sure, love?" Trent's words were slurred by his own drool and the half-chewed chocolate. Brent just pushed at him playfully and turned back to the fridge. Trent shrugged, turning to Charlie. "Come on, honey!"

Sitting at the coffee table, Trent pulled the rest of the chocolate block from his pocket, snapping off pieces for the both of them. "Did you find him?" Charlie asked, twirling her piece in her fingers.

"Sure did." Trent dug his phone out from his other pocket, swiping to unlock the screen and navigating to his photos app. "His birth name wasn't Albert, which might be why he didn't initially jump out at me. His legal name was Mersey Albert Hammond, and on his grave and in his burial records, he's listed as Mersey A. Hammond." She took the phone so she could observe the picture more closely. Albert's grave sat in a huge empty plot, surrounded by a short and well-aged metal fence. The plot was large enough to accommodate at least six full-sized adults, but his appeared to be the only stone. As though waiting, perhaps for Adelaide, perhaps for Beryl. The stone itself was cracked through at its base, and someone — perhaps even Trent — had leant the broken top upright against the fence.

"No sign of any of the others then? Adelaide?" Trent shook his head, sitting back on the couch, rubbing at his temples as if the day had fallen on him heavily. Or perhaps the chocolate. Charlie rehashed for Trent everything she and Raff had discovered about Adelaide and Albert's confrontation, and the additional context behind it.

"He was buried in the Catholic part of the cemetery," Trent began, as

Charlie's mind fluttered back to all those moments in the Dream. "His body would have been brought in by train. You know, there used to be a train station at the actual cemetery? After the mass was held at the church, usually the night before for those things, he would have been accompanied by mourners to the graveside for the Rite of Committal. Sort of like a procession. Made even more impressive by the train, right?"

"Hmmm..." Charlie grunted distractedly, still thinking about Raff sitting by Tess's bedside as they spoke.

"Fuck me, Charlie! A thank you might not go down too bad!" Charlie jumped at Trent's raised voice, shocked back to giving him her full attention. She'd never heard him speak like that before.

"S-sorry. Thank you, really," she said. Brent popped his head through the entry from the kitchen to check what the yell had been about. "For all of it, and f-for letting me stay here too." The shame that had been building in her all day bubbled over, and her face reddened and burnt brightly. She wished she could cover it, or even leave the room. With her house only thirty minutes away, she even briefly considered leaving.

"No, no, I'm sorry..." Trent put his head into his hands, massaging at his temples. "I just have a bad headache, and it's been a long day." Brent came in and put an arm around Trent's shoulders reassuringly, leaning over to press a kiss to the top of his head.

"It's okay! I'm not the best company right now, either. My mind's all over the place, and I'm so worried about Tess."

"Of course," Brent said soothingly. "Trent too. We all are. Now, let's crack open a bottle of red and forget about everything else for a while."

* * *

Lying in the crowded spare room, her feet hanging from the end of the small single bed, Charlie stared at the ceiling. She had a nice buzz from the two bottles of wine they'd shared, which had successfully numbed her emotions in good company. Alone, though, everything came pushing back. *Surely, these feelings are just because of the Blacks,* she thought, trying to convince herself as another stab of shame and jealousy poked at her stomach sharply. The hot sensation, coupled with her mild wine buzz, made her feel nauseous.

She rolled onto her side and focussed her thoughts on Albert. Or Mersey, if that's who he really was. She might not be able to do anything about Beryl on her own, but she sure could try again with Albert. Closing her eyes, she concentrated on her breathing and intent. Willing herself to connect with him; to discover something that might help her move him on. And to allow her to get back to Tess.

As Charlie sank into the Dream, she felt herself emerging not in her Waiting Place, but in Sandgate Cemetery once again. It was night. Or at least, it seemed to be. She looked to the sky but could see no stars, no clouds. Just a deep expanse of nothing. A soft light, similar to the moon, seemed to glow from the very air itself. Ever so softly casting shadows everywhere she stepped, in concentric circles around her. *Mersey*, she sent this time, moving to the Catholic segment without thinking. *Mersey.*

My love? Mersey rippled from the corner of the church like a thick mist, bubbling and warping as his form took shape. It was like he had effervesced to being from the very walls themselves. His eyes — his spectacled moon-eyes — were the last to emerge. They seemed to pull themselves together from the light in the air, making everything else fade ever so subtly to deeper darkness. She could feel that blackness, that nothing, creep closer and push at the edges of not just her sight but her very being. The coldness crept through too, so deep she began to forget what it was like to be warm.

Mersey, it's Charlie. I'm here to help.

Where are you, my love?! Mersey's howl came from every direction at once, like needles sprayed from a million invisible holes. He began to fade back into the bricks, his face the last thing to hang on, extending wobblily on a liquid neck.

Wait, Mersey. I know. I know Beryl was your love. I know you were tricked, that you wanted to marry her, but you ended up with someone else. The howl began again, his eyes glowing even brighter, making everything else around them dim to nothing. *I know she died, and you were left all alone. To lose her, have her come back to you, and then lose her again... I can't begin to imagine what you're feeling. Anyone might take their life in those circumstances.*

Mersey bellowed again. This time, instead of his cries, it was his emotions that hit her like a barrage of needles. Anger, grief, frustration, embarrassment, jealousy. *I lost everything. And then they tormented me at the end; laughing, gossiping, ridiculing, spitting. I couldn't stand it anymore. I just wanted to be with her again. It was supposed to be worth it. This mortal sin, this defiance of God's position as the sovereign master of life... But* where *is she? I am alone in this purgatory!*

Mersey... She gasped as she was drawn yet again to the moment he had hung himself. *Why does he keep showing me his death?* she wondered. They were here again in that small, dark room in the Sanatorium that stank of mouthwash, copper and bleach. The vague outlines of the corners, every inch bathed not just in that smell but in Albert's absolute anguish. He appeared in the dark as she thought of him, as though seen by the light of a small candle. He alone was visible, and barely, the light fading around him and flickering over his face. He carried a stool with him, which he placed centrally in the room, beneath the noose that awaited him. She noticed for the first time a piece of paper and his thick oak pen were held in his trembling hands.

Tears ran down his cheeks, which were even more stubbled than before. Hairs had begun to curl around themselves in the very rough beginnings of an unkempt beard. She wondered if some of the stink of that place might have come not from the air, but from Albert himself. With trembling hands, he began to pen his suicide note. Charlie eased closer, staring down as the words scratched and formed onto the page. It was surreal watching this, like a helpless spectator in the most morbid of tragic plays.

Adelaide

This past year, and these last months in particular, have been a torment to us both. Nothing I want is here for me any longer. Nothing but suffering and pain.

I go from this life with full awareness of the Catechism of the Catholic Church. 'We are stewards, not owners, of the life God has entrusted to us. It is not ours to dispose of. I know I shall walk this earth forever in purgatory for my sins, for her sins, and for yours.

If you have any love left for me, do this one thing for me. Send my body to Sandgate in Newcastle. Let me be buried with my love and my child. Let me not walk this purgatory alone.

Mersey

My child, Charlie thought as Mersey put his pen down, and the paper, and went about the task of securing his noose once again.

Beryl lost the baby, Mersey sent in the barest of whispers. *Before she died. I lost my love. I lost my child. I lost everything.*

36

Let It Be

Charlie sniffed at her armpit. It was musty, but tolerable. And it was better than Raff's odour in any case. She'd considered popping back home for more clothes, or even buying another packet of singlets, but she hadn't bargained for Tess being in hospital so long. *Today*, though. Today, Tess got to come home. A twinge of panic fluttered down her throat, landing firmly in her sternum. She still worried that Mersey would attack Tess again; try to finish what he'd started. But she felt *so close* to ending things now. So long as she kept Tess safe inside their white-enclosed cottage, she reasoned everything would be fine. She'd begrudgingly accepted Raff's offer to sleep in his caravan, in case things heated up at night. It was either that or continue staying with Trent and Brent… and Kent the black-and-white cat. For Tess, she would put up with anything.

Trent had messaged their new group chat that morning, agreeing to drive Charlie home so Tess could ride in more relative safety with Raff. Tess would even leave fifteen minutes after Charlie and Trent, so there was no chance of any accident if they drove in convoy. They were taking no chances after the fire. Raff agreed with Charlie that the final confrontation, as he liked to put it, was drawing closer. Making things even more unpredictable. With Charlie's brown-paper-bag of smelly clothes clutched in one hand, and her purse in the other, she stepped quietly out into the living room. Despite being quite early, Trent was already up, fully dressed and standing in the kitchen. He was staring off, completely lost in his own thoughts.

"Morning, Trent," Charlie smiled as she softly closed the spare room door behind her. "I stripped the sheets off the bed and left them with my towel in a pile. Hope that's okay." Trent turned to look at her and smiled, knocking away the final cobwebs of lingering doubt after their small tiff the night before. It made her feel incredibly happy, but slightly sad as well, for some reason she couldn't quite fathom. Without thinking, she dropped her bags to the floor, strode purposefully to the kitchen, and gave Trent a firm hug, burrowing her head into this chest. Just like she had after their first minor argument the year before, when Trent had unwittingly sent the cops to Charlie's house for an 'intruder'. She sighed happily as Trent's arms encircled around her, feeling her joy and that small bubble of sorrow beating together like a second heart in her chest. "I *am* sorry I wasn't more grateful."

"And I'm sorry I snapped. Brent reckons I've been pushing it too much at the library, and with all my own pet projects…" Charlie just shook her head into his chest, refuting his apologies. "This is much nicer. No more fighting?"

"No more fighting," Charlie agreed, finally releasing him and stepping back.

"I couldn't sleep last night, so I did a bit more research. Just on my phone. But I found Adelaide's obituary."

"What?! You did?!" Charlie's excitement was perhaps overblown. But she'd thought that piece of information was a lost cause.

"Yeah, I was looking in the wrong decade. I'd assumed she was a Black spirit so I'd kept my search narrowed to the 1910s-30s. More in line with the time period you'd described in your dreams."

"And?"

"Turns out she died on 13 March 1980, in Newcastle, aged 89. She lived a nice long life after her husband and sister passed."

"Hopefully racked with guilt for what she did to them. Is she buried in Sandgate as well?"

"No, actually. Her daughter had her cremated and interred at Wallsend, according to the obituary anyway." Trent looked off again, his eyes going vacant, as he recalled the information.

"I'm kind of glad Addie didn't end up with Albert at the end," Charlie sighed. "I suppose we'd better get moving, if you're ready? The more distance we can put between Tess and I on the drive, the better. And I'm *dying* for some clean clothes."

* * *

Charlie was relieved to be back in her own house, with a fresh set of clothes on, and smelling of her own soap and shampoo. It had been as though Marie were waiting to welcome her home as well. Not only were all the cupboard doors open (though, thankfully, without any cups removed), but each-and-every dining chair was spun facing the other way. She'd bid Marie a silent 'hello' as she'd raced through to the bathroom, leaving Trent to make cuppas in the kitchen.

What irked her now was that she sat almost pinned between Trent and Raff, across from Tess. They'd not had any trouble with Mersey attacking Tess *inside* the cottage, but Tess still hung back. With her skin peeling, and the blisters crusting over, Charlie could understand why she was anxious. Charlie still felt like her heart was ripping in two, though. Raff squirmed in his seat, his shoulder rubbing against Charlie's. She could feel every fibre of her knit sweatshirt brushing against her skin and repressed a visible shudder. She leant closer to Trent, now feeling well-and-truly claustrophobic between them.

"We're close now," she said stubbornly, defiantly, into the awkward silence. "We *almost* have the full picture. I can feel it."

"We just need to confirm what it is that's making them imbalanced," Raff added, shifting his shoulders again. Charlie's own shoulder tingled uncomfortably where it touched his. "Adelaide betrayed them both, lied to them both, so she could have Albert to herself. I expect that's what drove them to become Blacks. But I've seen much worse fates with other spirits, and they've not been so...disturbed."

"I feel like it must be something to do with Mersey's suicide note." Charlie pinched her shoulders together, holding her hands between her legs. She and Raff weren't looking at each other as they spoke, and she could see Tess's eyes flicking between them like a ball at a tennis match. "There's more there. And why would Beryl be with a man who abused her? Maybe that's got something to do with what's upset her spirit?"

"Yeah, nah…" As Raff answered, it was Trent's turn to fidget. Obviously picking up on some of the animosity and tension between the other two. "I mean, I have a strange feeling about Beryl's physical abuse. I agree, we need to know more, but something isn't sitting right with me. It doesn't line up."

"We need to go back to the Dream."

"I agree." Raff did turn to look at Charlie now. "But this time, as partners. I won't lead, and you won't lead. We do this together if we want to finish things." Charlie's breath rose up from her stomach like a gust of hot wind, twanging in her throat around the lump that was forming there. She wanted to disagree, but she could *feel* he was right about this too. And oh how that irked her.

"Fine."

"Fine."

* * *

This time as Charlie entered the Dream, she did it in partnership with Raff. Neither entered before the other or pulled the other with them. It was in almost pure synchronicity that the two of them entered, the weight of each other drawing them effortlessly into the Dream and straight into Albert and Adelaide's staff cottage at Waterfall Sanatorium. They stood in a short hallway. To their right, the hallway ended in two open doors leading to a master bedroom and a little girl's bedroom. To their left, an open door showed just a glimpse of a small sitting area, dominated in the back corner by a warm glowing fireplace. Behind them was a closet and another door that led into a large pantry — no doubt hanging off a kitchen. It was a narrow hallway with low roof, but from their vantage point, they could see more of the house than they'd seen yet. Before them stood a closed door, a small child crouched before it with her ear to the wood.

Little Sarah Hammond was still barely a child, her squat chubby legs clinging to their baby fat. She held a soft toy bunny tightly in one hand and a square blanket in the other. *Perhaps she's supposed to be napping*, Charlie thought to herself, but saw Raff nodding at the observation. She'd need to guard her thoughts carefully here. She marvelled at the small child's willpower not to barge straight through the door to where her parents loudly quarrelled. Barely muffled shouts could be heard from the other side, and Charlie felt a pang of sorrow for Sarah. This might have been an all-too-common occurrence for her, and perhaps why she'd learnt just to loiter and listen at such a young age. Charlie again thanked her lucky stars that her childhood had been, for the most part, a happy one.

Raff took a step forward and it was Charlie's turn to nod back at him, understanding he intended to enter the room. Charlie joined him, and once again they stood in the pale-yellow-walled room that was a study, a library and a sitting room. "Where is she?!" Albert yelled, throwing a stack of papers from his desk in frustration. Adelaide flinched, but barely, steeling herself. She wore black from head-to-toe and was drenched from heavy rain.

The day of the funeral, Charlie sent to Raff. *She's only just buried Beryl in the Waterfall Sanatorium Cemetery.* He nodded.

"It doesn't matter now," Adelaide said so softly that Charlie could almost see Albert's ears straining and pricking. Addie's mellow tone was even more frightening than Albert's screams had been. "She's *gone*, Albert. *Gone!* And this time, she won't magically reappear." Despite her sarcasm at the word 'magical', Charlie could feel — as could Raff — the sorrow that Addie had buried beneath it all. Beryl had still been her closest sister after all. Not just her flesh-and-blood, but her truest companion and friend for the majority of her life. They'd shared the type of bond that Tess and Charlie had; one that most people could scarcely think to dream of, let alone experience.

It's why my Black is after Tess, and Raff's Black is after me, Charlie suddenly realised. *We two share a link just like Addie and Beryl did. Only...*

Only you would never betray Tess, Raff sent, finishing her train of thought. Charlie was again shocked at how closely connected the two of them were in the Dream, as partners. At how he could hear her thoughts as easily as if she'd spoken aloud. But her surprise was quickly replaced by a brief flash of appreciation for him. For understanding.

Albert broke down, falling to his knees with his hands thrown behind him as his head heaved backwards. He bellowed before breaking down into great bursting sobs. He drew in air in ragged moans, as though reluctant to keep breathing. Adelaide walked slowly to his side, not crouching to comfort him, but standing over him. Looking down at him as if assessing, reasserting her ownership. "*Please*, Adelaide," Albert's words were thick with sorrow and mucus as he craned his neck to look up at her. "It's like you said. She's *gone*. Just tell me where you buried her. I have to know. I have to know…"

"I've sent her to Sandgate," Adelaide lied, her words as stiff as her pinched lips. "So don't even bother going after her, *dear* husband. My family will make arrangements for a quiet burial. It's more than that harlot deserves. No tombstone, so don't even think of trying to find her. Only we'll know where she is. Now what's left of her memory and her betrayal can simply fade away."

"Sandgate?" Mersey mumbled, his sobs easing, but his shoulders still heaving with the strain of his sorrow.

"It's time to stop this silliness, husband. Let it be. Let it be."

37

Not Too Deep

The Dream skipped, like an old record player struggling to find its place, distorting the world around Raff and Charlie. The world rematerialised in staccato bumps to reveal Adelaide facing Beryl in the small, two-bed room in the nurses' quarters. They'd gone back in time. Charlie could almost hear the scratching of a skipping record as Addie's contorted face emerged. "Get out." The words, like they had been with Albert, were low but laced with venom and ice. A wisp of another nurse fled from the second bed, pulling the door closed behind her with a slam. There was a long pause. "I know you haven't stopped, sister."

"Addie, I—"

"No." Adelaide held a single hand aloft to silence her, her face turned slightly downwards and her eyes held firmly shut. She let another pause grow between them, giving off the air of a predator. Every muscle was flexed and braced beneath a calm, cold and composed exterior. "Let's do away with the attempts at explanations, diversions or denials this time. Charles saw you two heading off into the bush again last night. And that whimpering fool of a roommate confirmed you didn't come home. She ratted you out almost before I could finish asking the question." Beryl's face — her whole upper body — fell forward. With her knees buckled, it was almost as if she was held up by an invisible rod at her lower back. Like the slightest gust of wind would make her crumple.

"I'm sorry…" Beryl's whispered words were so faint.

"You're what?" Adelaide tilted her head the other way, fixing a steady gaze on her. "Speak up."

"I'm sorry." The words were barely any louder.

"Ha!" Laughter filled the small room from corner to corner. Derisive, belly-thrusted guffaws. Beryl stiffened, ducking her head even lower between her shoulders as though each laugh were a ghostly blow. "I don't think so." Each word was forcefully enunciated. "If you were *sorry*, by the very definition of the term, you'd have remorse. You'd be contrite. You'd *stop*. But oh no! You two are like crazed animals. Like two dogs in heat." Adelaide took a step towards her sister, and Beryl shied away, pulling her chin into her shoulder. "No, talking won't do, will it? I'll have to treat you like I would a wayward bitch that can't keep her tail between her legs."

"P-please…I-I—" The words were wheezy, like Beryl couldn't quite catch her breath.

"No." And without raising her voice once, Adelaide lifted her hand and began beating her sister with an open palm. First her face, then as Beryl fell forward, the back of her head, her arms, her chest — any part of her that Adelaide could reach. Addie became the crazed animal. Beryl tried to keep her voice from calling out, and instead sobbed loudly.

"I'm sorry," she repeated, between the flurry of Adelaide's arms. "I'm sorry. I'm sorry. I'm sorry."

Charlie felt a hand lay itself on her shoulder and she jumped as she turned to stare at Raff. Fully absorbed in the horror of this moment, she'd almost forgotten he was there. *Time to go*, he sent softly. She nodded, raised her hand to encircle his, and together they pulled away.

But the Dream was not quite finished with them yet. Charlie felt almost nauseous, despite lacking a physical body. It was as though the filaments that spun together to form her here were shaking, bending, twisting as she entered yet another layer of the Dream. *Not too deep*, she willed aloud, warning herself as much as setting her intent.

Not too deep, Raff affirmed, adding his intent to her own. Charlie baulked as she realised where they were. The scent hit her first. Mouthwash. Copper.

Bleach. The cold crashed into her next, and her nausea solidified in her centre like a cold, wet, slimy stone. Mersey Albert hung there, the shadows of morning light dancing over a bulging purple and grey face. He hung so unnaturally. *Charlie... Do it now...* Realising what Raff meant — that he thought she could release Mersey's spirit — she put a firm hand back on his shoulder.

Not yet. He won't let me. He's not ready. In that moment, Albert's spirit puffed out of every orifice of the hanging corpse. Through his nostrils, his ears, around the swollen tongue, even out and around those bulging grey eyes. Two round moons of light bloomed on Mersey's spectacles, which had fallen to the floor, rising up in a liquid motion to join the mass of oily smog as it formed into the hook-nosed spirit of Mersey. He positively brimmed with malice. With hate and pain and shame. With jealousy thick as bile. Through it all, a burning rage and lust for vengeance made his black mist quaver. This had to end soon, Charlie knew, or he would do something far worse than he had yet. Pull Charlie's cottage down atop them stone by stone. Set the whole grasslands ablaze. Make Sandgate a mortal danger to anyone within fifty feet.

The single door to the room creaked as it was sluggishly forced open. Raff turned to see who it was, but Charlie knew. She didn't spin this time, knowing that soon enough a chubby-cheeked three-year-old girl would awkwardly push her way into the room. The heat of the summer day outside was still unable to touch this cold, damned place. "Found d-you Papa!" Raff flinched at the forced bright voice, laced with knowledge that something wasn't right. "Founded d'you!" the loud, confused and frightened little voice yelled. *"Papa!"* Sarah marched up to her father and began tugging forcefully at the trousers on his hanging legs. "Papa!" Her little fist began pummelling his leg. "Come down! Come down! *Come down!*" And then she screamed. A high-pitched wail that could break glass, shatter eardrums, and smash a soul in two.

Through the still open door, Charlie could see the edge of a red-brick cottage. They must be in some sort of garden shed. Addie was suddenly in view of the door, racing towards them, her long dark skirts hiked up to reveal her pumping legs. Her white shirt crinkled as her arms pumped. "Sarah!" She burst through the door gasping for breath, the sweat beading her forehead seeming to freeze as the coldness of the room, of death, and of the reality in which she found herself, slammed into her. She fell to her knees just before Sarah, her skirts tangling in the dirt and debris of the cold floor. *"Albert!"* Her scream forced whatever breath was left in her lungs to flee. Sarah immediately turned and burrowed her head into her mother's breast, wrapping her tiny arms as far around her as they would go.

Addie's arms were as still and lifeless by her side as Albert's. The quiet as all breath was expelled, just before Adelaide could draw breath to continue screaming, was stifling. She screamed again. A hoarse, endless cry of despair, anger, disbelief and pain. Amongst it all, Albert hung there, twisting and swinging from the force his little girl had exuded on his legs. In-between gasps and cries, the only sound that came from him was the twisting and squeaking of the noose.

We need to go, Charlie's words were almost lost in the cacophony, they held such little conviction. As she felt Raff forming his will to agree, Mersey's Black spirit was suddenly all around them, obscuring not only the sight but the sounds of his crying wife and child. Even though the smog of his body encircled them on all sides, those huge white eyes remained before them, above them, glaring down with fierce intent. *There's more...?* With just that tiny crack in her resolve, Mersey swept the two of them up, depositing them even deeper into the Dream.

Here, just as it had with Taylor's fractured spirit all those months ago, the Dream distorted. The edges of the memories blurred by *nothing.* By profound emptiness. Charlie and Raff clung so close to each other she wasn't sure whose fear was whose. Each knew that to touch that nothing would be to fall forever. To *become* a conscious part of that emptiness. They clawed at each other to reassure themselves of something else that was real, tangible. Adelaide materialised before them in the Medical Superintendent's office, Dr Palmer sitting in his chair across from her. A black veil obscured much of Adelaide's face, and her shirt and skirt were as black as Mersey's spirit.

"I know it's a lot to ask," Adelaide was whispering, whimpering. She pulled a white handkerchief to dab at her eyes beneath her veil. "And I shall contribute the full cost from Albert's estate, which he has left to me in trust for Sarah." She was babbling, as Dr Palmer stared at her stony faced, unmoved by the crying widow. "You can see, from his letter, it's what he wanted."

Dr Palmer pulled the letter to him now, across his desk, and read it aloud in slow, carefully enunciated sentences. *"If you have any love left for me, do this one thing for me. Send my body to Sandgate in Newcastle. Let me be buried with my love and my child. Let me not walk this purgatory alone."*

"You see, it was his last wish."

"So he repented in the end, then?" Dr Palmer's calm words were as much a judge's inquiry as a statement. He raised one bushy eyebrow as he stared Adelaide down.

She hesitated only a moment before replying, "Yes. Yes, he repented. He must have been so wracked with guilt at what he did to us that he couldn't face it. But you can see, clear as day. He wants to be buried with Sarah and I, in Sandgate, our families' home."

* * *

It had taken Raff and Charlie's full combined intent to dig themselves out of that deep layer of the Dream. With as much will, and fear-driven longing, as the two together could muster. They emerged, a sweating, relieved mess into Charlie's dark cottage. Charlie lay against Raff, who lay against the corner of their couch. Trent had made himself up a makeshift bed on the rug on the floor and was snoring softly. Tess was still in the armchair, curled up small, her head nestled in a pillow and a warm blanket tucked caringly around her.

Charlie had hurriedly pushed herself off of Raff, her whole body still shaking. Despite the sweat that ran rivulets down them both, and the warmth to the air courtesy of the heater, she felt unbelievably cold. The sweat was like ice leaching up from the pit of her stomach and running in melted droplets down her goosebumped skin. She shivered all over, trying to get to her feet, and falling instead. The thump as she landed on her knees woke the other two. Trent shot up like lightning, his face pale as he swivelled to take in the whole room. Tess blinked herself awake more calmly, moving slowly to sit upright, dragging her blanket with her as she did so.

"Charlie?" Raff asked. She ignored his thickly worded concern, putting a hand up and waving it to indicate she was fine.

"*Ma chére?*" Tess put both legs down firmly on the ground and shifted towards the edge of her seat. Trent stood, letting his own blanket fall in a crumpled mess, taking a couple of steps towards her to help her up.

"We have it," Charlie whispered, pulling herself to her feet and stumbling again. "We know what happened."

"Not now, Charlie," Raff put a light hand on her shoulder as he stood as well. "Rest. We all need rest." He sounded as though he'd just climbed the frozen, unforgiving peak of Mount Everest. It certainly felt like they both had. It was almost all she could do to nod.

38

Fluttering Wings

Charlie woke, her eyes itching, her nostrils trembling. She knew, even though her body had somewhat gotten used to the smell as she slept, that she was surrounded by the must and musk of Raff's hobo caravan. She pushed his blankets off her sharply, despite the cold, and shuffled quickly to the edge of his bed, letting her feet land with an echoing thud on the caravan floor. The whole thing shook slightly with her movements, making the nausea from the night before return in a gross, wet burp. She put a hand to her mouth, waiting as she steadied on her feet. She then stabbed her toes into her sneakers and left the caravan as quickly as she could.

Frost clung to the edges of the grass, crackling as she landed on them. The fence that Tess had erected around the cottage was also laced with a fine layer of ice, glinting in the early morning sun. The fog, too, that hung around the cottage sparkled in the first light of day. It was a little colder than normal for the time of year, but not unseasonably so. With the soft yellows of the grassland around her, and the deep — almost blue — of the hills in the distance, it was beautiful. She wished she could stand and appreciate it for a moment. But the need to end things, let alone the sharp cold, drove her forward to the cottage door. As did the sensation of eyes boring into her, watching her.

Once inside, she strode past Raff sleeping on the couch, and the closed guest bedroom door behind which she could hear Trent snoring loudly. She almost ran the final steps to the bathroom, throwing her clothes from her as though they were Raff's scratchy, filthy blanket. She spun the taps to the shower, desperate to wash away the previous night's sleep.

* * *

The four of them sat at the dining table, strong coffee in hand, and a pile of Trent's banana pancakes largely untouched in the centre. Not because they weren't good — they could *almost* rival Dot's — but because no-one had an appetite for anything but the stiff, bitter brew.

"It's almost like this is how it's meant to be," Tess broke the silence. She held her mug gingerly by its handle to avoid too much heat on her recovering, sensitive skin. "Four chairs. The four of us. It feels complete now, *non?*" Raff and Charlie stared at each other across the table. Not with animosity; maybe perhaps with a little kinship, following what had happened. But certainly not with a sense of fated friendship. Trent laughed nervously and buried his face in his mug.

"Thanks, Tess," Raff smiled up at her, reaching across the table to lightly stroke the back of her hand. Charlie's heart and stomach twanged disharmoniously. "But it'll be back to the three of you soon enough. This business is nearly done now, and then I'll have to get back to my own duties, and Charlie to hers." Tess just gave an unconvincing shrug, still smiling.

"We think we know what's unbalanced Beryl and Mersey," Charlie explained. "Do you remember me telling you that I saw Albert sitting by a sick bed, crying over a thin and emaciated woman? I couldn't see at the time if it was Adelaide or Beryl, but Albert was telling them how much he loved them, begging them not to leave him. Then he promised her he would ensure they would be buried together, so they could be together always, in death." The three of them, even Raff, nodded. "Now we know it was Beryl who died of Consumption, it's obviously her he was speaking to. We also know that Albert thought Beryl had been buried at Sandgate. Adelaide lied to him, not wanting him to go and see her. So when he wrote that suicide note, that he wanted to be buried with his love and his child in Sandgate—"

"He meant Beryl and the unborn baby!" Tess gasped. "Not Addie and Sarah."

"Yes. When they died, both Beryl and Albert thought they would be buried together. And as Raff told us, spirits are almost always tied to specific places after they've died. They can't just haunt anywhere. Unless they get attached to a Keeper, like me."

"They've been kept apart in death... Addie couldn't keep them apart in life, so she ensured it happened when they died. Not knowing just how successful she would be. *L'Agonie de Jésus. La Flagellation. La Couronnement d'épines. Le Portement de la Croix. Le Crucifiement...*"

"She was raised Catholic," Charlie explained to a confused Raff.

"But what does all of that mean?" Trent asked, still rubbing at his temples. "How do we fix this?"

"We have to bring their bodies together," Raff said matter of factly. "Someone has to go to Sandgate, dig up Albert, and bring him to Waterfall."

"No way!" Charlie spat in disgust, as the other two squirmed back in their seats. They'd had enough of dead bodies when dealing with the convict spirits. And enough close calls with the law. Charlie was not willing to add grave robbing to her list of criminal activities.

"We *must* bring them together."

"What about Albert's tombstone instead?" Trent asked.

Raff sat back, rubbing his chin as he thought it through. "It could work... You know, I think it might! One of the Blacks I helped when I first started all this was upset because her grave had been disturbed. There'd been a flood that washed away the tombstone. As soon as I could convince the locals to get her a new one, she settled down and continued on her not-so-merry way."

"That's settled then. The tombstone it is. We'll go today," Charlie said firmly, feeling Mersey's eyes still boring into her back. He might not be able to enter this house, *yet*, but he was certainly present. Staring and waiting, impatiently.

"I know exactly where it is," Trent declared as he got to his feet. "I'll come with you, Charlie." Charlie felt the familiar twanging inside her as

231

she watched Tess and Raff exchange glances. They'd spent so much time together lately...

"It makes sense," Raff agreed. Charlie looked to Tess, her eyes almost pleading with her to disagree. To ask her to take Raff instead of leaving him behind with her.

"It's fine, *ma chére.* It's good. Go."

* * *

Charlie had driven to Newcastle while Trent had continued to sleep in the passenger seat, saying he hoped a bit more shut-eye might rid him of his headache. She'd driven in silence, excepting the odd snore, her mind racing as it so often did when things were coming to a head. Racing with everything she had to do, and the *need* the spirits pummelled at her when time was running low. This time, she also kept seeing Raff stroking the back of Tess's hand. The jealousy was like a living thing that fluttered between her throat and her chest, beating its wings in painful twitches. She knew the relationship she and Tess had was beautiful. It was strong and unbreakable. But was it immovable? Tess had never looked at Charlie the way she looked at Raff. An acrid taste grew in the back of her throat. She repeated a mantra to herself in her head, focussing only on this to avoid facing the cancerous jealousy inside her. *Tess's safety is all that matters. As soon as the Black goes away, she'll be safe. And Raff will be gone.*

Charlie drove through the gates of Sandgate, her tyres crackling against the gravel driveway. There was only one other car parked here, but not a living soul to be seen. Only the flocks of cockatoos, parakeets and crows could be seen, squawking and cawing in the trees as if in anticipation of their arrival. She continued passed the first carpark and on down the road, towards where she knew the Catholic section with its towering church waited. The trees passed on either side of them like towering guards. She marvelled, again, at the sheer number of graves that rose and fell like the waves of a sea around her.

At the other end of the cemetery, she pulled to the side of the road, just beyond the path leading down to the church. Mersey was nowhere to be seen, yet, though there were certainly enough shadows beneath the church's looming walls for him to hide in. Charlie patted Trent on the arm, causing him to jerk awake. "Sorry!" he spluttered, rubbing at his face and at the drool that had rolled down his chin. "I slept the whole way?" Charlie nodded and then unbuckled herself. Stepping out of the car and into the cold. She stretched, rubbing at her lower back as she gazed up at the church.

"It's down this way," Trent led her, weaving through the stones, to a quiet edge. The fence and tree line cast such deep shadows here that the air grew even colder and damper. Mosquitoes whined around them in a frenzy in defiance of the weather. Charlie recognised the low metal gate from Trent's photo as they approached. The soil was dark and heaped, and a single, broken stone lay in the centre. It was, as the photo had shown, a large family plot. Yet Albert had been left to rot alone, surrounded on all sides by nothing. An emptiness as profound and terrifying as that of the deepest layers of the Dream.

No wonder he's so confused and upset, Charlie thought to herself as they came to the fence, resting their hands on the cool metal. Trent carried a blanket with him, in which to wrap the stone. The two of them looked around each other. Despite how huge the grounds were, and how many tens-of-thousands of loved ones rested here, they were alone. They'd seen no one else. It made the place feel even more lonely.

"I wish we'd come at night," Trent muttered.

"No time," Charlie breathed, tightening her grip on the fence and lifting her first leg over it. Once on the other side, she added, "it's less suspicious doing it now, right?" Trent joined her, looking over his shoulder at every opportunity, and the two of them walked through the shadows and to the already damaged stone. "Thank God it's already broken free."

"We're taking you to Beryl, honey," Trent whispered, as he lay the blanket reverently over the top of the stone. Some of the jealous butterflies that had continued to beat in Charlie's chest, along with her fear, fluttered away. Instead, she felt her chest warm with appreciation for Trent; the beautiful soul who'd come with her. She was instantly glad it was him with her, and not Raff. Even if that meant Tess had more time with the dashing bogan. She smiled up at Trent as she took one edge of the blanket, grunting, and they heaved at the stone.

"For Albert and Beryl," she smiled at Trent.

"For Albert and Beryl." The two of them lifted, arm joints creaking, as they crab-walked with the humongous stone to the edge of the fence.

39

The Forgotten

"No!" Charlie practically yelled in frustration.

"I'm *coming*, Charlie!" Tess planted her feet firmly between Charlie and the front door of the cottage.

"He nearly killed you! This will just give him the chance to try again. Maybe even succeed this time!" She could hear the pleading in her own voice. The panic that leached out of her at the thought of Tess in more danger.

"And Beryl attacked *you* the last time you went to Waterfall. Raff told me what happened, *ma chére*! All of it." Charlie glared at Raff, who was leaning against the living room wall as though without a care in the world. The slight lines at the corners of his eye told a different story, but in her anger, Charlie refused to acknowledge them. "Each Black thinks we're the other sister. Maybe you even *need* me there for this to come to a full resolution. I won't let you do this without me."

"My fucking life..." Charlie said. Trent placed a hand on her shoulder as she breathed out the curse. She could feel with that touch just how stiffly she was holding herself and let her shoulders collapse down.

"I'll ride with you," Trent said gently. "Let Tess ride with Raff. I don't like it, but I don't like you going either, so let's stick together." Anyone else might have smirked at having won this battle, but Tess just continued to drill into Charlie with her own stubborn and pleading eyes. It made her feel as though her heart were bursting.

"We'll meet where you and I parked last time," Raff said as he pushed himself off the wall. "You two take the head start. That way we can be sure that Mersey is well and truly gone before Tess and I leave the house. Hopefully the two of them will be distracted enough seeing each other that we'll be okay. We'll do this quickly."

* * *

Trent and Charlie had taken turns driving the three hours to Waterfall that Monday afternoon, hearing Mersey's tombstone sliding along the car boot with each corner. She'd breathed shallowly the whole time, scared to breathe any deeper with how tightly her chest was clenched. The nausea still sank deep into her stomach, and the cold was so deep into her skin now, it itched and burned. She was a bundle of discomfort and distraction. She'd kept looking over her shoulder, and in the rear-view mirror, for signs of Mersey. But he was gone. They'd made it barely half an hour before the sensation of his eyes boring into her had dissipated. Perhaps he'd fled back to Sandgate. He'd never wanted her to go to Waterfall in the first place.

With the end of Autumn approaching, the sun set early. It was already approaching the horizon when Trent and Tess pulled up behind them in the wide shoulder of the road. "Come on then," Charlie said to Trent as she opened her door, her feet grating on the gravel. The trees on each side of the road seemed to have twisted further into each other, making an almost impenetrable barrier. She held her phone tightly in one hand and a torch in the other. On her phone screen was a map of Waterfall Cemetery that Trent had been able to hunt down. The cemetery was surrounded and cut through the middle by a road, with nine distinctly defined sections. Church of England was the largest, followed by Roman Catholics. Then there was Presbyterian, Methodist, Baptist, Jews, Congregational, Unsectarian, and Unallotted. They had no idea where Beryl would be, but at least it gave them a map to work from.

"People came to New South Wales from all over Europe for TB treatment,"

Trent said as he got out of the car, nodding at the map on her phone. "In the 1800s, doctors in England were even prescribing a sea voyage and months in New South Wales as effective treatment. They thought there was something about the Australian air that was *'conducive to a cure'*. That's why you had so many different denominations in the cemeteries, and sections for those that didn't fit the standard mould."

"It won't take as long to walk to the cemetery," Raff said briskly, cutting Trent off. He blew on his hands to warm them. "But we'll be slow going with that gravestone. Even with the sled I whipped up for it." Charlie opened the boot to her car, and the others crowded around behind her. Tess trailed nervously, looking around at the twisted trees and the road. With the sky covered in clouds, there'd be no moon or stars to guide them this time.

Staring into the boot, they saw that Raff had used the old blanket and an elaborately knotted rope to form a harness for the tombstone. The stone was wrapped tight, likely to keep it as safe as possible on what would be a rough journey through the bush. "It's rained lately," Raff thought aloud as they looked down at it. "That'll make it slippery going, but it might help with moving this thing."

"And you're right, the cemetery isn't as far as the hospital," Trent added, pointing a finger at Charlie's phone, which still had the cemetery map open. The two boys shouldered their way into the boot to heave the stone out. Tess and Charlie nervously watched the road, using their backs pressed together to hide the boys from view whenever there was a passing car. All going well, anyone would think they were just having car trouble and selfishly speed on their way rather than stopping to offer assistance. The boys carried the stone across the road rather than dragging it and fumbled their way up the rutted dirt driveway to the gate which warned of severe fines for trespassing. Working as a team, they managed to manoeuvre the stone across the gate and then gently laid it down, ready to begin their onwards trudge.

Night fully closed around them as they left the road, everyone but Tess taking turns with the makeshift sled. All was silent except for that grating, sliding of the stone, their fevered breaths, and the thumping of their hearts in their ears. Charlie longed to hear even a bird call, or a cricket, but it was as though the night had swallowed not just the light, but all signs and sounds of life as well. They began to shiver; even the poor sweaty soul pulling the stone couldn't warm themselves with their exertions. The walk was mostly flat, and likely only one kilometre or so, but with the stone they found themselves stumbling for close to an hour before Trent finally stopped them.

"We're here." The other three looked around and at each other, flashing their torches at the white and grey barked trees and down the poorly kept trail. They stood alongside what looked like simply more of the same dense, overgrown bush.

"Where is it?" Tess shivered as she spoke, wrapping her arms tightly around her chest. She was shorter of breath than she should have been, and Charlie felt a flash of anger that neither of the boys had helped her to convince Tess to stay behind. "I see nothing but trees." Trent motioned his head towards the thick row of gums and walked to their edge, laying a hand on the pale bark of the tallest. He peeked his head into the dark void between them. There was no fence. No gate. No signage. Just the never-ending bush.

"You remember me telling you a while ago that gum trees are some of the fastest growing in the world?" Trent asked rhetorically as he stepped beyond the tree line and made his way through. The others followed, Raff dragging the stone behind him. "Well, most people had forgotten this cemetery even existed until recently. Loved ones rarely came to visit those buried here; at the time, people with TB were like lepers. And the local council didn't even know it was responsible for this place until it was too late. So the bush reclaimed it. It wouldn't have even taken twenty years of neglect. To top things off, a fierce bush fire ripped through here at one point, so anything wooden — like the crosses on those graves for people who had no money — all went up in flames."

Charlie fell against a nearby tree as the reality of the challenge hit her. Not just stumbling around in the dark without a clue where in the cemetery Beryl was buried. But stumbling about in the dark, through an overgrow and dense bush, without a clue where she was buried, and most likely no tombstone to let them know they'd found her. Raff shook the ropes off his shoulders, the deep and red indentations around his neck visible just for a moment as his clothes shifted. He joined Charlie in leaning against a tree, pulling his long black hair from the nape of his neck to let some of his sweat dry in the chill air. It was colder here, Charlie realised. Now she wasn't walking, it closed around her just as fully as the night had. Like an invisible wall, welcoming and then holding them here in the forgotten cemetery.

Trent had continued to walk in, through the trees, his torchlight occasionally visible. "I've found one!" The excitement in his voice was palpable. Raff and Charlie exchanged a similar glance; all they could feel in this moment was tension. It rippled in the air, along those freezing currents. Beryl was close. Mersey may have fled for now, but they were not alone. Leaving Mersey's stone by the edge of the bush, they followed Trent's light and the sound of his shuffling feet. The grave wasn't obvious at first, but when they spotted it, it seemed to loom up and out of the ground. Reminding them with sudden impact of its existence. Clusters of broken stones marked the grave's edges, which were disturbed in one place by a tall gum tree, growing up and through the grave itself. Its roots had burst behind it, toppling and splitting the gravestone in two.

Charlie was breathing shallowly again, her stomach no longer simply nauseous but twisting. As though those tree roots were growing through *her* corpse, rather than the ones below their feet. She felt a knot in the muscles of her back and looked over her shoulder surreptitiously. *Nothing yet*, she thought. The sight of this grave unnerved her beyond words. She'd seen graves that had been poorly kept before, but this was beyond anything she'd encountered. Her imagination ran wild as she glanced at the trees, knowing just how many people had been laid to rest here. Literally thousands of people not just left to rot in this place, but to be completely forgotten. Their very existence erased. The knot in her back tightened further, painfully, seeming to join with those roots in her stomach.

"There's more…" Trent whispered, allowing his torch beam to dance around them. And there were. *Dozens* of them. Some visible merely by a vague outline of stones. Some by cracked and overgrown tombstones. She could even see the darkened stumps of what might have once been wooden crosses, peeking out from underneath the groundcover. It was like the graveyard of a graveyard.

"We'll never get anywhere like this," Charlie whispered, looking up to see Raff staring at her intently. Once again, their thoughts had synced. It was getting unnervingly common.

"One last time to the Dream, then," Raff agreed.

* * *

Beryl, Raff sent through the Dream. They were standing in Raff's Waiting Place this time, not Charlie's. Just as he'd described, everything was black here, and everything was moving. There were no moments without movement. The sky heaved with black roiling clouds above them, and the ground was constantly shifting sands. This wasn't a desert, though. It was more like they were standing in the middle of a crashing black ocean, waves of sand constantly rising and falling. She hugged close to Raff, not wanting to be left behind in this place. *Beryl!* Before them, the sand shifted back on itself. Swirling like water around a drain, to open into a vortex that dropped down to an even deeper blackness. Raff approached its edge and turned his now-blackened head over his shoulder to Charlie. *In we go.*

Charlie much preferred her doors, archways and stairs to the gaping, gnawing hole she and Raff had to jump through. It pulled at her like a vicious storm, like it was literally trying to rip her apart, before spewing them unceremoniously back to Waterfall Cemetery. The ground still seemed to shift beneath her feet for several moments as she reoriented herself; even though they were back in Waterfall, they were still in the Dream.

Beryl stood before them. Charlie felt a tightness in her chest as she stared them down. Seeing Beryl here, Charlie realised how fully she seemed to belong in this abandoned place. The way her emaciated frame twisted like the roots of the trees that had overtaken everything. The way she oozed and dripped like the mud they'd trudged through. Her empty, black eyes bore into them. *Where are you buried?* Raff sent strongly, commanding this bent and warped woman to lead the way. The silence was so complete it seemed

240

to crackle and spark in the air. The anticipation was almost worse than the fear, and the feeling in Charlie's chest bloomed outwards.

Finally, Beryl lifted a single bent claw of a finger to point to her left, to their right, and she disappeared. Bleeding into the darkness of the night so suddenly and completely Charlie wondered if she'd ever fully been there. Or if she was still there and had simply become part of the darkness around them. They followed her directions, moving forward through the bush. Occasionally Beryl would re-materialise from the night, leading them with her crooked finger to the bottom, right corner of the cemetery. The unallotted section. Here the trees grew thicker, and signs of any graves grew sparser. Adelaide really had wanted her sister not just gone, but completely lost. A forgotten corner of a lost and forgotten cemetery. Beryl finally stood, facing them, between two tall white gumtrees. Her feet disappearing amidst a tangle of scraggly bush. Her clawed finger pointed down.

Thank you, Charlie sent, lifting a hand to Raff's feathered shoulder to indicate they should leave, and quickly. Get this done. Beryl screamed. Her mouth opened inhumanly wide and long, black mud spewing from her like projectile vomit. The sound was deeper, but higher, than any Charlie had heard. Screeching so profoundly that it momentarily knocked away her sight, let alone her hearing. And then Beryl was upon them, those clawed talons digging into their upper arms, her dripping eyes practically pressed against them, as she drew them further into the Dream.

40

The Marriage That Might Have Been

We missed something. It was the first time Charlie had heard real fear in Raff's tone. And it stabbed terror deep within her too. Not for herself, but for Tess, who they'd left unprotected in the night.

Keep your connection with Beryl, no matter what, she sent as calmly, but firmly, as she could. *Don't let her go. Don't let her get back to Tess and Trent.* Even though it was Albert who had been attacking Tess, Charlie didn't like the thought of the woman getting closer to any of her friends. She merely felt Raff's affirmation like a ripple in the air. This was a deep layer of the Dream again. There had been no pretence at making their way down slowly, layer-by-layer, this time. Her mind flicked back to *L'Inferno*, and Dante's layers of Hell. How deep were they? The nothing around them shimmered slightly, and they drew close to each other, Charlie steeling her intent with Raff's. *Don't let Beryl go.*

Show us, Beryl, Raff commanded, and she felt the fear in him grow. *What did we miss?* The scenes flashed around and above them; a tunnel of memories. It was almost exactly as it had been with Taylor, but less fragmented, clearer. They were pictures of Beryl in her sick bed in every memory surrounding them. How it had started, when it had just been a cough, and how it had progressed. It wasn't just that Beryl had grown thin; beyond thin, every bone protruding. Her eyes had sunk, her lids had darkened. All colour and vitality had drained from her face, her lips. She became slack, her mouth hanging open, all lines in her face deepening and pulling downwards. Her beautiful hair grew sparse, wiry, and flecked with greys.

They watched the disease consume not just her body, but her vitality. Seemingly her very soul. *There,* Raff nodded. Adelaide shifted through one of the pictures. At first it wasn't clear what she was doing, although by her furtive movements, it was obvious she didn't want to be seen. *That's Beryl's veil,* Raff realised before Charlie could. Adelaide was rubbing it against the piles of dirty linen, the darkened patches of dried vomit and phlegm. The scene skipped forward, Adelaide rubbing a washcloth on any soiled items she could find. The sickest patients, those not just with tuberculosis, but an array of maladies. Diarrhoea, bed sores, the common cold. Anything she could get her hands on.

And then she sat by Beryl's side, kindly tending her sister as she wasted away, with those soiled and contaminated cloths. Not just ensuring she got sick with the White Plague — the curse upon the women of their family — but with any minor ailment that would speed the process along and hinder any chance of recovery. A sickness that would force Beryl to miscarry her child, before succumbing to the disease herself. Charlie was speechless as the realisation dropped on her. *She killed you,* Raff almost whispered the message out. And then the spirit of Beryl was there again, before them. Not just angry, not just afraid and hurt, but *ashamed.* Ashamed of the love she'd had for her sister. The trust she'd put in her. *I've got her,* Raff sent to Charlie, keeping his eyes fixated on Beryl. *Go get Mersey. Bring him back to Waterfall Cemetery. Now.*

* * *

No matter how much practice Charlie had pulling herself from those deep layers of the Dream lately — unwillingly — it still hurt to extricate herself. The deep layers pulled like they didn't want to let her go. She felt the exhaustion setting in and tried to draw additional reserves of energy from the Dream itself. It buzzed painfully too, reinvigorating her, but she sensed now — this came at a cost. *Mersey!* The command flew from her as soon as she entered Sandgate Cemetery. She soared to his Catholic haunt, sending her intent and her message again, forcefully. *Mersey!* He appeared, even more melted than before. He was barely able to extricate himself from the corner of the church in which he'd entrenched his very being. *Out, Mersey. You are coming with me. To Waterfall.*

He moaned. Not with words, though the meaning was clear. He was giving up, pulling himself into a dangerous puddle of despair and vengeance. Revenge not just against Adelaide and those like her — but against the world. *We found Beryl.* His descent into himself halted but did not reverse. *We know where they buried her and her child. We know what Adelaide did to her. To you. Not just stealing you from each other through lies and manipulation. Not just sending you to purgatory, away from her. Not just dooming Beryl to be forgotten. But* murdering *her and your unborn baby.* Mersey moved now. Exuding from the puddle in tense and turbulent ripples. His moon-eyes shone even brighter as he continued to grow, to loom, as tall as he once had. As domineering as the first time they'd met. *Come with me.*

* * *

Charlie awoke in the forgotten cemetery, laying on the ground. She could feel twigs, stones and rough mounds of dried mud digging into her back where her shirt had lifted. She sat groggily, seeing marks in the ground where she'd been dragged through the bush, away from the tree. A torch lay on its side by her bottom, illuminating the ruts in the ground. She stood — stumbled — to her feet and cried out as her ankle seared in pain. She looked down to see three ragged claw marks raked through her jeans and sock, breaking the skin, fresh blood oozing from the weight she'd put on the leg. As she sucked in air to cry, she became aware of a deep pain in her back as well. Tentatively she put a hand under her armpit and to her shoulder, drawing it back slicked with blood.

Raff had obviously succeeded and brought Beryl firmly back with him to the cemetery. And Beryl must have attacked her while she still lingered in the Dream. She frantically felt about her now, feeling for Mersey, breathing in relief as she saw him looking down at her, beyond the torchlight. His piercing eyes were like a beacon to the primitive part of her brain, which wouldn't stop alerting her to the fact she was being watched by a dangerous predator. She heard a clamouring noise from behind her and picked up her torch, swinging its light into the bush. Torches flickered only a couple dozen metres from them, and she could now hear Tess, Raff and Trent's voices. Mersey surged forward in their direction.

"No!" *No!* Charlie screamed and willed as Mersey speared through the night. "Tess! He's coming!" The shriek ripped its way from her throat, it was so dry, desperate and high. She could feel the inside of her windpipe practically tearing. "Tess! *Tess!*" She lunged forward painfully, dragging her injured foot behind her. She gripped the torch with one trembling hand, while holding her chest with the other. It almost felt as though the claw marks in her back had reached all the way through her. The night blurred as tears of pain threatened and adrenaline forced the world to brighten. She barely breathed as she burst the last few metres into the clearing. This was the place where the two gum trees met, and the bush tangled together. The place where Beryl was buried.

Trent and Tess had worked together to heave the tombstone upright in that tangle of weeds, now free of its blankets. Raff was standing there, bent double and heaving at the obvious exertion of dragging Beryl away from Charlie. Exerting the full might of his will on a spirit that was loathe to listen. He must have used every reserve of energy at his disposal. The sight that stopped Charlie in her tracks was Mersey and Beryl. They stood together above Beryl's grave. Mersey's oily smog of a body fluttered now, rather than vibrated in crazed patterns around him. His shining eyes were bright, but with something other than malice. Beryl was still as terrifying as she'd been before, but the black mud that was dripping from her pooled with Mersey's own body, joining them together. She reached a taloned hand to his hooked face, and the sigh that left both of them was not audible, but physical. Like a breeze which tussled the leaves of the trees.

"Now!" Charlie yelled painfully, exhaustedly, to Raff. He barely nodded as each of them reached out to their respective Black spirit, giving them the nudge they needed to accept their fate. Beryl and Mersey didn't even resist. There was no need to anymore. They moved on together, disappearing from the cemetery, holding to each other, ready to haunt the ruined grounds and buildings of Waterfall Sanatorium, in purgatory, together.

Charlie limped to Tess and threw her arms around her. Tess clung limply back, and then Trent was at her back embracing them too. The scratch across her shoulder twinged, and she drew a sharp breath, but didn't cry out. She didn't want this to end. She let the three of them huddle like this, tears of relief finally running down her face, before squinting to look over at Raff. *Come on*, she sent not with words, but intent, and he joined them in their embrace. Charlie sighed herself, and felt something leech out of her, just as it had Mersey and Beryl.

The light of a dropped torch shone on the gravestone, which leaned against the scrub. And Charlie could see that Raff had taken the time to deeply scratch in new words:

Here lies Mersey A. Hammond and Beryl A. Morgan.

She was buried at Waterfall, where her baby sleeps,
  When he was a world away;
  And the sad old garden its secret keeps,
  For nobody knows to-day.
  But the haunting words of the dead to me
  Shall go wherever I go.
  We live in the Marriage that Might Have Been
  Do you think that we do not know?

* * *

Charlie stood with Tess on the veranda of their cottage in Greenfields, watching Raff leave. The four of them had returned to Greenfields as soon

246

as the ordeal at Waterfall had ended. Trent had continued on home, to Brent. Raff had stayed another two days to finish building the decks for Tess's tiny house empire. The home-and-contents insurance would apparently cover the cost of a replacement tiny house, and Tess was investigating options for something *new*. She seemed to have had enough of second-hand adventuring.

Two days in, just as Charlie was building up the courage to ask Raff what his plans were, he'd announced his departure. As he'd warned them at the start, his next Black spirit was already calling to him. Tess had withered, but understood. Charlie had surprised herself by feeling a little disappointment as well, mixed amongst the glee and relief. They now watched together as his beat-up 4WD — towing the even more dilapidated caravan —drove up their gravel driveway in a cloud of dust. Tess stiffened and sighed beside her as Raff reached the gate and disappeared. Charlie knew Tess would miss him; that he'd given her something Charlie would never be able to. And despite her misgivings, and her strong desire to dislike the man, he'd given something she'd needed too. A companionship in this never-ending cycle of purgatory.

Still, as Raff's dust began to fade, one emotion burst through all of them. Through the companionship, the concern and love for Tess, and the gratitude that this was over...jealousy. And a deep relief that he was finally gone. She grimaced at the thought that she and Adelaide might have anything in common.

Raff's next spirit had called to him so quickly after Beryl. *How soon until I'm called on again?* Charlie wondered, as she and Tess turned back to the house, both wounded and limping. *How much more of this can I take? Can Tess take?*

She thought back to her realisation in those final moments of confrontation, as she'd drawn on the Dream to re-energise herself. As she'd pulled on that white light, and it had hurt her as much as healed her. *Everything comes with a cost. How much, though? For myself and for those I love? And how soon until the bill must be paid?*

Acknowledgments

I acknowledge the traditional custodians of the land where this book is set, Australia's First Nations peoples, including the Dharawal, Gadigal, Awabakal and Worimi peoples. While many of the settings in this book — including the cottage and town of Greenfields — are fictional, the land is not. I pay my respects to their Elders past, present and emerging, for they hold the memories, traditions, stories, and hopes of the First Nations people of Australia. We must always remember that under the roads, houses, towns, cities, ruins, and in the history of modern Australia is a much deeper and much longer history.

I am deeply grateful for all that I learnt from the written works of Carol Herben OAM (1947–2020), former President of the Illawarra Historical Society. Her passion for local history and heritage shone from the pages of her works. Even after her passing, she taught me so much about the history in which this particular novel is grounded. I hope more people will pick up her book, *Forgotten Souls.*

Thank you once again to my family for all of their support, guidance and advice. This book hit me a little harder than the first two. There were moments, writing about the abuse, where I needed to take some moments to just sit and decompress. My family were with me for all of it — for the mood swings as I wrote, for the first drafts that needed gentle encouragement and soft touches, and for the story's final debut. You're with me every step of the way. I am eternally grateful.

Thank you to my editor, Greg, for pushing me to be my best. For testing each part of the story, ensuring its foundations stood true, and then polishing it for the world.

As we reach the halfway point in this series (yes, three down, three to go), I also want to say a huge thank you to *you*, the reader. Thank you for coming on this journey with me. Thank you for reading my stories. For loving my characters. For reliving the history. For feeling all these emotions with me.

Readers, it is you that these stories are written for. Every time I hear from one of you, it makes my day and gives me the nudges I need to keep on going. Please, keep reaching out. Whether it's through a review, a social media tag, or even a direct message — they all mean so much. *Je t'aimerai pour toujours.*

About the Author

JJ Carpenter has been writing books since she was six years old — a collection of kooky tales she would staple together and hide in a shoebox under her bed. She penned her first novel at the age of twelve; since then her love of all things creepy, supernatural and wild has never left her. Join JJ as she journeys through haunted places and chilling mysteries across the beautiful country, and rich history, of Australia.

JJ was born in Canberra, Australia. She spent her childhood in various locations, including the Barossa Valley, South Australia, and Hampshire, England. As an adult, she's spent much of her career living and working in the South Pacific: Solomon Islands (twice), Vanuatu, Fiji and beyond.

You can connect with me on:
- https://www.jjcarpenterauthor.com
- https://twitter.com/jjcarpenterbook
- https://www.facebook.com/profile.php?id=61554566154490
- https://www.instagram.com/jjcarpenterauthor

Also by JJ Carpenter

The Corner of Her Eye, Book One: The Keeper
Everyone dies. But what happens if you're not ready when it's your turn?

The spirits in Charlie White's new home are restless and not everything is as it seems. She left the city to try to escape her medical challenges, but instead ran into something even more peculiar. Charlie's life is not the only thing hanging in the balance. Her life, her sanity, her very connection to reality, are under threat.

She soon realises, **purgatory is all too real**, and she's not its only resident.

The Corner of Her Eye, Book Two: The Road

Charlie White thought this was the end. She thought once she'd accepted her fate as a Keeper of Purgatory, her story would conclude. But she's just scratched the surface; this is only the beginning.

As she grapples with an ever-expanding new world beyond the grave, she begins to draw imbalanced, disturbed and helpless spirits to herself in greater and greater numbers. How deep must she venture through the layers of purgatory? And who else — or rather what else — lurks in the shadows of limbo?

www.ingramcontent.com/pod-product-compliance
Lightning Source LLC
Chambersburg PA
CBHW070553120726
47909CB00007B/2335